# Forbidden Places

## DEANNA MADDEN

Copyright © 2017 Deanna Madden

All rights reserved.

ISBN-10: 1466332476
ISBN-13: 978-1466332478

Cover design by SelfPubBookCovers.com/FrinaArt

Flying Dutchman Press

2017

This is a work of fiction. Names, characters, places, and incidents either are the product of the author's imagination or are used fictitiously. Any resemblance to actual persons, living or dead, events, or locales is entirely coincidental.

*For Doug and Gypsy*

# 1

## Niʻihau, part 1

Peter was still feeling a little seasick when the barge pulled up to the dock. He had been warned that the crossing would be choppy, and it had been. He had never been seasick before, but then he had never been in such rough water before either. Still, he would have put up with even more to reach this island that few were permitted to visit. It was still dark and so he could not see much of the island. That would have to wait for daybreak. The barge banged up against the dock, and four men stepped out of the shadows and tied it. Ignoring him, they went straight to work unloading the supplies that had been brought from Kauaʻi.

"Well, you going ashore or not?" the skipper asked. He was a local man of indeterminate age, missing a few teeth, his skin weathered and eyes furrowed with crow's-feet. Peter sensed that the skipper found him amusing. He was not sure if it was because of the way he was dressed—the new polo shirt, jeans, and athletic shoes he had bought for the trip—or because he was so clearly ill-at-ease on the barge and didn't know how to keep his footing but lurched with the barge and felt repeatedly as if he were going to be flung over the side into what he suspected were shark-infested waters. Then too it didn't help when he puked over the rail. It wasn't easy to keep your dignity while losing your last meal.

He picked up his bag but hesitated to leave the barge. There should have been someone there to meet him. At the very least there should have been someone there to ask who he was and what he wanted. It seemed terribly lax for the dock to be so unguarded. Well, what had he expected—police with guns? Natives with spears? Of course not. But all the same, anyone could have come ashore. He glanced back at the skipper, now busy directing the dockhands as they heaved boxes onto shore and leaped nimbly after. They made it look easy, so he tossed his bag on to the dock and then jumped after it as they did, pleased with himself when he didn't fall on his face. Once he was on the dock, he saw a young woman walking toward him, materializing out of the dark. She was beautiful in the way so many Polynesian women were—a sculpted face with full lips and large languid brown eyes, long black hair pulled back in a ponytail, a white top with a V-neck where a small pendant glinted, slim hips hugged by jeans. She was young, late teens maybe.

"Peter Hoenig?" she asked as she came up to him.

"Yes," he said, startled.

She held out her hand. "I'm your guide."

He was surprised. He had expected a man. The fact that his guide was a woman and such a young one was one more sign that the island was not as secure as it ought to be. She barely looked old enough to be out of high school.

He shook the hand she had extended. It felt warm and firm in his.

"Follow me," she said.

Grabbing his bag, he walked after her to the end of the dock, near which stood an old blue pickup.

"You drive?" he asked.

"Of course I drive," she said with a toss of her head. "Why do you sound so surprised?"

"I didn't think there would be cars here. Or trucks."

"We don't have many, but we have a few. Most of the time we just walk, or on the ranch we ride horses. Should I have brought a horse for you?"

"No, of course not." He felt he was getting off on the wrong foot. He tossed his bag into the back of her pickup, then, after a bit of tugging, got the passenger door open and climbed in. He hunted in vain for a seat belt.

"I know it's not what you're used to," the girl said, starting the engine, "but it beats walking."

"I'm sorry," he said. "I wasn't aware you had vehicles here. It just came as a bit of a surprise."

"You were expecting a glimpse of old Hawaii, were you?" she said as they started down the dirt road. "Well, sorry to disappoint you. I don't know why they don't prepare visitors a little better before they send them here. We don't live in grass shacks or wear grass skirts. We have refrigerators and stoves and sleep on mattresses. Don't think they didn't try to take some of those things away from us when we received protective status. It practically caused a revolt. Everyone here was in favor of becoming a Forbidden Place until they heard they might have to give up their cars and TV's. Especially their TV's. Not too many people had cars. Finally they compromised. They agreed to give up some things if they could keep others. Reception wasn't all that great anyway."

"I thought this island was forbidden long before that," Peter said.

"It was. Since World War I. No one is allowed to visit without permission. And basically everyone stays here who is born here. If you leave, you can't come back. Except of course for the kids who go to Kauaʻi to attend high school."

"That's permitted?" he said, surprised again.

"I studied there. There was an unmistakable note of pride in her voice.

"But doesn't that—" He hesitated, uncertain how to say it. He didn't want to offend her. If young people were being allowed to go away and experience the modern world, then surely they were bringing back ideas to the people who stayed behind. The culture on the island would not be as pristine as he had hoped. It was disappointing and he wondered how valid the results of his research would be. He assumed Professor Rinehart, his dissertation adviser, didn't know about this; otherwise, the professor would surely not have suggested he include Niʻihau in his study.

"It's because I went over there that they let me be a guide," the girl explained. "They figure I already had my chance to choose and I chose to come back here, and so they think contact with outsiders is not going to make me want to leave."

"Well, I'm sure you'd regret leaving here," Peter said. "You're very fortunate to live in a place like this."

"You haven't even seen it yet."

He gave her a quick look, but her serene face offered no clue as to what was going through her mind. She really was beautiful. He wondered if she ever got visitors who tried to hit on her, and just as that thought surfaced, they jolted over a particularly bad bump.

"Sorry," she said. "They hardly ever bother to fix the roads around here. There aren't many vehicles anyway. No place to drive to. I think the Alliance is hoping we'll just give them up altogether one of these days."

"You know, you haven't told me your name yet," he said.

"Mele Keaulana."

When he tried to say it, she broke into laughter. She repeated it slower for him. "Meh-le-Ke-au-la-na. Just call me Mele."

"Have you been doing this very long?" he asked.

"About a year now. Ever since I came back from Kaua'i."

"And do visitors like me come very often?"

"You mean watchers?"

"I beg your pardon?"

"Watchers. That's what we call people like you. They come to watch. I suppose we get about one a month."

He felt relieved. One a month wasn't bad. And if visitors really were prevented from interacting with the islanders, then maybe Ni'ihau was still useful for his research project.

"What sort of things do they watch?" he asked, curious.

She shrugged. "Last time it was a birth. The time before that it was a death and a funeral."

Peter shivered. Both were traditional areas for anthropological research. However, he would have been embarrassed to watch women giving birth and he would never have chosen something as morbid as death rites for his dissertation topic. What kind of scholars were attracted to a subject like that? At least the topic he had chosen for his dissertation was preferable to watching someone die and be disposed of.

"So am I your first wedding watcher?" he asked.

The road turned sharply to the right and he had to brace himself to keep from being thrown against the door. As they bumped along, he found himself watching the girl's bare foot in its rubber slipper on the accelerator. In comparison his athletic shoes seemed large and clumsy.

Gradually the sky was growing lighter, and as it did, the bleached and barren landscape of the island emerged, strewn with rocks, pebbles, and scraggly plants, while in the distance the ocean shimmered.

"It's not much to look at," she said, as if apologizing.

"It's beautiful in its own way," he assured her.

She made a face. "That's what they say about a homely woman."

"Many people would give a lot to come here and see this."

She glanced at him curiously. "And where are you from? How far did you come to see our island?"

He hesitated, not sure he should tell her that. She was only supposed to show him the islanders, act as interpreter, and answer questions when he asked, not socialize with him. He couldn't remember anything in the contract he had signed about not telling where he was from, but it seemed kind of inappropriate for her to ask. She lived in a Forbidden Place, and he ought not to interact with her any more than absolutely necessary.

"What are you afraid of?" she asked, glancing at him. "Are you afraid I'll be so smitten by your description of where you live that I'll immediately want to leave Ni'ihau? I told you. I've been out there and I chose to come back. They trust me."

They may have trusted her, but he wasn't sure he did. She was so young, practically a kid. Was it possible the Association had hired her sight unseen?

"Look, I'm just saying, it would be interacting with the people—you're clearly one of the people—and interacting is strictly forbidden by the Association. You should know that."

"You're a very cautious person, aren't you?" she said,

looking amused. "I bet you're the sort who never breaks the rules."

He wasn't sure how the conversation had taken such an awkward turn, but he was not going to let this girl who was—what? maybe eight years younger than he was?—make him look like a fool. He broke rules. He'd smoked pot once, hadn't he?

"I'm from Boston," he said. It sounded ridiculously stiff. He half expected her to laugh.

"There, that wasn't so hard, was it?" She flashed him a smile that showed perfect white teeth. "So tell me about Boston. What's it like?"

He had a feeling she would keep pestering him until he told her, so he might as well get it over with. He couldn't imagine Boston would sound attractive to her anyway, not when she was from a place as undefiled as Ni'ihau.

"In winter it's cold," he said. "And the traffic is terrible. It has a population of about five million. It's not as big as New York, but it's larger than Honolulu."

"I've never been to New York or Honolulu," she said. "The biggest place I've seen is Lihu'e."

Lihu'e was the small town on Kaua'i where he had landed by plane yesterday afternoon.

"It's bigger than that," he agreed.

"I suppose there are lots of tall buildings?"

"Of course."

"And in winter it snows?"

"Yes, we get a lot of snow."

"I've always wanted to see snow."

He didn't know what to say to that. He couldn't very well say someday you'll see it, because she never would, not if she stayed on Ni'ihau. He couldn't say it's like you see in the movies because they didn't have movie theatres here either. They didn't even have TV she had said.

He tried to change the subject. "Look, are we almost there?"

"You certainly are impatient. We'll get there eventually. I want to show you something first."

"What?"

"You'll see."

In a few minutes she pulled to the side of the road and stopped. They were near the ocean. "Come on." She climbed out, and he had no choice but to do the same. She kicked off her rubber slippers and walked barefoot across a pale gold beach. He tried to follow, his shoes sinking at every step. She went right up to where the water lapped at her toes.

"Isn't it beautiful?" she said.

The sky was flushed pink with the dawn, and the ocean in the early morning light stretched as far as the eye could see.

"Yes, it's beautiful," he agreed. "You're very lucky to live here."

"This is my favorite place on the island."

"I can see why."

"I think if I left, this is what I would miss most."

"Well, since you aren't leaving, you won't have to miss it."

He expected some quick retort, but none came. She gazed at the ocean as if her mind were far away. It *was* very beautiful, he thought, but she wasn't supposed to be showing him the sights. He wasn't a tourist. He had permission to watch a wedding and that was all. He had signed a contract agreeing not to do anything else. Well, of course it hadn't said anything about watching the sun come up over the ocean; it had only specified not interacting with the local people. And there were no other people around besides Mele. If she insisted on talking to him, was it his fault? He couldn't very well be rude. Not when he was a guest on her island.

"Maybe you should take off your shoes," she said, looking down at his half buried sneakers.

He didn't relish plowing his way back through the sand, so he did as she suggested and pulled off his shoes. Of course then he had to take off his socks too because he couldn't very well walk in the sand in socks. As they trudged back to the car, the feel of the sand between his toes reminded him of when he was a kid and his family had vacationed at Cape Cod. It had been a regular summer ritual he had looked forward to until one year when he was twelve and they had suddenly stopped going.

Back in the truck, Mele was much quieter, lost in thought. He found himself wishing that she would start talking again. He liked it when she talked. He stole glances at her when he thought she wouldn't notice. It was incredible really to find himself sitting here with this young woman from a culture so unlike his own. He had not foreseen anything like this. When he got permission to visit some of the Forbidden Places to do primary research for his dissertation, he he had only thought of it in terms of what he would see. He never dreamed that he would have as much interaction with any of the people as he had already had with Mele.

As they approached a cluster of houses which he assumed must be Puʻuwai, the only town on the island and home for most of its two hundred inhabitants, he had his first glimpse of the people who lived here. A few children playing in the dusty street turned to stare as they passed. An old man with a broad brimmed straw hat sitting on a porch lifted a hand in greeting. A woman sweeping her front steps stopped to gaze curiously after them. He saw chickens in one of the yards and a skinny mongrel roused itself on a porch to bark at them but didn't bother to get up and give chase. They passed a quaint old white church with a steeple and three wood-frame buildings that Mele said were the elementary, junior high and high school.

"Here we are," she said, stopping in front of a low bungalow-style house nearly identical to all the others.

"Is this where you live?" he asked.

She nodded. "They said I should bring you here instead of taking you to the ranch. This way you'll be closer to the church."

He retrieved his bag from the back of the pickup and followed her to the door. She didn't pull out a key, he noticed, just opened it. It flashed through his mind that this would be one of those things he would tell about when he returned to Boston and people asked what Niʻihau was like. Imagine living in a place where people didn't have to lock their doors, he would say. He looked around at the neatly arranged little living room. The furniture was old and worn, but the effect was homey. A cheery orange-flowered throw covered the sofa, and framed family photos and half a dozen seashells, including a conch, sat on top of a crudely-made bookcase crammed with paperback books.

"It's nice," he said.

She made a face. "No computer, no TV, no phone, not even a radio."

"You have books." He immediately went to them, curious, and spotted *The Adventures of Huckleberry Finn*, *Pride and Prejudice*, and *The Odyssey*. Impressive. He wouldn't have expected to find books in a place like this, especially works of literature.

"If you ask my mother, she'll tell you I spend too much time reading."

"What else do you do besides read books?"

"I work at the ranch, like everybody else."

He had read about the ranch in the information packet he had been given before his trip. It belonged to a family from Scotland that had bought the island from a Hawaiian king in the 1800's. The islanders worked on the ranch and also raised crops and fished. It didn't bring in much money. In fact, they made just enough to make ends meet.

"This is where you'll sleep tonight," she said, showing him a small bedroom, which appeared to be the only bedroom in the little bungalow.

"What about you?" he asked.

"I'm sleeping at my grandmother's."

"Is it near here?"

"Everything's near here," she said with a wry smile. "Why? Are you afraid to stay alone?"

"Of course not. I only meant—" He stopped. She was teasing him, of course. He could see her trying to hide a smile. She must think he was an idiot.

"Are you hungry?" she asked.

He hesitated, trying to decide how to answer. He had eaten breakfast early that morning, then had thrown it all up during the rough crossing, but he didn't intend to tell her that.

"Come on," she said. "I'll fix both of us some breakfast."

Soon she was making pancakes and pouring hot coffee in mugs for them to drink.

"You didn't bring a laptop with you, did you?" she asked after his first sip of steaming coffee. It was just what he needed after the arduous crossing from Kauaʻi and the bumpy ride in the pickup.

"Of course not," he said. "They're not permitted here, are they?" He had brought a notebook, prepared to take all his notes by hand.

"Or a cell phone?"

"No. I couldn't have used it anyway. There's no signal, is there?"

"No," she said with a little sigh of disappointment. "But all the same, I thought you might have brought one. Sometimes watchers do."

"You should report them. The contract clearly said no cell phones." He was shocked that other researchers did not abide by the rules. The Association ought to set up more rigorous safeguards. Visitors should not be allowed to bring in forbidden items that could be adopted by the local people. That was the whole point of having Forbidden Places. Visitors could leave their cell phones in a locker at the Honolulu airport, just as he had. He planned to use it in between Forbidden Places to keep in contact with people back home, but he would not have dreamed of bringing it to the island.

"The last watcher smuggled in a cell phone," Mele told him, "but people noticed right away and it was taken away from him. He was really upset. They wouldn't give it back to him when he left either." She smiled, remembering.

That helped to reassure him. "What happened to it?"

"Oh, it was confiscated, of course."

"By the Alliance?"

She shrugged.

"Well, I didn't bring a cell phone," he said.

"You can use a small camera though. That's permitted."

"I have one in my bag."

"You came prepared."

"Yes, I think I did." Again he had the feeling she was making fun of him.

"Are you married?" she asked, watching him with those amused dark eyes.

Now this question was a little too personal, but not to answer might seem strange, or rude, or stiff, none of which he wanted her to think him.

"No, I'm not."

"Do you have a girlfriend?"

She was like a child who thought there was nothing wrong with asking any question that popped into her mind, no matter how personal. No doubt it was the result of belonging to a simpler, more naïve social system than his own.

"What does it matter if I have a girlfriend or not?" he said, trying to sound off-hand.

"I think it matters a great deal," she said. "If you're not married and you don't have a girlfriend, why are you so interested in weddings?"

It was a good question. He had to admit she seemed fairly intelligent in addition to being attractive. "It's just a topic my adviser suggested. I needed a research topic."

"And so you aren't really interested in weddings?" she asked, her dark eyes never wavering.

"No. I mean yes." Why did she make him feel so awkward? He wished she would stop staring at him. It was unnerving.

"I see," she said, although what she saw he had no idea. Perhaps he should tell her the truth, be absolutely up front about his unavailability, even though it was none of her business. There was no possibility of anything developing between the two of them. Even if he were available, she was absolutely off bounds. He didn't need the contract to tell him that. But he also didn't want her to get the wrong idea.

"Just for the record, I do have a girlfriend," he said.

This bit of information didn't seem to discourage her. She leaned forward with interest. "What's her name?"

"What?" He had taken a rather too large bite of pancake and she had caught him with his mouth full.

"What's your girlfriend's name?"

"Why do you want to know?" he asked when he had managed to gulp down the oversized mouthful and follow it with a swig of coffee. "What does it matter what her name is?" This was ridiculous. He knew he should put an end to it, but he didn't know how.

"Why won't you tell me her name?" she asked. "What are you afraid of? It's not as if I'll ever meet her."

That was true. They would never meet. Why was he being so cautious? Oh, very well, he would tell her. What could it hurt?

"Her name is Rosemary."

"Rosemary," she repeated thoughtfully. "What's she like?"

"What do you mean, what's she like?"

"Do you have a picture of her?"

"No." Actually he did have one in his wallet, but he wasn't about to show it to her. There was no reason she needed to see it.

"Well, describe her then."

He sipped his coffee to stall for time. Describe Rosemary? She was just Rosemary. He could see her in his mind. Blondish-brownish hair. Or maybe reddish-brown. Her eyes were—what were they? Hazel? He couldn't remember. It wasn't important anyway, was it? He could see her clearly in his mind even if he couldn't remember the color of her eyes. She always wore blouses with stiff little collars and practical low-heeled shoes. He could hear her voice in his head: 'Peter, what are you *thinking*? Peter, we're going to be late.'

"Is she pretty?" Mele asked impatiently.

"I suppose so. I mean, yes, of course."

"Are you going to marry her?"

Why couldn't she understand that his personal life was none of her business? He hardly knew her, and he did not intend to bare his soul to a young woman he hardly knew, especially not one who thought he was slightly ridiculous.

"I don't know. I really have no idea."

"Well, you must know if you love her or not. In fact, I think the first time you meet someone, you can tell, just like that." She snapped her fingers.

It wasn't like that at all, he could have told her, but why bother? She had a teenager's view of love. No doubt she believed in love at first sight and thought everyone had a soul mate. He felt infinitely older and more experienced. What did someone her age know about falling in love?

"Oh, so you're an expert on love?" he said, unable to resist a little sarcasm. "I suppose you're speaking from experience?"

"Maybe," she said, sipping from her mug of coffee.

"You have a boyfriend?" he asked, just to show her how it felt to be grilled about one's personal life.

"Yes, I do," she said, unruffled.

"So what's his name?"

"Mano."

Of course he could continue to barrage her with questions, as she had barraged him, but he didn't think questions would faze her and he hesitated to go farther. What would Professor Rinehart say if he could hear this conversation? Even worse, what would Rosemary say? He shouldn't let this young woman get under his skin. She was just a guide, and after this was over, he would never see her again. He should be careful not to say anything he might later regret.

"I think it's a very good subject for your research," she said. "Weddings, I mean. If I were a cultural anthropologist, that's what I would choose to study too."

He had the urge to laugh. All she had was a high school diploma. Did she even know what a cultural anthropologist was? He stopped himself in time, reminding himself that he was a guest here and must behave accordingly. It was a shame actually that a young woman as intelligent as Mele appeared to be would live out her life in a Forbidden Place. She would marry one of the men on the island and spend her life in this narrow world, working on the ranch, bearing children, her only contact with the outside world her books and the occasional watcher. He felt sorry for her.

"Have you finished?" she said suddenly, setting down her mug. "There's someone I want you to meet."

At once he was on his guard again. "Who?"

She rolled her eyes. "Are you always so suspicious?"

"You know I'm not supposed to interact with your people," he reminded her.

"It's okay." She gave a dismissive wave of her hand. "It's just my grandmother."

"Your grandmother?" he repeated, not understanding.

"No one will know," she said in a low conspiratorial voice. "It'll be our little secret."

Everyone would know, he thought with an inward groan. They couldn't step outside that door without half the town noticing.

"I don't think it's a good idea. It's against the rules." As soon as the words were out, he regretted saying them, but it was too late to take them back.

"You worry too much about rules. Look, will you ever come to Ni'ihau again? Probably not. This is a once in a lifetime experience. You need to reach out and grab it." To illustrate, she plucked an orange from a bowl of fruit on the table and pressed it to her, that little valley between her breasts.

Her dark eyes stared at him. "Do you understand? Otherwise you may never have the chance again."

He had to admit she had a very graphic way of making a point. And it wasn't done salaciously. She clutched the orange to her as innocently as a child might have. That was the thing about her that struck him the most. She was so young, so guileless. What did she know of the complexities of life beyond her island? Compared to her, he supposed he *was* too cautious. She was right, sometimes you did have to reach out and grab hold of life. And it was his one opportunity to experience Ni'ihau. What could it hurt to meet her old grandmother? Besides, he didn't want her to see him as bound by rules. Not that her opinion really mattered. But he would show her that he too could act on impulse.

"All right," he said. "Lead the way."

She grinned at him and tossed him the orange.

When they stepped outside, Peter noticed it was warmer now although it was still early morning. He glanced at his watch as they crossed the street. It was a German watch with a black face and an expandable silver band, a gift from Rosemary at Christmas. It was only 8:30 a.m., and the wedding would not take place until afternoon.

"Where is everyone?"

Mele shrugged. "Sleeping. Or getting ready for church."

"What about your grandmother?"

"She's an early riser."

Her grandmother's bungalow was directly across the street. As with her own house, Mele merely pushed the door open. When they stepped into the living room, he saw an old woman sitting in a rocker near a window. Her gray hair was neatly done up in a braided bun. She wore a muumuu and flip-flops on her gnarled feet. Mele greeted her in Hawaiian and kissed her cheek. It took Peter a minute to notice that the old woman's bright eyes never focused on them but gazed unseeing into space.

"Here, give her your hand," Mele said.

Peter took the old woman's fragile hand.

"Is he handsome?" the old lady asked.

Mele glanced at him and smiled. "Yes, he's handsome, Tutu. Here, let her feel your face. You don't mind, do you?"

He let the old woman take his face between her hands and slowly explore it with her fingers.

"He's not from the island?" the old woman asked.

"No, Tutu. He's a haole."

"Why is he here?"

"He's a watcher. He came to watch Noelani's wedding."

"Ah," the old woman said, nodding. "What's your name, young man?"

"Peter Hoenig," he said.

"What do you think of our island, Peter?"

"It's a very special place. It's like I've stepped into a different world."

She nodded her head, pleased with his answer. "Are you coming to church this morning?"

"Yes," Mele said, answering for him. "But we'll have to sit in the back."

They stayed a few more minutes while Mele talked to her grandmother in Hawaiian. Then she leaned down and touched her forehead to her grandmother's in a gesture that struck Peter as beautiful. He felt he ought not to be watching and yet he could not look away. Then she kissed her grandmother lightly on the cheek, patted her hand one last time, and they left.

\* \* \*

"Why did you tell your grandmother we were going to church?" Peter asked as they walked back to her bungalow. "You know I can't go anywhere except to the wedding."

"The wedding is not until three o'clock this afternoon," Mele said. "It's very boring to just sit around until then. Why not go to church? As a cultural anthropologist, you should find it interesting."

He glanced at her face to see if she was teasing him again, but she looked completely serious. "I'm not supposed to interact with people."

"We won't interact. We'll just sit in the back and be quiet as mice. No one will notice we're there."

He doubted that, but in the end he gave in, in spite of his better judgment because he was curious to see what he could of the life of this isolated community. Mele was right. It was the chance of a lifetime. He would probably never again have an opportunity like this.

And so by ten o'clock they were seated in the last pew of the little white church down the street. They had waited until nearly the last minute, but as Peter had feared, that didn't stop nearly every head from turning to look at them. Mele sat there in a pretty flowered dress and simply pretended not to notice all the attention they were attracting. The old minister was a little nonplussed at first but soon launched into his sermon, and his congregation ceased to crane their necks to look at Peter. The sermon itself was in Hawaiian, so he had no idea what it was about. There were songs too, also sung in Hawaiian. As the service dragged on, he began to wonder if Mele had really urged him to go because she thought he would find it interesting or because she wanted to show him off. He had a deep suspicion it was to show him off. All the same, the service was interesting, even if he didn't know what it was about. There was a lot of congregational enthusiasm, especially during hymns. Some of the children got restless and twisted about to communicate with other children farther back. The service lasted for about an hour and a half. Just before it ended, Mele gave him a nudge and they slipped out of the church. They walked briskly back through the deserted street to her bungalow.

"There. That wasn't so bad, was it?" she said, smiling as the screen door closed behind her. "You didn't interact with anyone. No harm done. The Alliance could not possibly disapprove."

Peter didn't bother to contradict her. He was learning that it was difficult to oppose this headstrong young woman. He supposed eventually the Alliance would find out she was a less than ideal guide and she would lose her job. But for now he would gather what information he could and hope the other three sites he was scheduled to visit were more isolated. He pulled his notebook out of his bag and sat down on the sofa.

"What are you doing?" Mele asked, immediately curious.

"I need to ask you some questions. For my research."

"All right. Would you like some guava juice?"

"No, thank you."

"Suit yourself." She disappeared into the kitchen.

He wondered if he should follow her. "Are you coming back?" he called to her in the other room.

"I'm just getting some guava juice."

He heard the refrigerator door open and close.

"But I said I don't want any."

"Oh, but I do," she said, reappearing with a glass of pink juice in her hand.

He sighed and looked at the questions he had written out in advance. Was she really prepared to take this seriously? "What is the average age at which people marry on Niʻihau?"

"Well, that depends." She looked up at the ceiling. "Kauilani and Keoni married when she was fifteen and he was seventeen, but then there was my Auntie Lani, who married Big Joe when she was fifty-five and he was sixty. That was after her first husband died of a heart attack and his wife from cancer. What would that make the average age? She closed her eyes, lips moving. "Thirty-five?"

"The average age of a *first* marriage." He saw he would have to be specific.

"Why didn't you say so? In that case, about seventeen or eighteen. Some wait to finish high school and some don't. If there's a baby on the way, they try to make sure they tie the knot before the baby's born. It's more respectable that way."

"So would you say the girl is usually not a virgin?" He felt a little embarrassed asking this question, but he told himself there really wasn't any need to feel embarrassed. It was all part of his research.

Mele gave him a look that made him drop his eyes to his notebook. "Some are and some aren't. If a boy has talked her into it, then she's not. After all, there's not a lot to do here. We don't have movies or restaurants or concerts. On the other hand, there's a lot of pressure to wait for marriage. We hear it in church all the time. And if a girl has given in, everybody knows it. You can't keep a secret in a place where everyone knows everyone else."

"Would you say more than fifty percent are not virgins?" he asked, his eyes resolutely on his notebook.

"Would you say more than fifty percent in Boston?" she countered.

"Maybe. Probably." He decided to move on to the next question, which was less sensitive. He had assumed he would be asking a male guide these questions. It was a little awkward to have to ask a female guide the virginity question. "How long would you say the average couple is engaged before they marry?"

She looked at the ceiling again. "Noelani and Keoki have been engaged about a month I think."

"Would you say that's about average?"

She shrugged and looked bored.

"How many children in the average family?"

"Five or six, I suppose, although some have as many as twelve. We like big families. I'm sure you already knew that."

"Do married couples argue much?"

"Is that really one of your questions?" She came over to where he was sitting on the sofa and tried to see his list of questions. "It doesn't sound very scientific."

"Well, it leads into my next question."

"And what's that?"

"Is there much domestic abuse? You know, men beating their wives, that sort of thing." Another question he felt uncomfortable asking her.

"I know what it means."

"Sorry. Well, does it happen often?"

"What's often?"

He thought a minute. "Once a week?"

She sipped her guava juice and stood there with her head tilted to one side trying to read the questions scrawled in his notebook.

"What about divorce?" he asked, moving on to the next question. He would come back to the domestic abuse question later.

"What about it?"

"Do couples here ever get divorced?"

She wrinkled her nose. "If they did, they'd have to leave, and not many are willing to do that."

"Why would they have to leave? Is that a rule?"

"Think about it. There are only about two hundred of us living here, and more than half of those are children. If you got divorced, every day you'd have to put up with people making comments about how you and so-and-so broke up and what a shame it was, and if you could put up with that, why not stay married?"

"I see your point." He wrote down, 'no divorce.' "What about infidelity?"

She stared at him.

"No infidelity either?"

"Well, not that anyone is supposed to know about. We have to live together here you know."

"I suppose there's a lot of—" He hesitated. "Inbreeding?"

"Well, almost everyone is related somehow to everyone else, but we're not savages. We don't practice incest or anything like that."

"I didn't mean to imply—"

She put up her hand to stop him. "I answered your questions. Now I think you should answer some of mine."

He looked up apprehensively after writing down 'inbreeding but no incest.' "I'm not supposed to—"

"I could tell the Alliance you made unwanted advances to me."

He looked at her, shocked. Would she do a thing like that? And, more important, would they believe her? There would be no witnesses. And if asked, everyone on the island would probably swear she was telling the truth. He was the outsider. Who were they going to believe?

"What questions?" he asked cautiously.

She smiled. "First, what places have you been to?"

At least it wasn't a personal question. "Do you mean Forbidden Places? This is my first. I have three more to visit as part of my field study for my dissertation."

She shook her head. "No, I mean places in the world."

He hesitated only a few seconds. What could it hurt to answer her question? "I've been to London, Paris, Rome, Madrid, and Mexico. My parents took me to Tokyo when I was a kid, but that doesn't really count. I hardly remember it."

"Tell me about them," she said, settling herself cross-legged on the floor in front of him, eyes shining, like a child eager to hear a story.

"What do you want to know?"

"What were they like?"

"Well, when I was in London it rained most of the time."

She rolled her eyes. "What did you *see*?"

"Well, the Tower, and Buckingham Palace, and Westminster, the British Museum and the National Gallery. In Paris I visited the Louvre, saw the Eiffel Tower and the Arc de Triomphe. In Rome the Colosseum of course."

"I want to see those places someday."

He looked down at his notebook, uncomfortable. This was why there was a rule against interacting. It could sow seeds of discontent and put ideas in her head that shouldn't be there. She would never be able to visit those places. Her world was a seventy-square-mile island. He should not be encouraging her to think about places where she could never go.

"What were the people like?" she asked eagerly. "Tell me about the people."

The people? How was he supposed to answer that? He really did need to put an end to this. He shouldn't have allowed himself to be pulled into this conversation in the first place. It was unprofessional. "I don't know. I didn't really meet any people."

"How could you not meet people?" she asked incredulously.

"Well, of course there were people. It was summer, the height of the tourist season. At the Tower, for example, it was elbow-to-elbow."

There was a knock at the door. Peter started guiltily, as if he had been caught doing something he should not have been doing. Beyond the screen stood several women. Mele sprang to her feet and in a few steps was at the door. She opened it a few inches.

"What do you want?"

"We brought you a cake," said the big woman in front. "Pineapple cake." She squinted, trying to see past Mele into the interior.

"You don't fool me, Lala. You just want to meet the watcher, but he's busy, so go away. Shoo."

"Mele Keaulana, is that any way to treat your neighbors?" the big woman demanded. "Only the other day, Ailani was saying, Mele's getting very uppity, getting herself hired as a guide, but I said, she's a good girl, she won't forget who she is."

"You know the rules," Mele said. "He's not allowed to talk to you. If I let him talk to you, I'd lose my job. Do you want me to lose my job?"

"You could just introduce us. It wouldn't hurt anything. We're just giving him a warm welcome."

"You'll meet him later. He'll be at the wedding and at the luau."

Muttering, the women turned away. Mele came back holding the cake. "Want a piece of pineapple cake?"

The words were hardly out of her mouth when there was another rap on the door. "For heaven's sake, what now?" she said, whirling around.

There was a little girl about seven years old standing beyond the door, hands cupped around her eyes, trying to peer through the screen. "Mele!" she called, then swung the screen door open without waiting for permission and stepped tentatively inside.

"What do you want?" Mele asked, hands on hips.

The little girl looked at Peter without saying a word.

"Okay, now you've seen him. Satisfied?"

The girl just stood there watching him.

"Hi," Peter said.

She broke into a shy smile.

"What do you want?" Mele repeated. "You know you're not supposed to be here."

The girl said something in Hawaiian.

"Oh, no," Mele said, closing her eyes.

The girl ducked back outside, letting the screen door bang, and ran off.

"What did she say?" Peter asked.

"My mother's coming."

"Is that bad?"

"I told her to stay away!"

"Well, just introduce me to her. The Alliance doesn't have to know."

"You don't understand." Mele paced nervously.

"Well, explain it to me."

"My mother doesn't want me to be a guide."

"Why not?"

She shot a look at the door. "Shh, here she comes. Let me take care of this." She flew to the screen door, opened it a few inches like before and again blocked the opening with her body.

He listened as she argued with her mother in Hawaiian. He guessed she was trying to persuade her mother to go away and her mother was refusing. Evidently her mother won because in a moment Mele reluctantly stepped aside and a tall imposing woman entered. There was a definite family resemblance. She was thicker bodied than Mele but still attractive with a firm, straight back. She smiled broadly at Peter, showing white teeth with a glint of gold.

"So you the watcher," she said, holding out her hand. "I'm Mele's mother."

He stood quickly and shook her hand.

"Mother, you know you're not supposed to be here," Mele said.

"And why not? Don't I have the right to be here? Aren't you my daughter?" She turned on the smile again for Peter. "What you think of our island?"

"Very beautiful."

"I bet you never see such beautiful place before."

He hesitated, uncertain what to say but not wanting to offend her. "Uh, yes, it's very beautiful."

"Why you here?" The smile vanished.

"To watch the wedding this afternoon."

"And why you do that? Don't they have weddings where you come from? You never see a wedding before?"

"Mother!" said Mele.

Her mother held up a hand for silence.

"Yes, of course they have weddings where I come from," Peter said. "And I've been to weddings before. But I'm interested in how weddings take place on Ni'ihau."

"Why?"

"Because it's the subject of my dissertation."

"What you mean—disser-tation?"

"A book, a paper I'm writing to finish my degree."

"Why you not find a wedding where you come from to write about? Why you come here?"

"Because weddings here are different from where I come from. I want to understand how they're different."

"Why?"

"Because they help me understand your culture."

"Why you need to do that? We don't care if you understand."

He looked at Mele for help, but she merely shrugged and left him at the mercy of her mother.

"Ha! You don't know," her mother said. "I thought so."

"But I do know," he objected.

She raised her hand again. "What your mother think about you coming to Ni'ihau?"

"My mother?" he said. "What's my mother got to do with this?"

"Just answer question. What your mother think about you coming to Ni'ihau? Why she let you do this?"

"Well, actually she wasn't in favor of me coming, but I don't see what that has to do with. . . ."

"Ha!" Mele's mother said. "Why you not listen to your mother?"

"Because I don't happen to agree with her. Besides, this has nothing to do with my mother."

"Children should listen to their mothers. It's important to respect your *kupuna*."

He glanced at Mele.

"Elders."

"Why you have to come here?" her mother asked. "Why can't you leave us alone?"

"I only want to watch," he said.

"Why?" she demanded again. "Are we so strange? Are we so different from *haoles*?"

"Of course not." This was a word he knew. Originally it had meant foreigner, but now it meant a white person. He was a *haole*.

Slightly mollified, she glanced at Mele. "What you think of my daughter?"

"She's very . . . nice."

"Ha! She's uppity Miss Know-it-all. It was mistake to send her to Kaua'i. I was against it. I said no good will come of this, but her father could not say no, and she beg him, and this is what happens."

"She doesn't approve of me being a guide," Mele explained. "In fact, she doesn't much approve of me in general."

"You can't deny it," her mother said, turning on her now. "Ever since you come back from Kaua'i, you've had your nose in the air."

"I have not."

"You think you too good for us."

"That's not true."

"Why you take him to church today? Tell me that! You had to show off, Miss Uppity, didn't you?"

"That was my fault," Peter said, trying to come to Mele's defense.

Her mother ignored him. "Why they make her a guide? Tell me that. Whoever heard of a girl guide?"

"They made me a guide because I asked to be a guide," Mele said.

"Did she tell you what happened to last guide?" her mother asked. "Did she?"

He looked at Mele, who had flung herself into the armchair and now was sitting, head thrown back, studying a spot on the ceiling.

"No, she didn't, did she? He was punished by Ukanipo." Mele's mother nodded significantly.

"Are you done now?" Mele asked. "Have you said what you came to say?"

"I have," her mother said. "You are swimming in dangerous water. You can laugh if you want, but I know what I know. Nothing good will come of this." Then her mother turned and marched out, as stately and dignified as a queen taking her leave.

"Sorry about that," Mele said when she was gone.

"What happened to the previous guide?"

"He went out in a canoe and never came back. People think sharks got him. Ukanipo is the shark god. Personally I like to think he made it to another island."

## 2

## Niʻihau, part 2

The wedding took place that afternoon in the little white church they had attended in the morning. At Mele's insistence Peter wore a blue and white flowered aloha shirt she had borrowed from one of her brothers. When she had seen the black suit he planned to wear, she had burst out laughing.

"You can't wear that," she had protested.

"Why not?"

"You look like you're going to a funeral, not a wedding. You're supposed to blend in."

"Then what should I wear?"

"I'll find something," she said, heading out the door.

Five minutes later she was back with the blue and white flowered aloha shirt.

He was glad now that she had borrowed it for him. Even sitting inconspicuously in the back of the church, he would have looked ridiculous in his black suit. The church was full of brightly colored shirts and dresses. Mele was wearing a long white and pink flowered dress that showed the curves of her body and had tucked an orchid behind one ear. Her bare arm brushed against him as they sat side by side in the last pew. He had brought along his camera, but he doubted he could get any good shots from where they were sitting and as a watcher he was not supposed to draw attention to himself or in any way interfere with the event so he couldn't exactly leap into the aisle or slip down front. Mele pointed out her family sitting farther up, but all he could see was the backs of their heads: her father, mother, and a row of stair-step children. The room buzzed with excitement until it was time for the ceremony to begin. There was a hush as the minister took his place at the altar and the groom and his best man took their places. The groom was wearing a flowered shirt and a braided lei of green ti leaves. He fidgeted nervously, consulting with his best man. Then the chords of the wedding march were struck on the old piano that stood to their right. All heads turned expectantly to watch the bride come down the aisle.

There was a collective "aah" as she appeared in the doorway. She wore a white muumuu with a lei of small white shells around her neck and another of white flowers crowning her dark hair. She was a pretty slender young woman who smiled radiantly as she walked slowly down the aisle on her father's arm.

The ceremony took place in Hawaiian, but this time Peter had no trouble understanding what was happening, especially since Mele whispered in his ear if she thought he might not understand. The wedding began with a blessing bestowed on the couple by a thick-bodied middle-aged man in a white shirt and white trousers with an orange lei around his neck. Mele told him this was a *kahuna*, a Hawaiian wise man. The minister then spoke about the solemnity of the marriage ceremony, and the couple said their vows and exchanged rings, just as they might have in a church wedding in Boston. The bride had a white flower tucked behind one ear, and when her new husband kissed her, he moved it to the other ear and everyone applauded wildly. The couple beamed as they walked back up the aisle hand-in-hand, and the guests tossed white flower petals at them.

Peter had hoped to get out of the church without having to talk to anyone, but that proved impossible. Almost at once they were surrounded by people who wanted to talk to Mele, and each time she insisted on introducing him. He couldn't very well be rude but tried to respond by merely nodding or shaking his head instead of talking. In that way he was interacting only minimally with the people.

He couldn't remember everyone she introduced him to. Many of the names were unfamiliar and confusing. He got the impression she was related to nearly every person there. She introduced them as aunties, uncles, or cousins. Most of them were speaking in Hawaiian, but sometimes he heard a word or several words in English.

As they left the church the wedding guests all seemed to be walking in the same direction—toward the ocean.

"Where are they going now?" he asked Mele.

"To the luau, of course. There's always a luau afterward."

"But I can't go to that," he objected. "I only have permission for the wedding."

"Don't be silly," she said. "If the Alliance gave you permission for the wedding, they gave you permission for the luau. It's part of the wedding. You can't very well write about the wedding if you don't go to the luau too. Ask anyone here. They'll tell you the luau is just as important as the wedding ceremony. It's unheard of to have just the wedding and no luau."

In the end he gave in and they joined the stream of gaily-dressed people flowing toward the ocean. As they walked along, she continued to introduce him to people. A boy of about thirteen ran up and spoke to her in Hawaiian. Peter got the distinct impression from the glances the boy threw at him that he was the subject of the conversation.

"You better watch out," the boy said to Mele in English before darting off.

"What was that all about?" Peter asked.

"Oh, don't pay any attention to him. That's one of my brothers."

"What did he say?"

"Nothing important."

"What did he mean—you better watch out?"

"Just forget about it."

He stopped, forcing her to stop too. "Is there a reason I shouldn't go to this luau?"

"This isn't really about you. Of course you should go. We should both go. We have a perfect right to be there."

Now he was worried. Were there going to be people at the luau who thought he was intruding? He didn't want any complaints to get back to the Alliance.

"Maybe we should go back," he said uneasily.

She stood even straighter, her eyes flashing defiantly. "You go back if you want. I'm going to the luau." She started walking again.

He didn't like to leave her like that, and so he fell in step beside her again.

"What's your brother's name?" he asked, trying to get past their little misunderstanding.

"Kimo," she said, eyes straight ahead.

"How many other brothers and sisters do you have?"

"I have three brothers, two sisters. That was one of my sisters, Lani, you met earlier today at the house."

"You're very lucky. I think it'd be great to be part of a large family." It was true. He had only one sister, his younger sister Susan. The eleven years difference in their ages had kept them from being close. He had always envied other people who had a lot of brothers and sisters.

She stopped suddenly and faced him. "All right, I'll tell you what he said. He said my boyfriend is going to be waiting there for me."

"Mano?"

"Yes, Mano."

He pictured a muscle-bound young man with a jealous disposition. He definitely didn't want to get into a confrontation with her boyfriend. "Then maybe I should go back."

"No," she said firmly. "I asked you to come. This is part of your research. This is what you're here for."

"I don't mind. I probably shouldn't go there anyway, and I don't want to cause trouble for you." He saw how it would look if he showed up at this local gathering with Mele. She was an attractive young woman and of course her boyfriend would be jealous if he saw her with another man. Why had the Alliance hired a pretty young woman to be a guide? Couldn't they have foreseen how awkward it could be?

"He has no right—" Mele said, anger in her voice. "We aren't married. He just assumes—"

Peter didn't know whether he should turn back or keep going. "Look, maybe this isn't such a good idea."

She put her hand on his arm. "Please come. Do this for me. I know you don't know me. I'm a stranger. After today you won't see me again. But do this one thing for me. I'll be forever grateful."

She was beautiful in her long white and pink flowered dress with the orchid tucked behind her ear. And those imploring eyes! How could he possibly say no? He would have had to be made of stone.

The luau took place on a nearby beach, where several long tables had been made by resting boards on sawhorses. Once there, he soon began to lose his qualms. The people were friendly, the food was plentiful, and there was beer to drink. A gentle breeze blew from the ocean, and the waves broke with soothing regularity along the shore. A pig that had been roasted in a pit was now the centerpiece on a table crowded with food. He had a choice of pineapple, papayas, bananas, and passion fruit. There was poi, which Mele told him to eat with his fingers, and yams and some kind of raw fish. She heaped his paper plate with far more than he could possibly eat, insisting he must try everything. People urged him to try the *opihi* and the *laulau*. Everyone seemed happy. Men clapped him on the back and women flirted with him. Even Mele's formidable mother seemed to thaw a little, and the boyfriend, a young man with tattoos on his arms, kept his distance, just glowering at him from time to time.

When they were done eating, Mele's father and several other men strummed ukuleles. Everyone fell silent while a young woman sang the Hawaiian wedding song in a high sweet voice that made Peter shiver. Then, barefoot, the bride danced a hula for her husband, her hands and body moving languidly as the waves crashed behind her. Peter thought it was one of the most beautiful sights he had ever seen.

After the sun went down, a fire was lit and there was more dancing. The younger children lay down on blankets and fell asleep.

"Let's go for a walk," Mele said, rising gracefully from the mat on which they had been sitting.

"Where to?"

"Just along the water."

It felt good to stand up and stretch his legs. No one seemed to notice them strolling away. For a few minutes they walked in silence on the wet packed sand in their bare feet. Every so often the water slithered over their feet or caused them to hop back out of reach.

"Now aren't you glad you came to the luau?" she asked.

"Yes," he said, looking out at the ocean and thinking how there was something so timeless about it. It had been flinging waves against the shore since long before he was born and would do so long after he was dead. It was terrifying and beautiful all at the same time. He thought he would always remember this moment. It was as if the world were holding its breath.

"What are you thinking about?" she asked.

"This, today, the wedding, your island—all of it."

"And tomorrow you'll leave and go back to your world."

"Well, not exactly. I have to go to some more Forbidden Places."

"What other Forbidden Places?"

He didn't know if he should tell her, but it seemed churlish not to after she had done so much to help him. What could it hurt?

"China. And then India, and Afghanistan, and Africa."

She sighed. "I wish I could go to places like that."

"Well, I'm only going because I have to. I need the field research to finish off my dissertation."

"You make it sound like a chore."

"It is, in a way."

"Then what happens afterward?"

"I go back home."

"To Boston."

"Yes, to Boston."

"To me Boston is as far away as the moon."

They both looked at the pale half-moon hanging over the ocean. The fire was farther down the beach now, but they could still hear the laughter and the music.

"I guess we should go back now," he said.

She gave another small sigh and turned back toward the fire.

As they approached, he saw that the crowd had thinned. The bride and groom had disappeared, but others were still celebrating. He turned his watch toward the fire to see it better. It was past ten.

"How much longer will it last?" he asked.

She shrugged. "Some of them will stay all night."

"Maybe we should leave. I have to get up early in the morning to catch the barge back to Kauaʻi."

He thought she would protest, but she didn't. Her mood had changed, and he wondered if something was bothering her. She seemed lost in her thoughts as they walked back to her bungalow. Just by the low rock wall that ran along the street outside her bungalow, she stopped.

"Look," she said, clutching his arm and drawing his attention to a profusion of large white flowers. That was strange—he hadn't noticed them before.

"What are they?"

"Night-blooming cereus. They only bloom at night. When morning comes, they'll be gone."

"They're beautiful."

"Can you smell them?" She took a deep breath.

"Yes." They had a strong perfume that scented the air and almost made him dizzy.

"Can we just stand here for a minute?" she asked.

"Of course." He felt magnanimous. In two weeks he would be back in Boston, and moments like this would seem unreal. They belonged to another world. The thought made him regret that his visit was almost over.

"Is it okay if I take a photo of them?" he asked.

"Why not?"

He hesitated. "Could I take a photo of you too?"

She stood beside the night-blooming cereus, and he photographed them together.

"Thank you for coming to the luau," she said.

"Thank you for persuading me to go." He no longer cared that he had violated the terms of the agreement. It had been worth it. Looking at her pale face in the moonlight, he had the urge to kiss her, just as if he were on a date back home, but he stopped himself in time. He felt as if he were still under the spell of the luau, as if the evening were somehow magical, but she might misunderstand, he told himself, and besides she had a boyfriend, a rather scary-looking boyfriend at that, and he had Rosemary waiting back in Boston.

So in the end they just said goodnight, and he went inside while she crossed the street to her grandmother's bungalow. Before going to bed, he jotted down his impressions of the wedding and the luau in his notebook. Even after he lay in bed in the dark, he felt too wide awake to fall asleep right away. He wondered what it would be like to live on this island, where the people were so warm and friendly, and everyone knew each other, in fact were practically all related to each other. It was so different from his world, an unspoiled Eden suspended in time. He fell asleep wondering if it was possible to just put his concerns aside, forget about the dissertation and not worry about getting a job when he finished, or marriage, or any of the rest of it.

"Peter, wake up. I have to talk to you."

Mele was standing beside his bed.

"What time is it?" he asked groggily. It was dark in the room except for moonlight streaming through the window. He looked at the clock beside his bed, wondering why the alarm had not gone off, and was surprised to see that it was only one o'clock. He didn't have to be at the dock until five. Why was she waking him in the middle of the night?

"It's not time to go yet, is it?"

"No, but I have to talk to you."

At one in the morning? What could be so urgent that it couldn't wait a few hours?

"Take me with you," she said, dropping to her knees beside the bed.

"What?" He was sitting up now.

"I want to go with you."

"I'm sure you don't mean that."

"I do mean it." She looked at him with shining eyes.

He wished she would get up off her knees. It was embarrassing. "Why would you want to leave? This is your home. You have family and relatives here."

She shook her head. "I don't care."

He knew she could not go with him and so he tried to reason with her. "You wouldn't like it out there in the modern world. It's an awful place. The stress. . . . Everybody rushing all the time. Traffic. Road rage. Crime. Lots of people would give anything to live in a place like Niʻihau."

"I could help you with your research. I'm a fast learner. I wouldn't be any trouble."

"I can't take you with me. It's out of the question. Besides, you said yourself, if you leave, you can't come back."

"I know that. I'll miss my family, my people. I'll miss Niʻihau, but if I stay here, I'll die. I have to leave this place. I want to learn things. I want to see other places. I want to go to college. Please, Peter, help me!"

Those desperate eyes, as if all her future depended on him.

"This is crazy," he said. "If you want to leave, can't you just go? Why involve me?"

"Because there's no way I can get off this island by myself. My mother and father would never give their permission. You have to take me with you. It's the only way."

He hated to disappoint her, but he had no choice. He couldn't possibly take her with him.

"You don't understand. It's not that simple. I doubt the skipper would let me take you on board. In fact, I'm sure he wouldn't."

"He would if we were married."

"What?"

Her eyes stayed fixed on his, two dark pools that he could drown in. "If we were married, he would let me go with you."

"I can't marry you," he said. This was insane. This couldn't be happening.

"Why not?" She said it like it was a perfectly reasonable solution.

"People don't get married just so they can leave home. Besides, you hardly know me." He did not add, and I hardly know you. Everything about this was so surreal. A beautiful woman on her knees beside his bed, begging him to marry her. He wondered what Professor Rinehart would say when he told him. *You got too close to the native people. You failed to maintain a professional distance.*

"Please. I'll die if I have to stay here. You have it in your power to save me."

If he could just get her to stop kneeling beside the bed like that. It was awkward. He swung his legs out of the bed and reached for his jeans on the chair.

"Besides, I'm engaged," he said, not looking at her as he pulled on his jeans and zipped up.

"I don't believe you."

"It's true. I am."

"Why didn't you tell me before?"

"I didn't think it was any of your business."

She lay down on the floor and stared at the ceiling. This was even worse than when she was kneeling.

"It's not so bad as that," he said. "Tomorrow you'll see everything differently."

"No, I won't. It'll be just like yesterday, and the day before that, and the day before that." Tears welled in her eyes.

He sat down on the bed and tried again to reason with her. "You would marry a complete stranger just to get away from here?" He couldn't imagine making such a choice. He knew Rosemary well and he still had doubts about marrying her. He had not told her so, but the thought of marrying her made him feel queasy. He assumed when the time came, he would do it. Probably all men felt nervous before they got married.

"You're not a complete stranger," she said. "In fact, I think I know you pretty well."

"After one day?"

"Yes." His irony was lost on her.

He looked at her as she lay there with her black hair spread around her head like a dark halo. He wondered how many men in his shoes would jump at her offer. In his whole life he had never had a girlfriend as beautiful as Mele. In fact, he had not had many girlfriends before Rosemary. He had been too busy studying, and he was not the sort of guy who attracted pretty women. He was not good at socializing, he wasn't witty, and he had two left feet on the dance floor. When he had met Rosemary, it had seemed meant to be. She was a scholar too. She understood him. She overlooked his shortcomings, which were many. They got along well together. Gradually they had fallen into a comfortable routine. They had only gotten engaged the month before. They had both agreed there was no reason to rush into marriage, but as Rosemary pointed out, after more than two years of dating, they weren't getting any younger, and if they wanted to have children, they should not put it off much longer. He agreed. As usual, her reasoning made perfect sense. They were going to set a date after he got back from his trip. Maybe around Christmas. Rosemary said that would give them enough time to get everything ready.

Even if he were free, what did he and Mele have in common? What would his parents say if he brought Mele home and introduced her as his wife? They would not approve. In fact, they would be appalled. He could almost hear his mother: *What were you thinking?*

"What are you thinking?" Mele asked. "Talk to me."

"I was thinking about my mother."

"She wouldn't approve of me?"

"Well, my mother—" He stopped. "No, I don't think she would."

She smiled. "And my mother wouldn't approve of you."

He smiled back. They might have been children who had found common ground. They were both oppressed by their parents. Was it so inconceivable that he and Mele should marry? Stranger things had happened to people. If Mele was his choice, his parents would have to accept her. With Rosemary his future stretched ahead predictably; with Mele it would all be unknown. It only took a little courage, like whitewater rafting or bungee jumping or skydiving, none of which he had ever tried, but who was to say he might not one day? And if this was the wildest thing he ever did, well, surely once in his life he could do something wild and unpredictable. Besides, didn't he have the right to marry whomever he wanted?

He reached his hand out to Mele, and still smiling she took it. It was that simple. She touched his hand to her cheek.

"So you'll do it?" she asked. "You'll marry me?"

He didn't trust himself to speak, so he merely nodded.

"Good."

He felt like he was in a dream. In a moment he would wake up. Or come to his senses. This couldn't really be happening. It was too strange.

"Quick," she said, sitting up. "Get dressed. We don't have much time."

He hesitated. Would she really go through with it? He wanted to ask her but was afraid it would break the spell. Let it last a little longer. Let him keep this feeling that his life was about to change in some weird and wonderful way. He would do whatever Mele asked. If she asked him to jump through fire, he would jump through fire. And so he pulled on his polo shirt and then his socks and shoes.

"What now?" he asked, turning to her.

Without a word she took his hand and led him out of the bungalow, past the night-blooming cereus, across the street to her grandmother's house. There were no streetlights, but they could see by the light of the moon. She was the one in charge now. He was content to let her make all the decisions. Where she led, he would follow. Inside, the house was dark, but moonlight seeped in through the windows and the open door. Mele led him to the old woman's bedroom.

"Tutu?" she called softly. "It's me, Mele."

Peter heard the old woman stir as he hung back in the doorway.

"Mele?" the old woman said, holding out her hand.

Mele took it. "I came to say good-bye."

"What time is it?"

"It's a little after one."

"Where are you going?"

"I'm leaving the island."

"Help me up."

"You don't have to get up, Tutu. I just wanted to say good-bye."

"Help me up," the old woman said again.

Mele helped her get out of bed and walk to a nearby chair, where she sat down. She was wearing a white cotton shift that made her look smaller and frailer than when Peter saw her before. Her iron-gray hair hung down in a braid.

"That's better," the old woman said. "Now what's this all about?"

"I'm leaving."

"And this couldn't wait for morning?"

"I'm leaving when the barge comes."

"Does your mother know?"

"No, she'd try to stop me."

"Are you going alone?"

"No, I'm going with Peter. You met him today. Don't you remember?"

"Ah, the watcher. The *haole* boy. Is he here?"

"Yes, Tutu."

"Young man, come here."

Peter came nearer and caught the gnarled hand she held out to him.

"Closer," she said.

He bent his head to her, and when his ear was close to her lips, she whispered, "Take good care of her."

"I will."

"Promise."

"I promise."

"We're going to marry," Mele said. "Everything will be okay, Tutu. I don't want you to worry about me."

"Go get the ring," she said. "I always wanted you to have it when you married."

"Don't, Tutu. You'll make me cry."

"Go get it. You know where it is."

Mele walked to the dresser and opened a drawer. She came back with an ornate gold ring.

"Give it to me," the old woman said, and Mele put the ring in her hand. The old woman turned it between her fingers, feeling it. Then she groped for Peter's hand again, found it, and pressed the ring into it. "Young man, you must put this on her finger and say these words after me. Aloha aku no, aloha mai no. Mau loa."

It was like a magic spell, he thought as, haltingly, he repeated the words and slipped the ring on Mele's finger.

"And now, Mele, it's your turn," the old woman said.

"Aloha aku no, aloha mai no. Mau loa," Mele said, looking into his eyes.

"Now kiss," the old woman said.

He bent down and kissed Mele's lips. They felt warm and soft against his. She had closed her eyes. Was that it? he wondered. Were they married now? Could it be this simple?

"I'll miss you, Tutu," Mele said, hugging the old woman.

"I want a hug from the young man too," the old woman said.

Peter felt awkward as he hugged her. She was so small and fragile. She used the opportunity to whisper in his ear again. "Remember, you promised."

His mind was churning as he walked back to Mele's bungalow to pack. She had stayed behind to help her grandmother back to bed. They were married. He still couldn't believe it. It had happened so fast. Maybe it was just a dream and he would wake up. I'm married, he kept repeating to himself. He had expected to feel different when the day came, but he felt no different, just dazed.

Soon Mele was there too, hastily packing a bag for herself. They said little, both feeling shy about their new relationship. He knew he ought to try again to talk her out of leaving, but he didn't want to spoil the moment. If she wanted to leave, didn't she have the right to? And if she wanted to leave with him, didn't she have the right to do that too?

Just before they climbed into the pickup, Mele paused to look back at her bungalow.

"Are you sure about this?" he asked. "It's not too late to change your mind. Only your grandmother knows. We could pretend it never happened."

She glanced down at the ring on her finger. "Are you having second thoughts?"

"No, not if you aren't." If she could walk away and leave her island and her people behind, why then he could step into the unknown too.

She drove them to the dock, where they slept a little in the pickup, her head on his shoulder, as they waited for the barge to come. It seemed strange to wake with her nestled against him. He tried to stay still so he wouldn't disturb her. It swept over him, the amazing wonder and strangeness of what had happened to him. This young woman so unlike himself had linked her destiny with his. She seemed terribly young and vulnerable as she rested her head on his shoulder. She trusted him and he must not let her down.

As he watched her, she stirred. Her eyes opened and she smiled at him.

"Is it time yet?"

As if in answer to her question, he heard the rumble of an engine and then saw the shadowy barge emerging from the inky darkness of the ocean. "Yes, it's time."

The skipper was skeptical when they said they were married. He didn't want to take Mele on board, not even when she showed him the ring.

"Anyone can put a ring on their finger," he said. "Anyone can say they're married."

"But we are," Peter insisted.

"Yesterday when I brought you over you weren't married, and today you say you are."

"That's right. I am."

"It's my grandmother's ring," Mele said, holding it out for the skipper to see. "She wouldn't have given it to me if we weren't married."

"Maybe you stole it," the skipper said. "How should I know?"

"I didn't steal it," she said, hurt.

"All I know is I could get in a lot of trouble taking you away from this island."

"I'm with my husband." She tucked her arm in Peter's. "I go where he goes. That's what married people do."

"You know, you can't go back once you leave."

"I know that," she said, lifting her chin. "I don't want to go back."

The skipper shook his head, giving up. "And you," he said to Peter. "You ought to be ashamed."

He grumbled, but in the end he took them back across the channel to Kaua'i.

# 3

## Boston, six weeks earlier

"This is a wonderful opportunity," Professor Rinehart said, touching the tips of his fingers together and looking at Peter over the rims of his glasses. "I envy you."

Peter had dropped by his office to give him the news. Final word had come through. He had received permission from the World Alliance for the Preservation of Cultural Customs to visit five Forbidden Places. The contract was signed and he had his flight schedule and hotel reservations.

"I remember my own field research among the Yanomami in the Amazon rainforest," Professor Rinehart said. "That was a very special time in my life. Nothing like that ever again. Of course it's a Forbidden Place now. With permission from the Alliance, anthropologists can go there. But it's not the same. I *interacted*. Can you imagine what that was like? I got to talk to the people—with the help of an interpreter of course—eat with them, really get to know them. I probably did irreparable harm without realizing it, but I learned so much!" He let out a happy sigh.

Peter waited patiently. He had taken several classes with Professor Rinehart and had heard a number of his Yanomami stories, some several times. They were interesting stories, but he always suspected there was more that the professor did not tell. So often there was that tantalizing little hint at the end that he was thinking of something he wasn't telling.

"Let me ask you something," Professor Rinehart said. "When was the last time you did something spontaneous? I mean, really spontaneous."

Peter tried to think of an answer, but before he could, Professor Rinehart continued: "It's what I most regret not having done enough of in my life. I should have been more spontaneous, gripped the bull by the horns, so to speak."

Peter listened respectfully. He wondered what Professor Rinehart was referring to. Did he mean doing something wild and crazy? Or did he mean just doing something without much thought? He had to admit he didn't usually do things that could be categorized as wild and crazy. He didn't think he saw the advantage to that. No, he wasn't the spontaneous type.

"Well, never mind," Professor Rinehart said, waving his hand. "You understand the rules, don't you? You don't want to violate the terms of the contract. They're very strict about it. That's how they preserve the past for future scholars. Without the Alliance's efforts, unique cultural customs would be lost in no time. It's invaluable what they're doing. Every bit as worthwhile as preserving gorillas and pandas. More really."

"I realize how lucky I am," Peter said.

"What does Rosemary think about this trip? She's a bright young woman. I'll bet she's one hundred percent behind you."

"Oh, she is," Peter assured him. "She thinks it's a great opportunity for me."

"Sometimes they don't," Professor Rinehart said.

"Rosemary's just as career-minded as I am," Peter said, wondering if there had been someone who did not approve of the professor's field research among the Yanomami. His wife? A girlfriend? He had recently divorced, but his field research in the Amazon had been years ago, and he might not have been married then.

"She seems like a fine young woman," Professor Rinehart said, although he hardly knew her, Peter could not help thinking.

"We're going to get married once I've got my Ph.D."

"Are you? Well, good for you. A young man needs a wife."

"We've gone together for two years."

"I understand. It's time to get married. You don't want to wait forever. You wait too long and then it's too late."

"That's what Rosemary says."

"I imagine you'll be wanting to start a family."

"That's right. Rosemary says we shouldn't wait much longer. Once a woman is past thirty. . . ."

"Oh, I quite understand. Ticking biological clocks and all that. Have you talked about how many children you want?"

Peter was touched that Professor Rinehart was interested in his future. His concern went beyond the dissertation. A sort of friendship had sprung up between them during this long period of working together on his dissertation. He felt comfortable enough with the professor to share his future plans. Yes, he and Rosemary had discussed children.

"She says we should have two—a boy and a girl."

"And you agree of course?"

Impossible to tell what he was thinking, the bright intelligent little eyes and benevolent smile.

"Yes, completely. It makes sense."

"Yes, it does. I see Rosemary looks ahead. Any idea how far apart you'll space these two children?"

For a second Peter thought Professor Rinehart was making fun of him, but no, there was only that look of mild amusement he so often had. He was just curious. After all, he had spent a lifetime studying courtship rituals and mating habits.

"Two years," Peter said. "That way they will be close enough in age to play together."

"Oh, yes, that's important. I suppose Rosemary thought of that?"

"As a matter of fact she did." Peter felt a little embarrassed, but why should he? Women thought more about these things than men, didn't they?

"She sounds like a remarkable young woman."

"There is one thing I wanted to ask you about," Peter said tentatively.

"Of course, ask away."

"I don't quite see how going to the Forbidden Places is going to help my dissertation. I know I'll be allowed to take some photos and ask a few questions if the local inhabitants don't object, but basically all I can do is observe, and since I'm not allowed to interact. . . ."

"Nothing matches up to field experience," Professor Rinehart declared. "It doesn't matter if all you can do is watch. It will bring these cultures to life for you in a way no amount of research in Mugar's stacks can. You'll see. When you write, it will be with the voice of experience. It will make all the difference."

Would it? Peter wondered as he navigated through traffic to get to the little restaurant where he was supposed to meet Rosemary. Every Wednesday they met at the Whistle Stop downtown to have lunch together. Rosemary liked it because it was close to where she worked and it had good salads. She was watching her weight.

Thirty minutes later he was seated across from her. Usually he hardly looked around him, but today he felt vaguely dissatisfied with everything. There were too many mirrors on the walls and he disliked seeing himself eating. It made him feel self-conscious. Also there were so many potted plants sitting about that he felt as if he were in a jungle, and the waiters never seemed to smile.

"Maybe next week we should try someplace new," he suggested as he glanced at the menu.

"Why?" Rosemary said. "We like it here."

It didn't seem worth arguing about so he let it drop. He was still mulling over his meeting with Professor Rinehart. He should have told the professor how he felt about the trip. He had intended to, but then face-to-face he just hadn't been able to explain how he felt. Professor Rinehart assumed he was thrilled about going to the Forbidden Places, but he wasn't. He knew he ought to be. It was a privilege. So few people ever got to see one. But it just seemed like a bother. What was the point? If he got to interact with the people, really study them, that would be different, but how much could he learn from just watching and taking some photos? And even the photos would be subject to many restrictions.

Rosemary tapped his hand with her menu. "Are you listening to me? I bet you haven't heard a word I've said."

"I'm sorry. What did you say?"

"I said I think they're going to let me help on that toxic dump case."

"That's great."

"I talked them into it. I told them they needed a woman

on the team. A woman's perspective. If they don't let me sink my teeth into these things, why then what was the point of taking me on?"

"So they agreed?"

She smiled, a look of satisfaction and triumph on her face. "The firm is kind of a boys' club, but that'll change."

He never ceased to be awed by Rosemary's ability to get what she wanted. For as long as he had known her—which now was about five years—she had been incredibly focused on her goals. She had just finished law school and was now a junior partner in an up-and-coming firm. She knew exactly where she was going—it was all planned out. She had it written down—a five-year plan and a ten-year plan. She had read somewhere that creating a plan was the way to achieve success. To leave your future to chance was to court failure. He had no doubt she was right. But forming a plan like that was exactly where he fell short. Planning ahead did not come easy for him. He worried that his plan could be wrong. What if he got five years down the road and decided it had all been a mistake? Maybe that's what was really bothering him right now. Not the trip to the Forbidden Places which Professor Rinehart had so painstakingly helped to arrange, but the dissertation topic—weddings. Why had he ever agreed to such a ridiculous topic? Professor Rinehart had suggested it when Peter had been stumped to come up with a topic, and it had seemed as good as any other at the time, so he had agreed. But now he saw it was all wrong. What did he hope to accomplish? Search committees would probably snicker when they read it on his resumé. But it was too late to change his mind now. He would just have to plow ahead and finish the damn thing, get his degree, find a job, and move on.

"Honestly, Peter. What are you thinking about? You're not

listening again. You're a million miles away." Rosemary tilted her head, looking slightly exasperated.

It occurred to him that he would be seeing her across a table from him for many years to come. He wondered how she would change. He couldn't imagine her any different than she was at this moment, her eyes resting on him in bemused contemplation, the little furrow between her eyebrows, her lips curved into a sardonic smile, her brown hair neatly framing her oval face. Was he really sure he wanted to marry her?

"Peter!"

"Sorry," he said, starting guiltily. "I keep thinking about my dissertation."

"Well, it's practically done, isn't it? You just have to visit those Forbidden Places, do a little revising, and defend the thing. Then you're done."

"You make it sound so easy."

"You're just having last-minute jitters. It's like how people get nervous right before they get married."

He looked down at his half-eaten sandwich, afraid to meet her eyes for fear she would read his thoughts. Was she right? Was he just having last minute jitters about the dissertation—and maybe about her?

"I just wish I didn't have to take this trip," he said.

"Do you know how many people would like to go where you're going? I don't see why you're complaining. If I had a chance like that, I'd jump at it."

"I wish you could go along." With Rosemary beside him, he felt his doubts would disappear. She would banish them with her practical no-nonsense approach to everything. It would be just a visit to cultural preservation sites and not a time when his mind would be free to question what he was doing there.

"That's sweet." She patted his hand. "But even if the Alliance would let me—which of course they won't—I couldn't take off right now, not when I've just gotten this chance to show the firm what I can do. And anyway you'll have your cell phone with you. When you're between places, we can talk."

"I suppose so," he said without much enthusiasm.

"Just think of it as a vacation."

By the time he got home that afternoon, he was thoroughly depressed. He just wanted to go to his room and take a nap before dinner. Unfortunately his mother heard him come in.

"Peter, is that you?" she called from the dining room when his foot was on the first step of the stairs.

"Yes, Mother." He paused with his hand on the smooth varnished wood of the stair rail.

His mother appeared in the dining room doorway, a magazine in her hand. She was wearing her pearls and a tailored green dress he had not seen before. As usual, she looked impeccable. Looking impeccable was something she worked very hard at and which required frequent visits to her hairdresser, manicurist, masseuse, and cosmetologist, not to mention many hours spent shopping in high-end fashion stores.

"Don't forget that the Bukowskis are coming to dinner tonight," she said.

That explained the pearls and the new dress.

"Again?"

The Bukowskis were friends of his parents. Ted Bukowski worked with Peter's father at AMG. He hated being present when the Bukowskis came to dinner. The talk was always of the DOW, the NASDAQ, and the S & P, of profits and margins.

"Well, it's our turn."

"Maybe I'll grab something out."

"You will not. What would they think?"

"I don't care what they think."

"Peter Hoenig! As long as you are living under this roof, you will act like you're part of this family. I expect you to be here for dinner."

He knew from experience it was useless to argue with his mother. And she was right about his living under her roof. He didn't want to, but until he finished graduate school and got a job, he couldn't afford a place of his own. He didn't like it, but that's the way it was.

"And change your shirt," she added. "Maybe wear your blue shirt."

He was twenty-seven years old and his mother was still telling him what to wear. How old did he have to be before she stopped supervising his wardrobe?

"Oh, there's mail for you by the door. Something from the World Alliance."

He turned back to the mahogany side table where the mail lay in a neat stack. The envelope on top was indeed from the Alliance. He picked it up.

"I suppose it's about that trip you're taking next month. Although why you want to go traipsing off to any place forbidden is beyond me. You'll probably come back sick with some awful illness that doesn't exist anywhere else. I'm sure those Forbidden Places are a breeding ground for germs. How could they not be without running water and electricity? I feel sorry for the people who have to live in them. I wouldn't want to live like that." She shuddered.

"Some people say the same thing about Boston," he muttered under his breath.

"I don't see why you chose that field." It was an opinion she had voiced many times before. "How do you ever expect to earn a living at it? You should be in management, like your father."

"I'll get a teaching job."

"Everyone knows teachers don't make much money. How will you support a family? Have you thought about that? Of course you haven't. You always have your head in a book. Oh, well, maybe Rosemary will make enough for both of you. I'm sure I don't know what she sees in you, but she sees something, so thank your lucky stars for that."

Peter fled upstairs. He didn't want to hear any more. He'd been hearing complaints about his chosen field for as long as he could remember. And it wasn't only from his mother. His father was just as bad. They both considered him a disappointment. Trying to persuade them that anthropology was a worthwhile field to pursue was a waste of breath. He would never convince them.

At least when he was married to Rosemary, he would not be living under their roof anymore and he wouldn't have to listen to his mother's complaints about his shortcomings.

They could pick on Susan for a change, he thought as he reached the top of the stairs. It would be her turn to take the brunt of their disapproval. Immediately he felt a twinge of guilt. He didn't really wish that on Susan, of course. But wish it or not, that was probably what would happen when he was gone. They would turn their attention to her, and it would be her future they would try to shape into their idea of success. He stopped at her bedroom door, which stood open. She was sitting in the middle of her bed, hunched over her laptop, earbuds in her ears, oblivious to the world. Poor kid, she had no idea what was waiting for her when he was gone.

He knocked, and she pulled the earbuds out.

"What's up?" she asked as he came in. Her blonde hair was pulled back in a ponytail, making her look even younger than her sixteen years.

"Did you know the Bukowskis are coming to dinner again?"

"Yeah, Mom told me. I have to wear a skirt." She made a face.

"I don't see why we have to have them over so often. They bore the hell out of me."

"I've got a theory about it. I think Mom invites them over because when they're here she and Dad don't fight. Must keep up appearances for the Bukowskis, you know."

Peter grinned. He liked his sister. She could always lift his mood. "You may be right about that. So what are you doing?"

"My homework. I'm writing a report about Machu Picchu."

"Machu Picchu?"

"Yeah, I want to go there someday. It's really neat."

"What's neat about it?"

"It's old, for one thing, and it's not like anything else in the world. It's one of the few places left by the Incas. They're gone but this place they built is left, and you can climb up to the top of it. That's cool."

"You like old things?"

She nodded. "I want to be an archaeologist, but don't tell Mom. I'll keep it from her as long as I can. I've seen how she goes on at you about your field."

"What's your opinion about the Forbidden Places?"

"What do you mean?"

"Do you think we should do away with them?"

She shrugged. "I wouldn't want to live in one, but it would be fun to visit. Why?"

"No reason. I guess I'm having second thoughts about my trip next month."

"You can send me in your place," she suggested. "I could dress up to look like you. Maybe no one would notice."

He grinned again. "You're a little short to pass yourself off as me. And your hair is a little too long."

"I could wear lifts and cut my hair." She twisted her ponytail into a ball to show him the effect.

"So, if you were me, you'd go?"

"In a heartbeat."

"I wish I could change my topic for my dissertation."

"Isn't it kind of late for that?"

"Yes. But I wish I'd chosen something else."

"Maybe it's fear of finishing. I've heard about that. People do all the work for their thesis or whatever and get almost to the end, but they can't finish."

"You think that's it?"

"Positive."

"How did you get to be so smart?"

"I suppose it runs in the family." She crossed her eyes and stuck out her tongue at him just like she had been doing since she was ten years old. He laughed.

# 4

# Honolulu

Mele had never flown before. She was as excited as a child about the prospect of boarding a plane. Peter, on the other hand, was a nervous wreck by the time they were strapped in for takeoff. His initial thrill at having Mele for his wife had now passed. She was not really his wife, he told himself. How could putting a ring on her finger in front of her grandmother and saying a few words in a language he didn't know possibly be binding? It was just more evidence of her naiveté that she accepted it as so.

He could not believe he had been so stupid as to get himself into this situation. What had he been thinking? And it wasn't just his own life he was messing up; it was Mele's too. He had taken her away from the only home she had ever known. She would probably end up hating him for that. He felt so guilty about it that he half expected to be challenged by every uniformed guard he saw as they entered the airport. Then when he tried to buy a ticket for her, he found the flight was sold out. Seeing his disappointment, the young woman behind the counter suggested she might be able to fly standby. He had his credit card out, ready to proceed when they hit the next snag. Mele had no ID. The young woman was polite but adamant: "She can't fly without an ID."

"What do we do then?" Peter asked. "She's from Niʻihau. They don't have ID's on Niʻihau."

"They must have something," the young woman insisted.

"Why?" Mele asked. "Everyone knows everyone else. We don't need a card which says who we are."

"Look, she's my wife," he said, and Mele held up her left hand so the young woman could see her ring. "I have to be on that plane, and she has to come with me."

"Do you have a marriage certificate with you?" the young woman asked.

"No," he admitted, the hopelessness of their situation looming before him. He supposed he would have to choose between leaving Mele behind in Lihuʻe or staying there with her. How would he explain *that* to Professor Rinehart?

In the end the young woman had to call for her supervisor, who in turn had to call his supervisor. Just as Peter was beginning to despair of getting on the flight, permission was granted.

Now they were in Honolulu, in Peter's room at the Ilikai. Mele was on the lanai leaning over the railing marveling at the droves of people walking by on the sidewalk ten floors below and the traffic.

"Let's go out," she urged, eyes shining with excitement.

He shook his head. "I have to make some calls first." He had been worrying all morning about how he would explain to Professor Rinehart about Mele. He was not looking forward to this call. And then he would have to let Rosemary and his parents know. He dreaded how they would take the news that he was married. He just hoped Rosemary would understand.

"Can't you make them later?" Mele asked.

"No, I need to do these now. Look, why don't you watch TV while I make my phone calls? I'll show you how the remote works."

"I don't want to watch TV. I want to go out."

"Well, I'm busy." He knew he sounded like a parent putting off an importunate child, but he couldn't help it.

She sighed. "Then I'll go out alone."

"No, it might not be safe."

"Why not?"

"You might get lost."

She laughed. "Don't be silly. I won't get lost."

"You might get hit by a car."

"I know about traffic lights. They had traffic lights on Kauaʻi."

"You might be robbed." How could he make her understand that there were dangers she couldn't dream of out there? She wasn't on Niʻihau anymore.

"I have nothing to take." She showed him her empty hands.

There was that ring, but why bother to mention it? He could see it was useless to argue with her. She couldn't conceive of the dangers of a modern city. He knew he should not allow her to go out alone. If anything happened to her, it would be his fault. But while he debated whether to go or stay, she breezed out the door. As soon as it closed behind her, he sank down on the sofa, relieved. It was the first time he had been alone since they had left Niʻihau. Now he would be able to make his phone calls in peace. He just hoped she didn't wander far from the hotel.

When they had arrived in Honolulu and he had retrieved his cell phone from the airport locker, he had told himself he would wait until they got to their hotel room before he made his calls. Now he could postpone making them no longer. He had to tell Professor Rinehart about Mele. Otherwise, he wouldn't be able to make arrangements for her to go with him to the other Forbidden Places.

When Professor Rinehart answered, he wanted to know all about Peter's visit to Ni'ihau. Peter told him as much as possible, omitting all mention of Mele.

"Well, good luck at Yunnan Province," the professor said. "I really envy you this opportunity. If I were a young graduate student, it's just the sort of thing I'd like to do. Make the most of it. You may never get an opportunity like this again. And remember what I said about spontaneity."

"Right," Peter said, screwing up his courage. "There's just one more thing. I was wondering, is it possible to arrange for a second air ticket? I would pay for it of course, but I'd like to take someone along."

"To Yunnan Province? I really don't think—" The professor stopped. "Who? Who do you want to take along?"

"You see,"—he took a deep breath and closed his eyes—"I met this girl on Ni'ihau. Actually she was my guide."

"Your guide?"

"We sort of got married."

"You *what*? Did you say you got married? Did I hear that right? Good heavens. You're not supposed to interact with the locals. Oh, my god. I can't believe this. You of all people. You did say married? Wait a minute. Does Rosemary know about this?"

His stomach sank. "No, I haven't told her yet."

"Well, you'd better. I don't think she's going to be too happy about it."

"So you'll make the arrangements?"

"I'll see what I can do. But I'm not making any promises. Married! You've got a certificate and everything?"

"Well, no. It was sort of informal."

There was a short silence on the other end of the line. "You do realize you've put the college in an extremely awkward position? The next time one of our students wants to visit Niʻihau, we could be refused because of what you've done. The Alliance takes its commitment to preserving these cultural sanctuaries very seriously."

"I know that," Peter said, feeling miserable. "I didn't mean for this to happen."

"They may rescind permission for you to travel to the other sanctuaries."

That hadn't occurred to him. If he could not complete his research, he might not be allowed to finish his dissertation. And if he didn't finish his dissertation, how could he get a job in his field? Why hadn't he thought about that before? Had he jeopardized his whole future by one reckless act?

"I'll see what I can do," Professor Rinehart repeated. "Let me talk to the Alliance people, and then I'll get back to you."

Peter felt depressed after the call ended but thought he might as well get the call to Rosemary over too. Sooner or later it had to be done, and it was probably better to do it while Mele wasn't there.

As the phone rang on the other end of the line, he tried to think how to break the news to Rosemary that he was married. Should he blurt it out or build up to it gradually? If he blurted it out, he would get the worst over all at once, but if he could build up to it gradually, it might seem more understandable. Maybe she would even see the humor in it. He had blundered into this marriage the way he had blundered into a dozen other awkward situations. *Oh, Peter,* she would say. *You're hopeless.* No, he doubted she would see any humor in it. In fact, she would probably be angry at him. Certainly she had a right to be. If she shouted at him, he deserved it, although Rosemary hardly ever shouted. And if she cried? Oh, god, he thought, please don't let her cry.

His heart stopped as a little click indicated the pickup and Rosemary's familiar voice greeted him. Then, a wave of relief swept over him as he realized he had gotten her voice mail, not Rosemary herself. He took a deep breath.

"Hi," he said after the tone. "It's me, Peter. I'm back from Niʻihau. Back in Honolulu, that is. Everything went smoothly. You were right about the food on the plane. It was pretty awful. Listen, there's something I have to tell you, but I don't exactly know how to begin." Get it out, he told himself. Otherwise, her voice mail will cut you off and you'll have to do it all over again.

There was another click. "Peter?"

At the sound of her voice he panicked and pushed the end-call button, then dropped his cell phone as if it had bitten him. He stared at it lying there on the bed. Then it began to play its insistent little ringtone. He made no move to pick it up. It had been bad enough trying to put the message on her voice mail; he was not ready to deal with Rosemary herself. The enormity of what he had done hadn't struck him until he had to make that call. Rosemary expected to marry him. He had let her down. He had *betrayed* her. She would hate him now forever. She would tell everyone that he was some sort of monster. And it would be true.

Of course he knew he should pick up the phone, confess what he had done, and let her rant. If there were going to be a scene, he should get it over with. But he couldn't bring himself to. After several minutes of listening to his cell phone ring, he fled from the room, leaving the offending object on the bed. He rode down the elevator, which was packed with tourists, then hurried through the lobby and out into the sunshine. People were striding past, cars rushing by. He was surrounded by noise and bustle and life. At once he felt better. The world was going on without any concern about what he had done. Maybe it wasn't so terrible after all. He hadn't murdered anyone. He had just gotten married. People did it all the time.

He looked around him. So where had Mele disappeared to? Now that he was outside, he supposed he ought to look for her before she got into any trouble. He looked first one way, then the other down the street and realized that it might not be easy to find her among so many people, so he simply picked a direction and set off walking. Maybe she would vanish, he told himself. Maybe she would just walk out of his life as suddenly as she had walked into it. She had wanted to escape her island and he had helped her do that. Now she was free. She could go wherever she wanted and do whatever she desired. She didn't need him anymore. Mission accomplished. He looked about him and tried to think what Waikiki must look like through her eyes. There were so many shops, restaurants, and hotels,. so many tourists, so much traffic. Would she have headed toward the beach, attracted by the sand and the sunbathers and the ocean? He scanned the people, trying to catch a glimpse of her. There were lots of women with long black hair like Mele's, but when he caught up with them or they turned, they weren't her.

Finally just as he was about to give up and walk back to the hotel, he spotted her across the street under a palm tree talking to an old homeless man pushing a grocery cart filled with plastic garbage bags. He felt relieved that he had found her but uneasy too. Why was she talking to a homeless man? He waited impatiently for the light to change.

"Oh, Peter, I'm so glad you've come," she said as he came loping up. "Can you give this man some money? He needs some change for coffee, and I don't have any."

Reluctantly Peter pulled out his wallet and handed the old man a five-dollar bill. He didn't ordinarily give money to homeless people, but he didn't want Mele to think he was stingy.

The old man stood blinking at the bill a minute with rheumy eyes before he tucked it into the pocket of his dirty shirt. Maybe he expected more.

Peter took Mele's arm and pulled her away. "You should be careful of people like that."

She looked back at the old man, still standing there. "Why? He seemed very nice. He said he was related to Queen Liliuokalani."

"And you believed him?"

"Why shouldn't I? Lots of my people are related to each other."

"I really don't think he was related to Queen Liliuokalani."

She tossed her head. "If I'd had some money, I'd have given it to him."

He saw there was a lot he was going to have to teach her. "You can't give money to every homeless person you meet."

"Why not? If they don't have money, and we do, we should share it with them. That's what we do on my island. Everybody helps someone who needs help."

"You're not on Niʻihau now. Besides, there are too many of them."

"That's because too few people share what they have. If everybody helped people like that old man, he would always be able to buy a cup of coffee."

Convincing her was not going to be easy. "It isn't that simple."

She shook off his hand and walked with a small space between them, letting him know she disagreed. She was like a child, he thought; she knew nothing of the world. He would have to guide her; he would have to explain everything. He just hoped she would be willing to listen. Maybe he should have kept his mouth shut. When he had given money to the old man, she had been pleased with him. He should not have said anything after that. If she stayed with him, there would be time later for her to learn about things like the problem of homeless people.

She hardly spoke all the way back to the Ilikai. They rode up the elevator in silence while a married couple with two children argued about whether to go to the beach or the zoo. The first thing he noticed when they were back in their room was his cell phone lying in the center of the bed, where he had dropped it. Almost at once the ringtone began again, as if the phone sensed they had walked into the room.

"Aren't you going to answer it?" Mele asked when he made no move to pick it up.

His mind cast about for a plausible excuse to offer her, but he could think of nothing. She was watching him with curiosity, and his caller appeared unwilling to give up. Reluctantly he reached for it.

He was expecting the call to be from Rosemary, so he was flooded with relief when Professor Rinehart's voice came on instead.

"Well, it's not going to be easy," the professor said, "but I think I just may be able to swing it so that you can take this young woman—your, uh, wife—with you to Yunnan Province."

"And to the other Forbidden Places too?"

"Yes, of course. We can't very well leave her stranded in

Yunnan Province, can we? It will take some fixing, but I managed to persuade the Alliance to let you do this—although they kept reminding me that it's most irregular—*and* against their better judgment. But if she really *is* your wife...."

"She is. I told you—"

"Now this is what you'll have to do," Professor Rinehart interrupted. "You'll have to get a license and be married by a justice of the peace or city clerk or someone like that and get it registered. That's the only way they'll let her go with you. I think it's a perfectly reasonable stipulation on the part of the Alliance. They're being very accommodating. I hope you realize that."

Peter glanced at Mele, now sitting on the edge of the bed. He was not at all sure she would agree to the Alliance's demand. She might be insulted if anyone hinted the ceremony with her grandmother had not been legal.

"Well? Are you willing to do this? Because if you're not—"

"I need to talk to Mele first."

"Who? Oh, the young lady, of course. Well, I don't see why she should have any objection. If you two really want to be married to each other, what does it matter if you go through it again? Besides, she surely won't want to stand in the way of your career. Explain it to her. Make her see how important this trip is for you. It's your research. It's your future. Everything you've worked for depends on this."

"I'll call you back." He pushed the end call button before Professor Rinehart could say anything else.

Mele was still watching him. He couldn't read her expression. Curious? Disapproving? Amused?

"That was my adviser. He said you can go with me to the other Forbidden Places if we get married again in a civil ceremony."

"What's a civil ceremony?"

"We go to City Hall and get a license and it would all be very official."

"But we're already married. Why does he want us to do it again?"

"It's not him. It's the Alliance. They want us to make our marriage official."

"Now it's not official?" Her dark eyes studied him. He had no idea what she was thinking.

He looked away. "Apparently not."

She got up, stretched, and walked to the window, where she stood looking out.

"I'm sorry," he said. "You don't have to do this."

"But if I don't, I can't go with you. Isn't that right?"

He hesitated. "Are you sure you want to go with me?" There, he had said it.

She turned to look at him, the blue sky and sunlight behind her. He was struck again by her tropical beauty. Surely she wouldn't want to stay with him. She could have dozens of guys. Why would she want to be married to him?

"What do you mean?" she asked, a slight furrowing of her forehead.

He had to be sure she understood the enormity of the step she was taking. "Maybe it's a mistake for us to get married. We're so different, Mele. We're from different worlds. How can I take you away from here?"

"You're my husband," she said simply, lifting her chin. "I go where you go."

"You don't understand. I'm trying to tell you that you're free. You can do anything you want. You can go back to your island. It's not too late. Or you could stay here in Honolulu and start a new life."

"I want to go with you," she said stubbornly.

"Are you sure?" Somehow it seemed far more complicated now than it had the night before on her island when she had asked him to marry her. He felt panic rising within him. Even if she felt sure, he didn't. Not by a long shot.

"We will do the civil ceremony. Then it will be official and I can go with you." Her matter-of-factness calmed him. If she could treat this so sensibly, maybe he could too. It was just a minor technicality to overcome so she could go with him. There was no reason to blow it out of proportion.

In order to be married in a civil ceremony, first they had to have a marriage license. This turned out to be a problem because of Mele's lack of an ID, so they spent the rest of the morning and part of the afternoon wandering from one government building to another, tracking down a birth certificate for her, and having her photographed and fingerprinted for a state ID, before finally satisfying the requirements for the marriage license.

It was three o'clock in the afternoon when they joined the line of couples waiting to be married at City Hall. At least ten couples were ahead of them. One young couple near the front of the line stopped talking every few minutes to lock lips in a steamy kiss. Several couples behind them, a short woman with a pink hibiscus tucked behind her ear and a tall man in an aloha shirt were engaged in a heated argument. Peter felt nervous as they waited in line. He was afraid something would go wrong at the last minute. It would turn out they didn't have all the necessary documents, or they would run out of time and be told to come back the next day, which would be too late since the plane left late tonight. He kept glancing at his watch, knowing the office would close at 4:30.

At last it was their turn.

"Next," called an impassive-faced male clerk.

Peter handed across their papers and ID's, and the clerk looked through them in a bored fashion. He explained the ceremony in an equally bored voice, then said, "Ready?" and glanced from one to the other.

Mele slipped her hand in his. Maybe she was as nervous as he was, but there was no time to think about that now. He had to concentrate on what the clerk was saying.

"Peter Hoenig, do you take Mele Keaulana to be your lawfully wedded wife?"

"I do," Peter said, hoping his voice didn't betray his nervousness.

"Mele Keaulana, do you take Peter Hoenig to be your lawfully wedded husband?"

"I do."

"All right, by the authority vested in me by the State of Hawaii I pronounce you man and wife. Sign here." He pushed a form at them and pointed where they should sign.

"That's it?" Peter said after they had signed. He could not believe they had gone to so much trouble for something that was over in less than a minute. He was not sure what he had expected, but this was so brief and impersonal that he didn't feel much more married than he had when Mele's grandmother had asked him to slip her ring on Mele's finger.

"That's it," said the clerk. "Next."

"That was fast," Mele said as they went out the door. She touched her ring as if to reassure herself that it was still on her finger.

Peter felt he ought to apologize. It seemed a shabby way to get married. He wished they had not had to do that. But at least they were officially married now, and they had a marriage certificate to prove it. Mele would be able to accompany him to Yunnan Province.

"Look," she said as they walked to the bus stop. She pointed at a quaint old stone church where a wedding had just finished. The guests in their finery were still milling about. The bride, a young Japanese woman in an elegant white wedding gown and veil, was posing for a photographer in front of a green hedge, her bouquet clasped in her hands.

"They're probably tourists," he said. "I think a lot of people come here to get married."

"She's very beautiful."

Peter took Mele's hand and squeezed it. He wondered if she regretted that they had not had a wedding like that.

# 5

# Yunnan Province

At the Kunming airport a young Chinese man dressed in an immaculate white suit and sporting a Rolex on his wrist was holding a sign with Peter's name on it as they came out of customs.

"I guess you must be our guide," Peter said, shifting his bag to his left hand so he could shake hands. The young man ignored his hand.

"You are Peter Hoenig?"

"Yes, and this is Mele, my wife."

"Wife?" The young man frowned and consulted a paper he whipped from his pocket. "There was no mention of a wife."

"Well, no, not originally. It happened very suddenly. But it's been cleared with the Alliance."

The young man shook his head. "The arrangement was for one person."

"But that was before I got married. Now it's for two. Look, why don't you call the Alliance and ask them?"

"I will," the young man said stiffly. He pulled out a cell

phone, turned his back to them, and a moment later began speaking rapidly in Mandarin.

"Don't worry," Peter told Mele. "I'm sure everything will be okay. It's just a little misunderstanding."

He wasn't sure she had heard him. It was crowded and noisy in the terminal, and she was looking around at all the people with wide-eyed curiosity. She seemed content to let him work out their problems. He just hoped he could work them out. What if their guide refused to take them to the Forbidden Place? They couldn't very well go there on their own. He had no idea how to find it since its exact location was a closely guarded secret, and even if they could find it, they would never be allowed to enter without permission from the Alliance. Nor would they get very far without an interpreter.

The more he thought about it, the more nervous he became. Five minutes passed, and then ten. Finally the guide ended his call and slipped his cell phone back into his pocket.

"They don't like it, but they say your young lady friend may accompany you if you will agree that she is not to interact with anyone in the Forbidden Place at any time."

"She's not my young lady friend," Peter said. "She's my wife. And don't worry. She knows the rules. She's a guide herself, or was, I mean, before we got married."

The young man, who had scarcely glanced at Mele so far, now shot her a look of disapproval. Peter immediately regretted having said anything about her background as a guide.

"Follow me," the young Chinese man said coldly.

He led them out of the terminal and into a parking structure. After a brisk walk they came to a shiny red compact. After packing their bags in the trunk, Peter and Mele squeezed into the back seat, their guide slid behind the wheel, and they were off. Their guide was wearing dark glasses, and every time Peter glanced in the rearview mirror he had the impression the young man was watching them, but since he couldn't see his eyes, he couldn't be sure. In any case, it made him uncomfortable.

"Have you been a guide for long?" Peter asked after they had been riding in silence for a while. He had hoped Mele would say something, but since she seemed absorbed in watching the outskirts of the city slip past, he would have to be the one to speak.

"I have been a trusted servant of the Alliance for almost two years," the guide said with obvious pride.

"Then you've been to the Forbidden Place lots of times?"

"No one has been there lots of times. It isn't the Great Wall or the Forbidden City. Only a privileged few ever see it."

"I understand."

"It is a great honor to be allowed to visit the Forbidden Place. Very few foreigners are allowed to see it."

"We know that and we appreciate the opportunity to visit."

"You must realize how rare this place is. It preserves old customs that don't exist anywhere else in China today."

"My field is anthropology. I'm quite aware of the value of the Forbidden Places."

"Then you are aware of how important it is that you do not interact with the people of this place. While we are there, you speak only to me. You say nothing to them."

"Of course."

"If they only speak Chinese," Mele pointed out, evidently deciding to join the conversation, "they won't understand us even if we speak to them."

"You must not speak to them," the guide said sternly.

"Did I not make myself clear? You're not supposed to talk to the people. It's strictly forbidden."

"We won't," Peter assured him. "We understand the rules."

"You must be invisible. You can only watch."

"We understand."

Mele grinned at him, slipped her arm in his, and entwined their fingers. They were in league against their guide.

"You aren't married, are you?" she asked, addressing the back of the guide's head.

"My marital status is of no consequence."

Peter looked down at her hand, slender, smooth, graceful, with her grandmother's ring on her finger. In comparison his own hand seemed overlarge and pale. Again he was struck by the wonder and strangeness of their union. As yet their marriage had not even been consummated since they had been so pressed for time. Their first night hardly counted; they had spent what little of it they had sleeping in Mele's pickup. The next day, back in Honolulu, they had had to rush about getting everything in order for the civil ceremony at City Hall. Then it was off to the airport to catch their flight to China. There had been no time for anything more. And even if there had been, he wasn't sure anything would have happened. They still felt too awkward with each other. They needed to get to know each other better. He would just be patient. Eventually they would be alone together and nature would take its course. Meanwhile this journey would serve them as a sort of honeymoon, and after all, how many people got to spend their honeymoon in a Forbidden Place?

\* \* \*

At midday they stopped to eat at a noodle shop in a small village. Then it was back in the red compact to endure more miles of the rugged terrain. Not that it wasn't scenic. There were green mountains, meandering rivers, and placid lakes. Sometimes they passed villages. Peter gave up asking how much longer it would be. Their guide, whose name they had learned by now was Yang Yi, stubbornly refused to tell them, as distrustful as if they had been foreign spies.

As it grew dark, Mele fell asleep against his shoulder, and he had to wake her when the car finally arrived at the remote village which was their destination. All they could see was the wall that had been built around it and a high wooden gate guarded by sentries in a small guardhouse. At least it had tighter security than Ni'ihau, Peter told himself.

Yang Yi parked the red compact in a dirt clearing where a dozen other cars were parked.

"We must walk the rest of the way," he announced. "No cars are permitted inside."

"Whose cars are those?" Peter asked.

Yang Yi shrugged. "How should I know? People who must come and go, like the guards."

Peter only saw two guards. That would not account for all the cars.

"But people inside the village don't leave, do they?"

"Of course not. I don't know whose cars these are. Whoever they belong to, it is not the people of the village, I assure you. And now will you kindly wait here a minute?"

Yang Yi climbed out, walked to the back of the car, and opened the trunk.

"What's he doing?" Mele asked.

"I don't know. Getting something from the trunk, I suppose."

"Can we get out now?"

"I think he wants us to wait."

But Mele apparently didn't want to wait. She flung open her door, stepped out, and stretched. Once she was out, Peter thought he might as well get out too. As he stood, he was surprised how stiff he felt from having been cramped up so long in the small car.

Yang Yi was standing by the trunk wearing a black traditional Chinese jacket, loose-fitting trousers, and a small black cap. With lightning speed he had transformed himself into a figure out of the past.

"If you have a cell phone or tape recorder, you must give them to me now," he said. "You are permitted to use a small camera if you use it discreetly, but you are not allowed to take any recording devices or other modern technology into the compound."

Peter had expected this. He pulled his cell phone from his bag and handed it to Yang Yi, who dropped it into the trunk. "That's all I have."

"And her?" Yang Yi threw a stern look at Mele.

"I don't have anything," she said.

"Fine." He closed the trunk. "Now we will enter the Forbidden Place. Remember—no talking. You must be invisible to the people who live behind that wall."

Peter picked up their bags and they followed Yang Yi. After he showed the guards their papers and took care of all the protocol, the gate was opened for them. Once inside, he led them through a maze of narrow streets past shadowy houses and high walls until they came to a large wood door flanked by a pair of Chinese stone lions.

"They guard the entry from evil spirits," Yang Yi explained.

He knocked on the door with the large knocker, and soon an old servant woman carrying a lantern opened the door for them. Inside all was still. The cluster of buildings that made up the compound might have been deserted. Were the people sleeping? Peter wondered. Or were they watching their visitors without being seen? The old servant woman handed Yang Yi her lantern, then shuffled away. He led them through a narrow open-roofed passageway, motioning them to follow as he opened another door. They stepped into a small room furnished with a low divan, a bed, a small vanity with a mirror, a black lacquered wardrobe, and a folding screen decorated with cranes.

"You must not leave this room or talk to anyone until I return in the morning," he told them. "In the morning someone will bring clothes for you to wear while you're here. You can't go around dressed like that."

"All right," Peter said.

Yang Yi cast a distrustful look at Mele.

"We'll be fine," Peter assured him. "Don't worry."

"And don't forget to put out the lantern," Yang Yi warned, setting it down near the door.

"We won't."

With a last reluctant look around the room, their guide turned and let himself out.

"Did he lock us in?" Mele asked.

"I don't think so." Peter opened the door an inch. "No."

"Well, here we are at last. Do you suppose there's a bathroom?"

"There must be something." He was eyeing the bed. He saw right away that it would be impossible for him to sleep in. It had not been made for a six-foot tall American. Nor would the divan give him space to stretch out. He would have to sleep on the floor.

"I wonder where that goes," Mele said, noticing a door on the other side of the room. "Do you think there might be a bathroom there?" Even as she spoke she was crossing the room.

"Don't—" Already she had opened it. He could feel cool night air waft into the room like a ghostly presence.

Mele turned her head and smiled at him. "Don't you want to know what's on the other side?"

"Yang Yi said we're supposed to stay in this room," he reminded her.

She shrugged. "You can stay here if you like, but I'm going to see what's out there." She stepped out into the darkness, leaving the door standing open.

Peter groaned. This was going to be more difficult than he had thought. Mele was not used to repressing her impulses. He told himself he had better go with her and make sure she didn't get into any trouble.

Following her out the door, he found himself in a small courtyard drenched in moonlight. He saw potted plants, large white flowers in bloom, and the smooth surface of a pool reflecting the moon like a mirror. Beside the pool knelt Mele, trailing her fingers in the water.

"Isn't it beautiful?" she breathed. "Now aren't you glad we looked on the other side?"

She looked like a fairy or a princess under an enchantment. As she rose, he kissed her. He thought he felt her shiver. Her eyes were closed and her face still lifted to his when he dared to look. Then an expression of alarm swept across her face and her eyes sprang open. She stared at the wall beyond the pool.

"What's wrong?" he asked, his heart racing.

"Did you hear that?"

"What?" His eyes strained to detect any sign of movement.

Maybe they were not alone. Maybe someone else was there, hiding in the shadows.

"I thought I heard someone crying."

He listened hard. "I don't hear anything."

"It's gone now."

"You're shivering."

"It's a little cool," she admitted. "Not like Niʻihau."

"Let's go back inside."

She looked at the wall again, hesitating. "All right."

When they were back in the room, she sat down cross-legged on the bed and hugged herself. "Do you think it could have been a ghost?"

He stifled the impulse to laugh. "There are no such things as ghosts." Then he wondered if she believed in ghosts.

"I'm sure I heard someone crying," she insisted.

"Maybe it was a cat."

"No, it wasn't a cat. I know what cats sound like. And I didn't just imagine it."

"Well, it wasn't a ghost."

He would have sat down beside her and taken her in his arms, but he was not sure she wanted him to. Her mind was not on him; she was brooding over what she thought she had heard.

"It was such a sad sound. A lonely sound. Someone all alone and crying."

Maybe it was her own loneliness that had made her think she heard someone crying. He had taken her away from her island and her family. In the dark night, far from home, she was missing them.

She took a deep breath. "We still haven't found the bathroom," she reminded him, her eyes roaming around the room. Spotting a narrow paneled door on the other side of the room, she hopped off the bed and went to it.

He followed her and looked over her shoulder as she opened the door. In a small space the size of a closet there was a single toilet sunk in the floor.

"What is it?" she asked.

"A squat toilet. You have to—"

"Never mind." She pushed him back. "I'll figure it out."

After they had taken turns using the squat toilet, Peter suggested they try to get some sleep since tomorrow would be a busy day.

Mele looked dubiously at the bed. "It's very small, isn't it?"

"I'll sleep on the floor."

She nodded and stretched out on the bed.

"You're not sorry, are you?" she asked, shooting him an anxious glance.

"No, of course not."

She nodded, satisfied, and laid her head down on a small silken pillow. Within minutes she was fast asleep. It had been a long tiring ride and she was exhausted, he thought as he pulled an embroidered coverlet over her. Then he put out the lantern, stretched out on the floor with his jacket folded under his head for a pillow, and soon fell asleep himself.

He was woken in the morning by Mele shaking his shoulder.

"Wake up. We have clothes to put on." She held up a blue silk dress and a black robe.

"Where did they come from?" he asked, raising himself on his elbows. He felt stiff from sleeping on the hard floor.

"I don't know. When I woke up, they were here."

"Someone must have brought them while we were sleeping." He said that to keep her from jumping to the conclusion that anything supernatural was involved in the sudden appearance of the clothes. However, she seemed uninterested in where they had come from. She had already ducked behind the folding screen and was putting on the dress that had been laid out for her. He glanced at his watch. It was 6:30. He wondered what time Yang Yi would show up.

"How do I look?" Mele asked, emerging from behind the screen in a clinging blue silk dress with a small high collar, her long black hair cascading down her back.

"Beautiful."

She surveyed herself in the small oval mirror over the vanity table. "Do I look Chinese?"

"Well—"

"Put yours on," she urged. "Don't you want to see how it looks?"

He would have preferred to wear his own clothes, but he knew he had to abide by the rule to blend in as much as possible with local customs of dress. It was in the contract he had signed. All the same, he knew the minute he saw the black robe and trousers that he was going to look ridiculous. He groaned inwardly but told himself he had no choice. He would have to wear the outfit no matter how ridiculous it made him look. However, he was not going to undress in front of Mele. He stepped behind the screen as she had to change. When he came out a few minutes later, she burst out laughing.

"That bad?"

"I'm sorry. It's just that you look so funny."

"I have a feeling these clothes belong to someone at least six inches shorter than me," he said, catching sight of himself in the small oval mirror. His wrists and ankles stuck out awkwardly.

"Maybe we can ask if they have something else for you to wear," she said, still smiling. "Shall I go look for someone?"

"No. We're not supposed to leave the room until Yang Yi comes back. Remember?"

She made a pouting expression. "I'm hungry. They'll give us something to eat, won't they? When watchers came to Niʻihau, I always made sure they got fed."

As if in answer, there was a light knock at the door. When Mele opened it, a servant woman bowed to them, her eyes on the ground.

"Oh, we're so glad you've come," Mele said.

"She doesn't understand English," Peter reminded her. "And besides we're not supposed to talk to her."

He might as well have saved his breath. Mele wasn't listening to him.

"Too short," she said, lifting his arm and showing the woman his exposed wrist. She pointed at his ankles. "Too short."

The woman glanced at him uncertainly.

Having made her point about his clothes, Mele moved on to her next concern. "Food?" she asked hopefully, making the motions of eating and drinking. He marveled at how well she could communicate without knowing a word of the language.

The servant bowed and shuffled away. Within five minutes she was back with two bowls of rice and tea on a lacquered tray. Mele thanked her with words and hand gestures, and after bowing, the woman shuffled away again.

Mele lost no time digging into her bowl of rice. She ate like an eager child, Peter thought, watching her use the chopsticks, then give up and use her fingers instead. He had to admit the rice tasted good. The tea was wonderful too. He could feel it warm his insides as it went down.

They were just finishing their meal when the door flew open and Yang Yi burst in. He was wearing the same black cap, jacket, and trousers he had donned outside the wall the night before.

"We have a problem," he announced dramatically after closing the door.

Peter thought he was about to be rebuke them for having left their room last night or for having spoken to the servant woman this morning. Had he been by himself, these infractions would not have occurred, but with Mele along he seemed destined to break half a dozen rules. He sighed and waited to hear what Yang Yi had to say.

Their guide looked from him to Mele and back to him again. "They don't believe you're husband and wife."

It was not what Peter had been expecting. He wondered why someone would doubt they were married. "They haven't even met us."

"Nevertheless, they don't believe you are husband and wife."

"That's silly," Mele said. "We've married twice already."

"I can show you the certificate," Peter said, reaching for his bag.

Yang Yi held up a hand to stop him. "They don't care about a piece of paper. You could have ten certificates, twenty even, and it would make no difference. They don't believe you are really married."

"Oh, for god's sake," Peter said. "That's crazy."

"The servants say the young lady slept on the bed, and you slept on the floor. Is that true?" He looked sternly at Peter.

"The bed was too short."

Yang Yi scowled and shook his head in disapproval. "That is unfortunate."

"Can't you explain to them?" Mele asked.

"What does it matter what I say? I'm only a guide. They judge with their own eyes. And their eyes tell them you are not husband and wife."

"But we are!" Mele held up her left hand to show him her grandmother's ring.

"So they won't let us watch the wedding today?" Peter asked. He suspected this snag to be more Yang Yi's fault than that of the servants. He had been opposed to them from the beginning. He hadn't approved of Mele, and now he was probably secretly pleased that they would have to leave without witnessing the marriage ceremony.

"I didn't say *you* couldn't watch it."

"You mean Mele can't watch it."

Yang Yi avoided his eyes. "It is Madame Zhang's decision, not mine."

Peter glanced at Mele.

"It's all right. You go ahead. It's for your dissertation."

"No. We both have permission to observe." He gave Yang Yi a hard look, determined not to be cowed so easily. "I want to talk to Madame Zhang."

Yang Yi shook his head. "That's impossible. You are not allowed to talk to anyone but me."

"Then I'm going to complain to the Alliance about how we've been treated," Peter said. "I'm going to complain about how rude you've been as a guide, and how you've denied us permission to see the marriage ceremony after they granted it."

"I didn't deny you permission," Yang Yi protested. "It's not my fault."

"If you deny Mele, you deny me."

"She has nothing to do with this."

"She's my wife."

Yang Yi glanced at Mele sitting on the bed in the blue silk dress. "All right," he said stiffly. There was a moment of silence in which his words seemed to hang in the air. "I'll see what I can do. But I make no promises. Understand? No promises."

After he left the room, Peter looked at Mele and saw she was smiling. If he lost this opportunity to observe the ceremony, he would probably regret it later, but for now he was glad he had stood up to Yang Yi. He had showed Mele that he was not going to be pushed around.

"You know, it's all right if you want to go alone," she said.

"I don't want to go alone. Besides, we both have permission."

Fifteen minutes later Yang Yi returned.

"Madame Zhang wants to talk to you," he announced.

"All right." Peter picked up the marriage certificate.

"Both of you." He looked pained to have to say this.

Mele sprang up from the bed, a big smile on her face.

"Remember, you don't speak to her," he warned as they walked down the hall. "You speak only to me. I'm the interpreter."

"We understand," Peter said.

"Does she speak English?" Mele asked.

"Of course not."

The room to which he led them was ornately furnished and dimly lit. In its center, like a queen on her throne, sat Madame Zhang in an elaborately carved chair with her small bound feet resting on a little footstool. She was a woman of about fifty, her hair still jet black, two ornamental chopsticks sprouting from it like antennae. She wore a black silk dress and held a black fan in one hand. A few feet behind her stood a servant woman with bowed head. Facing her were two straight-backed chairs, which Yang Yi indicated they should sit on. He stood between them and Madame Zhang but a little to the side so they could see each other.

After Peter and Mele were seated, Madame Zhang addressed them in Mandarin.

"She wishes to know where you are from," Yang Yi said.

"Boston," Peter answered promptly.

After Yang Yi translated his answer, there was an awkward silence in which Peter wondered if he should say something. Then Madame Zhang spoke again.

"And the young woman—where is she from?" Yang Yi asked politely.

"Ni'ihau," Mele said.

"Hawaii," Peter said.

Yang Yi translated their answers, and again Madame Zhang responded in Mandarin with a question.

"She wishes to know how you come to be married."

"I met Mele when I visited her island," Peter said.

Yang Yi translated, and Madame Zhang asked another question.

"She wishes to know why your parents arranged for you to marry this young woman."

"They didn't arrange it. Surely she must be aware that in other places marriages aren't arranged."

Yang Yi held up his hand to stop him, then translated what he had said. Madame Zhang spoke again.

"If the marriage was not arranged, she thinks it was not a proper marriage."

"I have the certificate here." Peter stood and held out the document to Madame Zhang.

"She can't read your certificate," Yang Yi said. "It has no meaning for her. Give it to me." He took the document.

Madame Zhang spoke sharply and with a bow Yang Yi passed it to her. She unfolded it, put on a pair of wire-framed glasses, and studied it carefully. Then she spoke again in Mandarin.

"She wishes to know why the young woman's parents agreed to a marriage for their daughter to a foreigner."

"I'm not a foreigner," Peter protested.

Mele laid a hand on his arm. "Tell her I asked Peter to marry me. I wanted to leave my island."

Yang Yi translated, and another question followed.

"You asked? What did your parents say?"

"I didn't ask my parents, but I did ask my grandmother."

After he translated her answer, Madame Zhang regarded Mele thoughtfully before handing the certificate back to Yang Yi and speaking once more in Mandarin.

Yang Yi returned the certificate to Peter. "She says you may go now." He made another stiff bow to Madame Zhang. Peter, standing, attempted a similar bow to show his respect.

"Well?" he asked when they were back in the hall.

Yang Yi sighed. He looked unhappy. "She said your wife may also attend the ceremony."

An hour later a small procession left the compound to fetch the bride, four servant men carrying the empty bridal sedan, a few more servants bearing gongs and drums, while Peter, Mele, and Yang Yi brought up the rear. By daylight Peter got a different impression of the village. It was larger than he had thought, a community of several hundred people, judging from the number of compounds he could see. And there was a wider street with shops that they had not seen the night before. People were out and about in the streets now, servants buying food, bicyclists sweeping by, and an occasional sedan chair carried by servants. People stared at them with open curiosity.

"The bride should be ready when we arrive," Yang Yi said. "By now she has had a bath to wash away bad spirits and a woman of good luck has put her hair up like a married woman."

"What is a woman of good luck?" Mele asked.

"She is a woman who has given birth to at least one healthy son."

"And what if she has only healthy daughters?"

"Then she is not a woman of good luck."

"That doesn't seem fair."

"The Chinese value their sons more than their daughters," Peter said. "Or at least they used to."

"Still today it is the same," Yang Yi said. "People say it is a blessing to bear a son, a misfortune to bear a daughter."

"Why a misfortune?" Mele asked. "I don't understand."

"She cannot work as hard as a son," Yang Yi explained. "And she must be fed. When she marries, she goes to live in her husband's household. A son, on the other hand, does not leave home, and his wife and children become part of the family, making it larger and more prosperous, just like a growing business. In old age his parents will have many people to take care of them, but parents who have only daughters will end up alone."

"How many people live here?" Peter asked.

"About three hundred, I believe."

"Is there concern about intermarriage in such a small community?"

Yang Yi shrugged. "They follow the old way, which dates back to Confucius."

"And what is that?"

"No one with the same last name can marry."

Peter pondered this. It seemed to him a rather risky way to ensure blood relatives did not marry. He was just about to point out the shortcoming of this method when they stopped before the weathered wood door of a compound that looked forlorn and neglected. A servant woman opened the door.

After a short exchange with Yang Yi, she admitted them while the sedan and the servants remained at the gate.

"You are very fortunate," Yang Yi told Peter and Mele in a low excited voice as they followed the woman through a series of passageways. "We have arrived early and you will have the opportunity to see the bride's tea ceremony. She serves her parents tea before she leaves her childhood home. You should find it very interesting."

The servant led them to a small room and gestured for them to stand near the door. In the center of the room stood the bride in a crimson jacket and skirt with gold embroidery, a headdress on her head with a curtain of red tassels hiding her face and crimson slippers on her feet. Her parents sat on the floor facing a low table. She knelt before each in turn, pouring and then handing them tea in small bowls. She spoke to them in a nearly inaudible singsong. Neither the bride nor her parents glanced at the three strangers who had entered the room. Peter raised his camera and snapped a picture. The bride's parents bowed their heads to their daughter as they accepted the tea she offered them and then sipped it while she waited patiently on her knees.

"She serves them tea to show her respect and thank them for having raised her," Yang Yi explained in a low voice.

When the bride's parents finished their tea, they set the bowls on the tray on the table.

"What happens now?" Mele asked.

"It's time for the bride to leave," Yang Yi said. "It's time for her to go to her husband's house and start her new life."

The bride and her parents now rose. There was more bowing. Then she walked toward Yang Yi, Peter, and Mele in the back of the room with mincing steps, her face concealed by the red tassels of her headdress, and left the room, followed by her parents, their eyes lowered, faces expressionless.

"We go now," Yang Yi said when they were past.

In the wake of the bride and her parents, they retraced their steps through the maze of walkways that led to the door opening onto the street. A small cluster of people waited by the door to say good-bye to the bride. Peter assumed they were relatives or neighbors. Yang Yi informed him that two young girls were sisters of the bride. Peter thought it strange that the mood was so somber. You would have thought a funeral was underway instead of a marriage. One of the bride's sisters looked as if she had been crying. Before leaving, the bride again bowed to her parents, and they to her. Then a middle-aged woman almost as small as the bride stepped forward from the cluster and the bride climbed on her back.

"What are they doing?" Mele whispered.

"She is the woman of good luck," Yang Yi whispered back.

"The bride's feet aren't supposed to touch the ground," Peter said, trying to snap a picture. "It's considered bad luck if they do."

The good luck woman staggered with her burden to the waiting sedan. There was a universal sigh of relief once the bride was safely deposited inside. The curtains were then lowered, hiding her from view.

"They are supposed to keep her from seeing anything unlucky along the way," Yang Yi said.

Now the servants who were not holding the sedan set off firecrackers and banged their gongs and drums as the procession started back the way they had come.

"What about her parents?" Mele asked, looking back at the gate where the bride's parents still stood, watching them. Of the people who had gathered to see the bride off, only the good luck woman had joined them.

"She leaves them behind," Peter said. "It symbolizes her

entry into a new life. Now she will be part of her husband's household."

"Yes," Yang Yi said. "She is no longer part of her parents' family. When she marries, she leaves her childhood behind."

As the procession made its way back through narrow streets past shops and houses, people stopped to watch, dogs barked, and children ran alongside.

"I like this custom," Mele said, "especially the firecrackers. I think it must feel wonderful to be carried through the streets like a queen and hear the music and celebrating."

"The firecrackers are supposed to scare away bad spirits," Yang Yi said. "They do not want bad spirits to follow the bride to her new house."

"Were there bad spirits at her old house?" Mele asked.

Yang Yi shrugged. "Who knows? But if there were, they don't want them to go with her."

"The Chinese believe bad spirits can cause the bride to sicken and die or have stillborn children," Peter told Mele. "She could bring bad spirits with her into the house if they don't take precautions."

"Of course Chinese people today don't believe such things," Yang Yi added. "They are just old superstitions."

When the wedding procession arrived back at the groom's compound, more firecrackers were set off and the good luck woman carried the bride on her back again, her feet never touching the ground until she was over the threshold of her new home. Once inside, they were led to a hall where several dozen people waited.

"These are relatives come to witness the marriage," Yang Yi informed them.

A short gray-haired man wearing a dark red gown with a black vest and a black cap stepped forward and bowed stiffly to the bride.

"Is he the groom's father?" Mele asked.

"Shh," said Yang Yi.

"I think he's the groom," Peter whispered in her ear.

"Isn't he kind of old?"

Yang Yi scowled at her.

The groom and his bride walked together to the ancestral altar and bowed several times.

"They are praying before the tablets of Heaven and Earth and his ancestors and the Kitchen God," Yang Yi said in a low voice.

"She is paying homage to his ancestors," Peter whispered. "Now that she's part of his family, she must show respect to his ancestors." Lifting his camera, he snapped a picture.

"Is the wedding afterward?" Mele asked.

"This is it. They're married now."

"I thought there would be more," she said, disappointment in her voice.

Their prayers finished, the groom turned to his bride and parted her curtain of tassels with his hands. A pale and lovely face appeared.

"She's so young!" Mele breathed.

Indeed, the bride could not have been more than seventeen, Peter thought. A pretty girl with dark eyes and porcelain skin who looked far more like she should be the groom's daughter than his wife.

Madame Zhang in her black silk dress now stepped forward, looking imposing, and the groom introduced her to his new wife. The women bowed politely to each other.

"Now he is introducing her to his other wives," Yang Yi told them, keeping his voice low.

"Other wives?" Mele said.

"Mr. Chen is a very wealthy man. It is not unusual here for

a wealthy man to have several wives. Madame Zhang is his first wife. She has the most power and must be shown the most respect."

"How many wives does he have?" she asked as a second woman, younger than Madame Zhang and dressed in green silk, stepped forward to be introduced. Again the women bowed politely to each other.

"The new one is number four."

"Four wives! Doesn't she mind?"

"Why should she mind?"

"I wouldn't want to be married to a man who already had three wives," Mele said indignantly.

"It is an excellent match for her," Yang Yi insisted. "Her family is poor. Now she won't be a burden for them. And to be a rich man's fourth wife is better than to be a servant."

Peter knew he was right. A servant's life in the past was a fate far worse for a woman than that of a younger wife. The labor would have worn away her youth and beauty, not to mention her health, in no time.

"Couldn't she find a rich *young* man?" Mele asked.

"Rich young men marry suitable wives," Yang Yi said. "They don't marry young women from poor families. It wouldn't be appropriate."

They watched as the bride was introduced to the third wife, who was younger than the first two, but not nearly so young as the bride. Peter wondered how many more wives the groom would accumulate before he became too old for such pursuits or satiated.

The introductions over, everyone moved into a large room with tables heaped with food. More people arrived, and children chased each other between the rows of tables while servants scurried about bearing trays of food. The groom and his new bride took their places at the head of the main table. Yang Yi led Peter and Mele to a table in the back of the room, where less important guests were being seated.

"Will you have four wives too one day?" Mele asked Yang Yi as servants set bowls of soup before them.

"Of course not. It's only allowed in the Forbidden Places."

"It's an awful custom." She gave a little shudder. "Why don't they get rid of it?"

"I don't think it's an awful custom," he protested. "It's a very ancient and honorable custom."

"Actually polygamy has been a common practice in many places," Peter told Mele. "Eighty percent of the cultures of the world have practiced it."

"Don't tell me you approve of it," she said, frowning.

"It's not a matter of approving or disapproving. It just is. I'm an anthropologist and it's my job to observe things the way they are."

"Well, I think there ought to be a law against it."

"There *is* a law against it," Yang Yi said. "One was passed in 1950. However, it doesn't apply to Forbidden Places. The whole point of a Forbidden Place is to preserve the culture of the past."

"I know that," she said. "I grew up in a Forbidden Place. But it wasn't anything like this."

"You don't understand our ways. It just shows I was right. You shouldn't have been permitted to come here."

"Mele is new to this," Peter said, jumping to her defense. "You might have warned us ahead of time that the young woman was a fourth wife. I could have explained to her."

"I can't believe neither of you see anything wrong with a man having four wives." Mele slammed her chopsticks down on the table. Heads of the other guests at their table turned to look at them.

"Please lower your voice," Yang Yi said. "You are calling attention to us."

"If we try to fix what's wrong with the past, we will lose the past," Peter explained patiently. "The wonderful thing about the Forbidden Places is that they are preserving the past. They are living museums. Of course they are going to be different from the present and there will be some things which strike us as wrong, but we can't pick and choose which customs we will preserve and which we will forfeit. If we start doing that, it won't be the past anymore. We will have lost it."

"Maybe some customs are better lost," Mele retorted.

Peter didn't want to argue with her. He tried to change the subject. "You should try the Peking duck. It's really good."

"I like the chicken," Yang Yi said, reaching for another piece.

Mele just stared moodily across the room at the bride and groom and scarcely glanced at the servants quietly setting more food on their table.

"There will be eight courses," Yang Yi said, "because eight is a lucky number."

Peter wondered if he could get a picture of the bride and groom from where he sat. He decided to try. Looking at them on his camera's LCD screen, he had to admit the bride did not appear to be enjoying the banquet. Her eyes were cast down, and she wasn't eating.

Having snapped his picture, he put away his camera and turned his attention to the noodles that had just been set before them.

"Long noodles signify long life," Yang Yi explained. "So they are very popular at wedding feasts."

"Can we talk to the bride after the banquet?" Mele asked.

Yang Yi shook his head. "You are forgetting. You are not supposed to talk to anyone. It's against the rules."

"We talked to Madame Zhang."

"That was different. She requested to talk to you."

"Then ask the bride if she would like to talk to us."

"May I remind you that you are only here because you were allowed to accompany your *husband*." Yang Yi reached for another piece of chicken.

Peter was trying none too successfully to lift long noodles to his mouth with his chopsticks.

"You tell her," Yang Yi said. "She's your wife. Tell her she can't talk to anyone. It's against the rules."

Peter sighed. He didn't like being pulled into the argument and he wasn't about to tell Mele she couldn't talk to anyone. All the same, he couldn't ignore Yang Yi. He turned to Mele. "If you could talk to her, what would you say to her?"

"Well, to begin with I'd ask if she minds being married to a man more than twice her age."

"You can't ask her that," Yang Yi objected.

"She'll just say she doesn't mind," Peter said. "How can she say otherwise?"

Mele twisted the ring on her finger, a stubborn look on her face. "And I'd ask her why she consented to being married to a man who already has three wives."

"I *told* you," Yang Yi said. "She had no choice. Her parents sold her."

"Sold her!" Mele stared at him. "You didn't say *sold* her."

"Did you try the long noodles?" Peter asked. "They're really good."

Mele ignored him. "What do you mean, *sold* her? Like for money?"

"It was a fair exchange," Yang Yi said. "A sort of trade. The groom gives money to the bride-to-be's family, and the family gives their daughter to him. It's an arrangement that benefits everybody."

"She is sold like a cow or a pig?" Mele said, appalled.

"It's called a bride-price," Peter said.

Mele looked at him now. "What's a bride-price?"

"It's found in many cultures. Buddhists do it and also Muslims. American Indians used to practice it too. Sometimes it involves money and sometimes property. In poorer countries it can involve giving the bride's family a certain number of cows or sheep."

"What kind of parents would sell their daughter?" she demanded.

Yang Yi picked up something small and round like an olive or an eyeball and popped it into his mouth before answering. "Parents who need money and parents who know it is best for their daughter to have a husband, even if she has to share him with other wives."

"I'd rather be a servant!"

"Servants live hard lives."

"You think it's better to be this man's new toy?"

"Maybe she will bear him a son." He popped another eyeball into his mouth.

"By the way, what is that?" Peter asked.

They both ignored him.

"And what difference will that make?" Mele asked.

"Men are grateful when they have a son."

"What if she bears him a daughter?"

Yang Yi shrugged. "There is an old saying, 'When a son is born, let him sleep on the bed, clothe him with fine clothes, and give him jade to play with. When a daughter is born, let her sleep on the ground, wrap her in common wrappings, and give her broken tiles for playthings.'"

"That's from the *Shih-ching*, the *Book of Songs*," Peter said, pleased that he had recognized it.

"Very good," Yang Yi said.

Mele was not impressed. "That's awful. Do people really believe that?"

"What's so awful about it?" Yang Yi said. "It's simply the way things are. I told you before. If a couple have a son, they will have someone to take care of them when they grow old, but if they have a daughter, they will simply lose her someday, she will be no use at all, and in the meantime she is a mouth to feed. That's why when people were restricted by the one-child policy, they chose to have sons."

"Chose?" Mele said. "What do you mean? How could they choose?"

"They aborted their female children," Peter said, "or practiced infanticide."

"They *killed* them?" She stared from one to the other.

"It's a very old custom," Yang Yi said. "It dates back to ancient China."

"I don't care how ancient it is," she said. "I think it's horrible. There ought to be laws against it."

"There are," Yang Yi said. "At least against infanticide. Abortion of course is perfectly legal. We have to have some means of controlling our population. Otherwise there would be too many people."

"You aren't eating," Peter said.

"I've lost my appetite," she said, rising. "I think I'll go back to our room."

He started to get up, but she stopped him.

"No, you stay here. This is what you came for. I don't want to interfere with your research."

Now Yang Yi was on his feet too. "I will go with you so you don't get lost."

"Thank you, but I can find my way back by myself," she said icily. "I don't need your help."

"Nevertheless, I must go with you," he insisted. "You must not wander about alone. It isn't allowed."

"I'll come too," Peter said, getting to his feet.

"Really, it isn't necessary."

No one spoke as they made their way through the maze of passages back to the room where Peter and Mele had slept the night before.

"You will not wander about?" Yang Yi asked nervously, lingering at the door.

"No, of course not," Peter said.

Yang Yi glanced distrustfully at Mele, who had thrown herself on the bed and closed her eyes. "Very well. I will return after the banquet. I'm sure you will want to see the ceremony of the bed."

"What's that?" Mele asked without opening her eyes.

Yang Yi's face lit up. "After the banquet the bride and groom are escorted to their bed and everyone goes along to celebrate. There is toasting and drinking. It's a lot of fun. I'm sure you won't want to miss it."

"Peter can go if he wants. I think I've seen enough."

"As you wish," he said with a hint of a bow, cool again. "And now, if you don't mind, I will return to the banquet. I don't wish to appear rude. Besides, it would be a shame to let so much excellent food go to waste." At that he turned abruptly and left, pulling the door closed behind him.

"I'm sorry." Peter sat down beside Mele on the bed.

"I feel sorry for that girl," she said. "It's her wedding day, but it's not a happy wedding day. Her parents sold her, and her husband is old and already has other wives. What does she have to look forward to?"

He leaned down and kissed the top of her head. The scent of her hair reminded him of tropical flowers.

"I'll be glad when we leave," she said. "I don't like this

place. Can you imagine how many baby girls have died here because their parents wanted boys? Their ghosts must be everywhere." She shuddered.

"There are no such things as ghosts. You know that, right?"

"You're wrong. I've seen them. And I've felt them."

Again he didn't want to argue. There would be time later for her to learn the difference between superstitions she had grown up with and scientific facts. In the meantime he must be patient.

"Want to go in the courtyard?" he asked, thinking that would make her feel better. They had promised Yang Yi they would stay in their room, but he doubted anyone would mind if they went into the courtyard, and since everyone was at the banquet, no one would know.

She hesitated only a moment, then sprang off the bed.

This time when they opened the door, they stepped into a gray world beneath an overcast sky. The courtyard looked different by day. It was smaller than he had thought, with chrysanthemums in bloom and orange carp swimming lazily in the pool.

"It seems so strange to be here," Mele said, sitting down on a stone bench. "I always knew that one day I would leave home, but I didn't realize I would go so far away or that I'd miss home so much."

"You miss it?" Peter asked, joining her on the bench.

"Yes, I do. Very much." There were tears in her eyes. "I worry about my grandmother. I shouldn't have left her."

"Are you sorry you married me?"

"No." She touched his hand. "I'm not sorry about that."

He kissed her then and she kissed him back. Her lips were soft and inviting. Now he was glad that they had left the banquet. His dissertation no longer seemed so important. What really mattered was this moment in this place with Mele.

"There it is again," she said, turning away from him. "Do you hear it?"

"What? I don't hear anything."

"Someone's crying."

"You must be mistaken. Everyone's at the banquet."

She looked hard at the wall on the far side of the courtyard, where there were two doors.

"Where are you going?" he asked as she rose.

She skirted the pool and approached the first door.

"You can't go in there."

Ignoring him, she pressed her ear to the door.

"Do you hear anything?" he asked, joining her.

She shook her head and pushed on the door. To his relief it didn't budge. Then she went to the second door and pressed her ear to it, listening. When she pushed on this door, it slowly swung open.

He knew they shouldn't go in, but Mele wasn't easy to stop. He put his hand on her arm, but she pulled away and stepped over the threshold into the dark room. He couldn't allow her to wander around by herself, so he had no choice but to follow.

The room they entered was dim and shadowy with an unpleasant odor. A small black lacquered cabinet stood near the door and next to it a bamboo bird cage with a small bird sitting on a perch. Then he noticed a little girl beyond the bird cage sitting up in her bed staring back at them. She could not have been more than five or six years old.

"We heard someone crying," Mele said. "Was it you?"

"She can't understand you," Peter said.

The girl just stared at them, her face wet with tears. She didn't seem frightened.

"Why were you crying?" Mele asked gently.

"We shouldn't be here." Peter glanced uneasily about the room. Everything about it struck him as wrong—the darkness, the clutter, the child herself.

"Why do you suppose she isn't at the banquet?" Mele asked.

"I don't know. Maybe she's being punished. Seriously, Mele, I don't think we should be here."

The little girl spoke to them then, her voice ending in a sob. He had no idea what she was trying to say.

"Oh, Peter, get Yang Yi," Mele urged. "He can translate."

"I don't think that's a good idea. He'll have a stroke if he finds out we didn't stay in our room."

"Why are you crying?" she asked again, moving closer to the little girl. She wiped imaginary tears from her eyes to convey her meaning.

The child hesitated, then pointed to her feet. Her legs were stretched out straight in front of her and her feet were bound in wrappings. Mele leaned forward to examine them and gasped. "Her feet are bleeding!"

It hit him like a thunderbolt. He knew what they were looking at. "She's had her feet bound. It's an ancient custom to make the feet small. The Chinese admire women with small feet."

"But she's *bleeding*. She's in pain."

The little girl looked at them with pleading eyes and again tried to speak to them.

"We shouldn't be here," Peter said, laying his hand on Mele's arm again. If he could just get her out of there and back to their own room.

"We can't just leave her like this," Mele said.

"Yes, we can. Now let's go."

"Isn't there something we can do? Obviously her bindings are too tight. We should tell someone."

"We weren't supposed to see this. It has nothing to do with the wedding ceremony."

"But we have seen it, and now we can't just go away and leave her suffering."

"We can. We must. This is one of their customs, and we have to respect it. We have no right to interfere."

He tugged at Mele's arm, and reluctantly she let herself be coaxed back to the courtyard. Once they were back outside in the daylight and fresh air, he felt a wave of relief.

"I don't understand you," she said angrily. "How can you not want to help that child in there?"

"I'm an observer. We're both observers. We're not supposed to interfere. If everyone who came here as an observer tried to change these people's customs, then there wouldn't be any customs left for us to observe. It would all disappear, everything that makes them special and the past different from the present. Don't you see? We would lose it all."

"I see you turning your back on that little girl's pain." Mele looked at the carp standing motionless in the pool, as if under a magic spell.

He tried to put his arms around her but she pushed him away. He watched helplessly as she strode back to the door that led to the little girl with bound feet.

"Where are you going?"

"We have to help her."

"How? What can we do?"

She pushed the door open and vanished inside without answering.

He swore under his breath. Okay, he would have to go

back in there, and somehow he would have to persuade her there was nothing she could do.

The little bird fluttered nervously in its cage as Peter stepped back into the dark room. Again he noticed the foul odor. Mele was standing at the foot of the bed. The little girl drew back her feet with a cry as Mele reached her hand toward them.

"It's all right," she said in a soothing voice. "I won't hurt you."

The little girl seemed to understand her and slowly stretched her feet out again. Mele studied one foot carefully and then gently began to unwind the bindings. The little girl stopped crying, her eyes on Mele's hands. Mele removed the bindings one strip at a time. As she did, the foul odor grew stronger. Peter realized it was coming from the little girl's feet. They were abscessed. The bindings fell away stained with blood and pus. When the last scrap fell, Mele gasped.

"Oh, my god!"

Peter saw the child's broken and deformed foot and quickly looked away. It didn't even look like a human foot. He remembered now reading about how foot binding was done—they bent back the toes and broke the foot to make it look small—but seeing a foot to which it had been done was a lot different than reading about it.

At that moment a door on the other side of the room opened. An old servant woman carrying a basin froze at the sight of them, then turned and fled. Peter's heart sank.

"Okay, now the other foot," Mele said to the little girl as if nothing had happened.

"There's no time," he said. "We have to leave. They can't find us here."

"You go then. I'll come as soon as I've finished."

"I'm not leaving you here."

The wrappings came off, one by one, dropping to the floor in a soiled heap. The little girl was no longer crying, but Mele was.

"Look, what they've done to her feet. How will she ever be able to walk again? How could someone do this?"

The little girl was trying to tell them something and looking anxiously toward the door.

"I think she wants us to leave," Peter said.

But it was too late. The door flew open and Madame Zhang swept into the room with three servants in her wake. She took in the situation at a glance.

"What have you done?" she demanded, her voice cold with anger.

Peter stared at her. She could speak English?

"I took off her bindings," Mele said defiantly. "They were too tight and she was crying."

"They are supposed to be tight," Madame Zhang snapped, "and it doesn't matter if she cries. Her tears are of no importance, you stupid girl. Now we must bind her feet again. You just caused the child more pain."

"Please," Mele begged, tears in her eyes, "don't do this to her. She's just a child."

"She is old enough. If we wait longer, it will be too late. Her feet will be too big."

"But you're crippling her. Look what you've done to her poor feet."

"It is what needs to be done if she is to marry one day," said Madame Zhang. "She must have lotus feet. My own were bound when I was even younger than she is now."

Peter's eyes flew to Madame Zhang's tiny bound feet in their embroidered silk slippers. They were so little it was a wonder she could stand on them, even leaning on a cane as she was.

"It is our custom. Would you ruin her chances at marriage? If her feet are not bound, she will have big feet like yours—ugly feet—and no man will want to marry her."

"If you bind her feet, how will she walk?" Mele demanded. "How will she run?"

Madame Zhang looked at her with narrow cold eyes. "Eventually she will learn to walk on her lotus feet. She doesn't need to run. And when she is married, she will thank us for what we did. She will have beautiful lotus feet."

"They aren't beautiful," Mele objected. "They will never be beautiful. They're deformed and horrible. Can't you see that?"

Madame Zhang lifted her head proudly and glared at Mele. "You will leave now. Both of you. You're not welcome anymore. You have broken the visitor agreement."

"I'm sorry," Peter said. "It's my fault."

"I don't care whose fault it is," Madame Zhang said. "Your visit is over, and you are not welcome here in the future. We allowed you to come into our home and observe our venerable traditions and in return you abused our hospitality. I will let the Alliance know I am most displeased. Now return to your room and wait there until we can find your guide."

Peter stepped closer to Mele and took her hand, hoping she would say no more. It was clear that nothing was going to change Madame Zhang's mind. Arguing would only make the situation worse.

"Come on. Let's go back." He gently tugged Mele toward the door that led to the courtyard and she didn't resist.

As soon as it closed behind them, they heard a bolt slide into place.

"I'm sorry," he said when they were in their room again. He took her in his arms, and she didn't push him away.

"Isn't there anything we can do?" she asked.

"What can we do? It's their custom."

"It's horrible."

"To them it isn't horrible."

"Could we take her with us?" She looked up into his face with pleading eyes.

"Of course not. This is her world. This is where she belongs."

"We could find a doctor who can fix her feet."

"She's a child, Mele. We can't take her away."

"You could offer Madame Zhang money. Maybe she would take money for the girl."

"I can't do that. You know it wouldn't be right."

"How is it any worse than what they're doing? That girl who was married today was sold by her parents, wasn't she?"

"It isn't the same."

"How? How is it not the same?"

"Mele, be reasonable. We can't take that little girl away from here. I can't buy her. It would be wrong in so many ways. Madame Zhang would never agree to it. And even if she did, how would I explain when I got back home? Oh, by the way when I was in China I bought this little Chinese girl to save her from having her feet bound? I'm an anthropologist, for Christ sake. I'm not supposed to interfere or tamper with other cultures. My job is to study them."

"I don't understand you," she said, pulling away. "How can you not try to change what is clearly wrong?"

"We are their guests. We can't come here and just change what we don't approve of."

"Why not?"

"Because they have a right to preserve their customs, even if those customs seem strange or repulsive to us. You can't just go to a Forbidden Place and start changing it. Soon its uniqueness would be lost. The past would be lost. It would only be something you read about in books."

"And you would let a little girl suffer in order to preserve these terrible customs of the past?"

"Mele, please."

"Because I wouldn't," she said, lifting her chin. "And I will never understand how you could let this go on happening."

"It's not something I can stop."

"You don't want to stop it."

"Of course I do." He didn't look at her. He sensed that a chasm had just opened between them. He didn't know how big it was, but it was definitely big. He didn't understand why she couldn't see the situation from his point of view. She was being unreasonable. But what could he expect? She was intelligent, yes, but she only had a high school education. Even worse, she had almost no experience of the world. It wasn't her fault of course. She couldn't help it that she had these limitations. He had taken her out of her world and dropped her into a totally unfamiliar environment and expected her to think like an anthropology graduate student. Of course she couldn't.

With a sigh he started to walk toward the folding screen in the back of the room.

"Where are you going?" she asked.

"To get out of these clothes. You heard Madame Zhang. She said we have to leave."

They changed their clothes in silence, separated by the screen. Peter wondered if Mele would demand to go back to Niʻihau now. Could she go back? She had said once you left, you couldn't go back. Would she have to stay with him because she had no other choice? Would she be like the young Chinese bride, married against her will to a man she didn't love? But of course that was ridiculous. They could divorce. She could find somebody else. There would be lots of men who would jump at the chance to marry her.

They were dressed in their own clothes again when there was a sharp rap at the door. Peter's eyes met Mele's. Then he went to the door and opened it.

"What have you done?" a distraught Yang Yi demanded, rushing into the room. "Did I not tell you don't wander about? Do you know how much trouble you've caused? Never have visitors caused such an uproar. Madame Zhang is furious. She says you must leave at once."

"We know that," Peter said.

"But you will miss the bedside party and the morning rising ceremony." Yang Yi seemed almost in tears. Peter suspected he had been very much looking forward to these events himself.

"It can't be helped."

"And you will have no place to stay. Nor will I."

"We'll just have to drive back to Kunming."

"It's a long way, and when we get there, where can you stay? It will be too late to find a hotel room." Now that Yang Yi's initial disappointment was over, he seemed to resign himself to the situation.

"We'll think of something. You can drop us at the airport if you want."

Yang Yi shook his head. "What would the Alliance say? They would say I didn't take good care of you. What did you do to upset Madame Zhang so much? I have never seen her so angry before."

Peter glanced at Mele. He didn't want Yang Yi to blame her for what had happened. He tried to think of something he could say to explain Madame Zhang's anger without casting blame on Mele. He was about to say he had found the child and removed her bindings when Mele spoke up.

"I'm afraid it was me. There was a little girl in a room on the other side of the courtyard—"

"Her feet had been bound," Peter hastened to explain.

"I unwrapped them," Mele said.

Yang Yi winced. "Oh, now I understand. No wonder Madame Zhang was so angry. They change the wrappings of course, but each time it is very painful for little Su-Ling."

"You know about her?" Mele asked.

"Yes, of course I know about her. Her feet were bound just three weeks ago. I saw them do it although I had to leave the room. It's not the sort of thing I enjoy watching, not nearly as pleasant as a wedding."

"Wait a minute," Peter said. "You mean someone came here to watch?"

"That is correct. A woman from San Francisco writing a book about foot binding."

Mele stared at him in disbelief. "She watched?"

"That's right. And she took pictures too. For her book."

Mele's eyes flew to the little camera in Peter's hand. Feeling guilty, he hastily tucked it into his bag and zipped the bag shut. Surely she knew he would never have done such a thing.

The sun was setting ten minutes later as they climbed into Yang Yi's red compact and started back to Kunming.

"By the way," Peter asked as he watched the rugged landscape slip by, "how is it that Madame Zhang spoke such good English?"

"She majored in foreign languages when she was at university," Yang Yi answered promptly. Now that they were no longer in the Forbidden Place, he was becoming almost cheerful.

"So you knew she spoke English?"

"I knew but I let her speak Mandarin and she lets me translate. It is mutual respect, you might say."

"If she went to university, then she hasn't always lived in the Forbidden Place?"

"No, I suppose not."

"Just how old is that village?"

"Oh, very old."

"I mean, how long has it been a Forbidden Place?"

"Perhaps twenty years. But even before that it was a very backward place because of its remoteness. And that of course is why it was chosen to be a Forbidden Place."

Peter felt disappointed. Twenty years was not very long, not nearly so long as Niʻihau's isolation from the outside world. The community and its inhabitants might be quite influenced by modern culture. How truly traditional was it if it had only been given protective status twenty years ago?

"I'm surprised Madame Zhang would choose to live there when she has a university education," Mele said, speaking for the first time since they had left the compound. Until now she had been staring out the window. Peter suspected she was brooding about the little girl with the bound feet and thought it might be best to leave her to her thoughts.

"She believes strongly in preserving our heritage," Yang Yi said.

"I guess that includes foot binding," Mele said bitterly.

"Of course. It was a custom for over a thousand years and now you will find it only in the Forbidden Places."

"It shouldn't be allowed anywhere. It's cruel to do that to a child's foot—to cripple her for life."

"You are criticizing something you know nothing about."

"Have you ever seen a foot that has been bound?"

"Many times. In case you didn't notice, most of the women at the Forbidden Place had bound feet, including the servants."

"Have you seen a foot like that with the bindings off?"

"No, of course not. But such feet have been considered beautiful in my country for more than a thousand years. Poets have written about the beauty of the lotus foot. The smaller the foot, the more beautiful the woman. It is not her face or her figure that matters, as in the West, but the smallness of her feet. Bound feet are very sexy. They give a woman a sexy walk. And in the bedroom they give untold delights to a husband or lover, they say."

"What's a lotus foot?" Mele asked, frowning.

"The foot is bound to resemble a lotus bud, which is considered very beautiful. The ideal foot, they used to say, is just three inches long. They fit into tiny slippers that their wearers sew and embroider with their own hands. In modern China it is a lost art. Some of those slippers sell now to collectors for enormous sums."

"Does your girlfriend have bound feet?"

"Of course not. It's been banned for many years."

In the dark of the car Mele leaned closer to Peter and whispered in his ear. "I told you he wasn't married."

Peter reached for her hand. Had she forgiven him then? Were they allies again? He was relieved she was getting over her anger. From now on he would have to be more careful. They were from different cultures and they thought differently. He realized now he could lose Mele over a small misunderstanding. Their marriage might end before it had hardly begun, and she might pass out of his life as swiftly as she had entered it. If he wanted to keep her, he would have to be sensitive to the differences between them.

\* \* \*

It was past midnight when they got back to Kunming. Yang Yi took Peter and Mele to his apartment, which was on the fifteenth floor of a high-rise with a wonderful view of the city lights by night. They sat on stools at his breakfast bar sipping Coke from cans as he phoned hotels, trying to find them a room.

"Do you think my feet are ugly?" Mele asked, looking down at her bare feet. They had left their shoes by the door.

"I think your feet are beautiful," Peter said.

"Even though they're big?"

"They're perfect. I love your feet."

She laughed. "Well, you don't have to love them. I only meant, do you think they're ugly like Madame Zhang said. I know they're big. Everyone in my family has big feet."

"I fell in love with your feet the first time I saw them."

She laughed again. "Now *that's* romantic."

Yang Yi pocketed his cell phone. "It seems there are no rooms free. There is a convention of acupuncturists and they have taken all the rooms. I'm afraid you will have to stay here."

"I can sleep on the floor," Peter offered. "And Mele can sleep on the sofa."

Yang Yi shook his head. "No, that won't be necessary. I have made other arrangements for myself, and you may use my bed."

"But you said there are no rooms free," Mele objected.

"That is correct. I will stay with a friend."

"We don't want to put you out," Peter said.

"It is inconvenient, but I will manage."

"If it's inconvenient—"

Yang Yi held up a hand to stop him. "No, no, I insist. You are my guests."

Before they could protest more, he caught up a jacket and was out the door.

"He could have stayed here," Peter said when he was gone.

"I don't think he wanted to," said Mele. "Come on. Let's get ready for bed. I'm exhausted."

"Shall we flip a coin to see who gets the first shower?"

"No, I'm taking the first shower," Mele said, hopping off her bar stool. "You just try to stop me." She gave him a little push before making a dash for the bathroom.

Thirty minutes later, freshly-showered, they were nestling against each other in Yang Yi's queen-size platform bed.

"Did you notice there are two toothbrushes in the bathroom?" Mele asked.

"Maybe one's an extra," Peter suggested.

"I think it belongs to Yang Yi's friend."

"His girlfriend?"

"There are some women's clothes in his closet too."

"You looked in his closet?"

She smiled and touched her fingers to his lips.

"I wonder what she's like," Peter said. "What sort of girlfriend would Yang Yi have?"

"Would you like to know?" Mele switched on the light beside the bed, got up, and padded into the other room. A minute later she returned with a framed photo of Yang Yi and a pretty young woman on a motor scooter wearing a helmet, stylish boots and jeans.

"Not exactly the old-fashioned type," he said, examining the photo.

"Do you think he's taken her to the Forbidden Place?"

"I doubt it. Can you imagine him introducing her to Madame Zhang?"

She grinned. "No, I can't."

She set the picture on the stand beside her and switched off the light.

"About today—" Peter said. "I'm sorry.

She put her fingers lightly on his lips again. "Don't."

He kissed her fingers, then her lips, her closed eyes, her hair, her neck, her throat. And for a while in silence broken only by an occasional gasp or moan of pleasure, they got to know each other more intimately than before and at last had the wedding night that had been so long postponed.

# 6

# India

Dear Mom and Dad,
    I know you're probably still mad at me for leaving. But I hope someday you'll understand. I had to do it. If I had stayed any longer, I think I would have died. Or at least something in me would have. I just wasn't meant to spend my whole life on Niʻihau. I think I've known that for a long time. Remember how even as a kid I used to drive you nuts asking what it was like in other places? You'd tell me to stop asking questions, or you tried to discourage me by saying people weren't so nice out there, but it didn't stop me.

    You thought maybe if I went to school on Kauaʻi, I'd get it out of my system, but I didn't. That just made me want to see more. I tried to talk myself out of it. Honestly I did. When I came back home, I did my best to fit in. I tried to tell myself that I could be happy like that, living near all of you, working at the ranch, getting married to Mano one day, having kids of my own and growing old. But I still kept thinking about all those places I'd never see and how every day of my life, it would just be the same thing, and I'd be married to Mano, who wouldn't understand at all why I was unhappy.

*Working as a guide just made me all the more curious. I wondered about the watchers and the places they came from and asked questions when I could, but it wasn't enough. I'm not sure when I got the idea of leaving with a watcher, but it was before Peter came along. You shouldn't blame him. It's not his fault I left. He didn't talk me into it. In fact, I kind of forced him to take me with him. It could have been someone else I suppose, but it was Peter. I wasn't sure just at first. He seemed so awkward and uptight, but then that night at the luau, I made up my mind. I knew if I kept putting it off, pretty soon I'd be married to Mano and then it would be too late.*

*I know you don't approve of what I did, but I think if you got to know Peter, you'd like him. He's not an island boy like Mano, of course, but he's got a good heart and he treats me with gentleness and respect. Of course we're different. But with time we'll get to know each other better, and things will work out. Trust me. This wasn't a mistake.*

She stopped, pen in hand, and looked out the window of the train. The parched brown hills seemed to stretch away forever. Across from her Peter was typing on his laptop. Was that really true, she wondered, that part about it not being a mistake? She hoped it was, but she wasn't sure. They had not talked anymore about Su-Ling, the little girl with the bound feet. She wondered if that would always be between them, a kind of stumbling block they couldn't get around, a rock in their path—no, a boulder. She didn't understand why he was not as disturbed as she was by what they had seen. How could he have witnessed little Su-Ling's suffering and not wanted to rescue her from that terrible place? She sighed and returned to her letter.

*We are in India now, and it's very different from China, although here too there are so many people. In Bangalore it was noisy and crowded—cars honking, people shouting, beggars everywhere, people on bicycles, hordes of children. We were met at the airport by our guide, a polite and very handsome young Indian man who bowed to us and apologized in perfect English for anything that might have inconvenienced us. He has such white teeth when he smiles and black eyes that look at me as if he can read my thoughts. He knows how to scatter the children and points out the temples and government buildings and knows so many things about them. He has been to college in England and he's very intelligent. I regret now that I didn't read more and learn more when I was in school. I feel so ignorant compared to Singh and Peter. But in Boston I'll have a chance to continue my education. I want to go to a university and take courses. There's so much I want to know!*

*Well, I must stop now. We're near our destination. I hope you are all well. Give my love to Tutu, and please forgive me for leaving. I will enclose Peter's address in Boston and hopefully you will write to me and when we get there, there will be a letter waiting for me. I miss you all very much. Tell Kimo not to get into too much trouble. Malia, take good care of my books. Kai, Makani, and Lani, I miss you. I send my love to everyone.*
*—Mele*

"Well, that's done. I got my notes about the China visit typed up." Peter closed his laptop. "Where's Singh? I thought he said he would be gone just a few minutes. That was half an hour ago."

"I imagine he's trying to give us some privacy," Mele said.

"Well, I think we're there now," he said as the train began to brake.

A moment later the door to their compartment opened, and Harjeet Singh, their Indian guide, gave them a warm smile as he helped gather up their bags.

"Did you finish your letter?" he asked Mele as they got off the train.

"Yes, thank you. Will there be a place where I can mail it?"

"I will mail it for you if you will trust me with it."

Their eyes met and she looked away. She wondered if Peter noticed the way Singh looked at her. She glanced at Peter, but he was paying no attention. She handed Singh her letter, then watched as he dashed away to mail it.

"Where's he off to now?" Peter asked, frowning.

"He's mailing a letter for me."

A few other passengers had also disembarked from the train and were busy organizing their bags or being greeted by relatives who had come to meet them. No one gave them a second glance.

"I hope he's not going to just leave us standing here," Peter said.

"I'm sure he'll be right back."

Peter set his bag down on the station platform. "What do you think of him?"

"He's very educated."

"I suppose so. But you'd think if he's so educated, he'd find some other job."

His comment surprised her. Did he think Singh was not a good guide or was he saying Singh was too good? Could a guide be too good?

"Do you think he's handsome?" Peter asked off-handedly.

"Yes, very."

"Don't you think there's something about him—I can't quite put my finger on it—he's too friendly. I don't trust him."

"He seems trustworthy to me," Mele said. "He's taking good care of us. He has apologized about the heat, the dust, the traffic, the people—and none of it is his fault. Why don't you trust him?"

"There's something about him I don't like."

She wondered if Peter could be jealous. Maybe he had noticed Singh's attentions to her after all. The idea that he might be jealous amused her. There was no need for him to be. Of course Singh was handsome, but Peter was her husband.

Within five minutes Singh was back. "It's done," he said, flashing a smile at her. "Your letter is mailed. I'm so sorry to keep you waiting."

"You really don't need to apologize," Mele said. "It gave us a chance to catch our breath, didn't it, Peter?"

Peter glanced at his watch and muttered something she didn't catch.

Singh reached for her bag. "We will take a tonga from here, if you don't mind."

"What's a tonga?" she asked.

Singh pointed at several open two-wheeled horse-drawn carriages waiting outside the station.

"We're riding in one of those!" She could hardly wait to board. She would have to tell her family about this in her next letter home.

"I hope you are not too uncomfortable," Singh said a few minutes later when they were settled in a tonga, cramped together, knees bumping. "Cars are not allowed here."

"I'm surprised they have train service," Peter said. "Surely that makes it difficult to keep the place isolated?"

Mele could detect an aggrieved tone in his voice and wondered if Singh could detect it too.

"Oh, it's quite isolated," Singh assured him. "Who would want to come here? But they need to get supplies. Without supplies they could not survive."

"It's very big, isn't it?" Mele said, looking around at all the buildings and people. "More like a small city than a village."

"Well, not so large as Mysore, of course, but not as small as many rural villages."

"It's larger than I expected," Peter said, still in that aggrieved tone.

"Regrettably they do not take the measures to control population growth practiced elsewhere in India," Singh said. "And so their population keeps growing. Always the women are giving birth, and if the village were not receiving help because of its importance as a cultural sanctuary, the people would no doubt be starving."

It was much larger than the little village in Yunnan they had just visited. Mele looked around her with interest, wanting to miss nothing. They passed women walking with baskets on their heads and toothless old men in turbans while barefoot children ran along beside them. Dogs barked at them, and they saw several ungainly camels being led by men in long robes and a few scrawny cows wandering through the dusty streets.

"They are sacred cows," Singh explained. "It is a sin to harm them so they are allowed to wander wherever they please."

Although their tonga had a roof to shade them from the sun, it was hot and Mele soon began to sweat. She noticed Peter was sweating too, dark spots forming on his shirt under his arms.

"Is it far?" she asked.

"No, not far at all," Singh said with that quick flash of a smile.

"How much contact does the village have with outsiders?" Peter asked.

"Very little. The village is much as it was fifty years ago. In the countryside things change slowly. You could find many other villages like this one. The main problem is to keep the young people from leaving."

Mele was surprised when their tonga turned into a leafy

tree-lined street of large houses with verandas. It was so different from the dusty marketplace, and the ragtag crowd of children that had been following them stopped as if they were not allowed to enter this street.

"It's quite beautiful, isn't it?" Singh said. "Almost as fashionable as the houses you might find in the better sections of Delhi or Bombay."

"Do the people speak English?" Mele asked.

"Of course. Even in places like this, English is spoken. It goes too far back in our history to root it out now. We have our local dialects, but anyone who is educated speaks English too. You can't very well tell people they can't learn English or go to university. What kind of village would it be then? Only a village of poor and uneducated, the lowest castes, and who would want to visit that? No, if we are going to preserve our traditions, it must be the traditions of all castes, not just those at the bottom."

Mele knew Peter would be disappointed. He had hoped to find places untouched by the modern world, but perhaps that was impossible. She laid her hand on his arm to show him she sympathized and smiled when she caught his eye. Ruefully he smiled back.

She thought she would like India. There was so much to see and it was so different from her island. Surely a wedding here would be quite unlike the wedding they had witnessed in China. But then as she remembered the unhappy young bride who had been sold by her parents to be an aging rich man's fourth wife, doubt crept into her mind.

"And does the bride wish to marry?" she asked.

Singh's black eyes met hers. Again she felt as if he were reading her thoughts. White teeth flashed as his lips parted in a smile. "Why do you ask that? Of course she wishes to get married. What young woman doesn't wish to get married? It's a very important day, maybe the most important day of her life."

"Then she is not forced to marry against her wishes?"

"Of course not. I assure you this marriage is something the young lady has looked forward to since she was a child."

"And so in India young women are never forced into marriages with men they don't love?" She wasn't sure what drove her on. Perhaps it was what she had seen in China. Perhaps it was Singh's dark eyes.

He grinned. "Ah, it's love you are wondering about. Well, I'm afraid I can't swear that they are in love. In modern India of course who can stop young men and women from marrying for love? It is the modern way. But in places like this village it happens less frequently. Marriages are more likely to be arranged the traditional way, by the parents, who often go to a matchmaker to help them find a suitable spouse for their child. Usually the young man's parents do the searching, not the young woman's. It isn't respectable for young women to search, or even for their parents to search for them. They must wait for a matchmaker to come to them."

"Sounds like a debutante ball in reverse," Peter said.

"What if they don't like the person their parents choose?" Mele asked.

"Good sons and daughters respect their parents' wisdom in making the right choice. The parents seek a young man or woman of similar background so the match will be a success."

"My mother would be all for that," Peter said dryly.

"And love has no part in it?" Mele persisted.

Singh gazed at her steadily and smiled again. "Love comes later when you get to know your husband or wife well."

She could meet his gaze no longer and glanced away,

wondering how much he could guess about her marriage to Peter. Could he tell just by looking at them that they had not known each other long? Could he tell that they had not waited to fall in love but had been just as arbitrarily matched as a couple in an arranged marriage? Of course it's not the same, she told herself. I *chose* Peter. My parents would never have chosen him. They would have chosen Mano or one of the other island boys.

Just then Peter startled her by catching her hand, lifting it to his lips, and kissing it. "Did you know we're on our honeymoon?" he asked.

Singh flashed his white teeth. "No, I didn't realize you were so recently married. I hope I didn't say anything to offend you."

"You didn't," Peter said.

"You are fortunate to have such a lovely wife."

"What about you? Are you married?"

Singh smiled and shook his head. "Ah, no, I regret that I have not been blessed in that way, although my mother talks frequently of grandchildren and scolds me often for waiting. I try to make her understand that first I must finish my studies. Then I can think about finding a wife."

"You're a student?"

"Yes, at the university in Bangalore."

"What are you studying?"

"Linguistics. An impractical choice, I fear."

"Your English is very good," Mele said.

"Thank you. I had the good fortune to study at Harrow on a scholarship."

"Have you been doing this long?" Peter asked.

"Ah, you have found me out. I am very new at this. In fact, this is only my second time."

At that moment the tonga stopped in front of a rambling old house shaded by trees and Singh leaped nimbly out and offered a helping hand to Mele before Peter could climb down. As he paid the driver, four Indian girls of varying ages in traditional dress and wearing saris burst from the house, ran laughing down the walk, and surrounded them. The girls smiled and giggled, glancing at Peter and Mele.

"Let me introduce you," Singh said. "This is the breaker of hearts, Parvani." The youngest girl, about six years old, ducked shyly behind her nearest sister. "Rarest of jewels, Jeevana." This sister, perhaps age ten, also shyly dropped her eyes. "The lovely Sevati." The third sister, about fifteen years old, was a striking beauty with mischievous eyes. "And the equally lovely Darshana." The oldest, who could not have been more than sixteen or seventeen, dipped her head to Peter and Mele and pressed her hands together in greeting.

"Singh! We thought you would never come," said Sevati.

"You're late," scolded Darshana. "We've been waiting for hours."

"Did you bring me something?" asked little Parvani, emerging from behind Sevati and eyeing the bag he was carrying.

"Yes, I brought something for all of you," he said, "but first you must take care of your guests. I'm sure they are hot and tired and would like some lemonade."

"He seems to be very popular here," Peter said in a low voice to Mele as they followed Singh up the walk to the house.

"He knows how to charm," she said, watching the girls vie for the honor of walking beside him.

"I thought you said this was only your second time to come here," Peter remarked as they mounted the veranda.

"That is true," Singh said. "Do not attach too much

importance to these young ladies, beautiful though they are. My predecessor told me that I should bring along silk from Mysore when I came, that it would be much appreciated. I did as he recommended, and now I fear they expect silk or other gifts when they see me coming. They are most demanding."

"Do they all live here?" Mele asked.

"Indeed they do. Mr. Bhattacharya has five daughters. No sons, to his disappointment. It means he must provide dowries for all his daughters and find them good husbands. It is fortunate that he is a wealthy man."

The girls giggled and whispered among themselves.

"Which of you is getting married?" Mele asked.

This question elicited more giggles.

"I believe that would be their older sister, Kamala," Singh said, "who is no doubt inside undergoing one of the many rituals decreed by custom prior to marriage."

"*Haldi*," said Sevati.

"Quite so," said Singh. "*Haldi*, a purification ritual. They apply turmeric to the skin."

"What's that?" Mele asked.

"A kind of herb or spice," he said, meeting her eyes. "Quite harmless." He smiled.

There was a neat row of sandals beside the door.

"If you don't mind, we should leave our shoes here," Singh said, slipping off his sandals.

Mele and Peter did likewise. The girls giggled as Peter sat his large athletic shoes next to their sandals.

It was cooler when they stepped inside the house, where shutters blocked out the light and a ceiling fan rotated slowly overhead.

"They have electricity?" Peter asked, looking up at the fan in surprise.

"Of course they have electricity," Singh said. "They would move to Bangalore if they could not have electricity. But of course not everyone in the village has it. Only the higher caste families like the Bhattacharyas."

While they talked, Mele looked at a picture on the wall of a blue-skinned man and a woman in a sari in a garden. Then she noticed a small statue on a low table near the door of a man with four arms balancing on one leg surrounded by an ornate circle.

"That is Shiva," explained Singh. "He is dancing in a ring of fire, the eternal dance of the universe."

"Why does he have four arms?" she asked.

"Because he is a god. Because he is more powerful than a man."

Mele thought the four arms were strange, but the idea of a god who danced appealed to her. Again she had the feeling she was going to like India.

"If you please, follow me," said the oldest sister, Darshana. She led them into a room where there was a sofa with colorful pillows and a window looked out on a lush garden of blooming flowers. A servant girl brought them a tray with a large pitcher of lemonade and poured it into tall glasses. She was just leaving when a short plump woman of middle age in a saffron sari rushed into the room. She wore rings on her fingers and had a small red dot painted between her eyebrows.

Peter and Singh leaped to their feet, and Singh bowed to her. "Mrs. Bhattacharya," he said, "we are most grateful for your hospitality."

"We are very pleased you can join us for our daughter's wedding," she said, looking from Singh to Peter to Mele. "I am sorry we cannot give you a private room. I'm sure you will understand. We have other guests too. We are spreading mats wherever there is space, and there are more relatives arriving tonight from Bangalore. So many people! I beg you to overlook the inconvenience."

"Thank you for allowing us to attend your daughter's wedding," Peter said. "We'll try not to be in the way."

"We are honored to have you here," Mrs. Bhattacharya said. "And now if you will excuse me, I must get back to the kitchen. We are preparing a special curry for our many guests, and I must be sure it is cooked properly. Oh, there is so much to do! If you don't mind, my daughters will entertain you."

"We don't mind at all," he said. "I'm sure they will be very helpful."

As soon as she left the room, Sevati fastened her dark eyes on Singh. "So where is the silk you promised to bring?"

"You brazen thing," he said. "Have you no patience?"

"I don't believe you brought anything at all," she said, pretending to pout.

"Oh, very well. If you must have it now." He pulled several folded pieces of colored silk from his bag.

The girls burst into squeals of delight and leaned forward to touch it.

"I want the yellow," cried Parvani.

"Please may I have the blue?" begged Jeevana.

"Have you brought anything forbidden?" Sevati asked in a low voice, and they all glanced at the doorway to be sure their mother was not there.

"Of course I haven't brought anything forbidden," Singh said. "What a question! You will be giving Mr. and Mrs. Hoenig a bad opinion of this village."

"I don't mind if you take my picture," Parvani said shyly, looking up at Peter. "I like to have my picture taken."

"Don't pay her any mind," Singh said. "She's quite shameless."

Parvani ducked her head shyly.

"We have a camera and a gramophone," Sevati said proudly. "We have some jazz records too."

"Don't be telling them that," Singh said. "You want to have your records confiscated?"

"I don't see what it hurts," she said with a toss of her head. "We're ever so far behind the times. There are loads of things we don't have which our cousins in Bangalore have. Whenever they visit us, they pity us."

"It's you who should pity them," Singh said. "They are losing more of their culture every day, but you . . . you are growing up a living symbol of the culture of India. That makes you very special."

"You put it so beautifully," Darshana said. "Do you sit around thinking up things to say like that or do you think of them on the spur of the moment?"

The other girls giggled at her audacity.

"I assure you it was quite spontaneous," Singh said.

"Tell us about Bangalore!" Sevati begged.

"You know I can't."

"Can't you come visit us more often?" Darshana asked.

"Regretfully I cannot. I can only come when I have permission, and that is only when I have been asked to be a guide."

"Excuse me," Peter interrupted, "but just how isolated is this village? Their mother said they have relatives coming from Bangalore?"

"Ah, but their relatives had to get permission. Of course for something as important as a wedding, permission would not be refused. Otherwise, no one would want to live here."

Mele knew that answer would not satisfy Peter, but it made sense to her.

"I'm going to go to Delhi when I grow up," Jeevana announced.

"Not if Mama and Papa have anything to say about it," Sevati said. "You'll marry a boy they pick out for you and you'd better hope he won't have a mother who beats you."

Jeevana was about to retort, but Singh stood up just then, ending the argument as the sisters protested that he must not leave yet. "I must show Mr. Hoenig the purification ceremony for the groom. Will you be so good as to entertain Mrs. Hoenig while we are gone?"

"Oh, can't I go with you?" Mele asked, not wanting to be left behind. How could she help Peter with his research if she was not permitted to go with him?

"I'm afraid that would be awkward," Singh said. "The groom is being bathed and then they will rub *haldi* on him. The only women present will be his female relatives."

"I'm sorry," Peter said, turning to her. "Do you mind?"

"Of course not," she said, trying to hide her disappointment.

"I promise these lovely young ladies will take good care of you," Singh said, "and we'll only be two streets away at a neighbor's house where the groom is staying."

As soon as the two young men had left the room, the girls turned shy again.

"Would you like more lemonade, Mrs. Hoenig?" Darshana asked politely.

"No, thank you, and please call me Mele."

Darshana smiled, and they all seemed to relax a little. Sevati leaned forward, dark eyes shining.

"What's it like to be married?" she asked, lowering her voice almost to a whisper.

"You can't ask her that!" Darshana objected.

"Why can't I?"

"It isn't proper."

"Why isn't it proper? It's not about the outside world."

"But it's *personal*," Darshana said. "It's very rude to ask her such a question."

Sevati rolled her eyes.

"Have you got any children?" Parvani asked.

No one objected to this question. They all waited raptly for her answer.

"No," Mele said. "We only got married three days ago."

The girls exchanged quick looks, their interest piqued.

"Are you on your honeymoon?" Sevati asked. This caused everybody to break into giggles and glance nervously at the doorway again.

"I suppose we are."

"Do you know if Singh has a girlfriend?" Jeevana asked.

They all watched her, waiting for her answer.

"I have no idea. Why don't you ask him?"

"We did," Darshana said. "He said he doesn't, but how could he not have a girlfriend when he's so handsome?"

"He probably has several girlfriends," Sevati said. "Dozens even."

"Sevati!" Darshana said.

"Darshana wants to marry him," Jeevana said.

"I do not." Darshana tossed a small pillow at her, which she caught.

"Are you in love with him?" Mele asked.

"Most desperately," Darshana admitted. "But he treats me like a sister. I don't think he knows I'm alive."

"Why don't you tell him how you feel?"

"Oh, I couldn't do that!" She looked shocked.

"Besides, she has to marry whoever Mama and Papa want

her to marry," Sevati said. "We all do. The only way it could happen is if Singh's people came to them to arrange it, and what are the chances of that happening?"

The conversation halted abruptly as their mother sailed into the room. Her black hawk eyes swept over their faces suspiciously. Mele thought she could hear a collective intake of breath. Had their mother heard them talking about Singh? Then Mrs. Bhattacharya smiled. "Come, come. Your sister has finished her bath. They have just started *haldi* and then after that will be *mehendi*. You must all come watch."

Mele hesitated as the others jumped up, wondering if she was included. Darshana, noticing her hesitation, pulled her to her feet and linked arms with her. "You come too."

"Are you sure no one will mind?"

"Of course not. That is why you are here—to see a traditional Indian wedding."

Mele was surprised to find that so much activity was going on in a room not far from where they had been sitting. A number of women and girls were standing about talking while younger children ran in between people, playing their own games. In the center of the room a pretty young woman in a red-brown patterned Indian dress sat on a small stool. Several of the women were applying a yellow paste to her face and arms and feet while others offered good-natured advice and she tried not to laugh.

"What are they doing?" Mele asked.

"They are rubbing turmeric on her," Darshana explained. "It makes her clean, as Singh said, and also it makes her skin beautiful."

After the women had finished, another stool was brought forward and placed in front of the bride. The bowl that had held the yellow turmeric paste was taken away and another containing a brown paste appeared. One woman stepped forward and seated herself on the stool and the bride held out a hand to her. Everyone drew closer to watch. At first Mele thought the woman was giving the bride a manicure, but then she saw the woman was painting intricate designs on the bride's hand with a small pen-like instrument which she dipped into the brown paste.

"Can I see?" Parvani asked, trying to squeeze to the front.

"Yes, you can all see," Mrs. Bhattacharya said, "but don't bump Mrs. Pundir." Presumably Mrs. Pundir was the woman painting the bride's hands.

"Come closer," Darshana urged Mele. "You must see what they are doing."

"And who is this?" the bride asked. She was careful not to move, but her black-rimmed eyes lifted to meet Mele's.

"This is Mele," Darshana said. "She's come with her husband to watch the wedding. Singh brought them."

"Is Singh here?" the bride asked.

"He and Mr. Hoenig went to see Raj's *haldi* ceremony."

"Mele just got married a few days ago," Jeevana volunteered as she squirmed into position between Mele and Darshana.

"You look very different from the usual visitors," the bride observed.

"Different how?" Mele asked.

"Well, they aren't usually women, and if they are, they are not very attractive and they look as if they have no idea how to wear a sari. But you! If we lined your eyes with *kaajal*, you would look like one of us."

Parvani clapped her hands in delight. "Oh, can we do that?"

"Not unless she wants you to," Mrs. Bhattacharya said.

"Can I get *mehendi* on my hands too?" Parvani asked, holding out her hands.

"When you are older," Mrs. Bhattacharya said.

Parvani's face fell.

Mele debated whether to ask the bride a question that was on her mind. Maybe it would be better to ask it in private, but she might not get another opportunity. Leaning forward so hopefully only the bride could hear, she asked: "Are you happy you're getting married?"

"Of course she's happy," snapped Mrs. Bhattacharya, who evidently had excellent hearing. "What young woman is not happy the day before her wedding?"

The sisters and the other women laughed nervously, and no one contradicted her.

"Now let Mrs. Pundir have a little more space or we'll be here all evening."

Everybody took a step back. Mele watched in fascination as Mrs. Pundir's pen did its magic and flowers and whorls gradually proliferated on the palms of the bride's hands and then the backs of her hands, filling every inch and moving up her slender fingers.

"When she is finished with Kamala's hands, she will paint her feet," Darshana explained to Mele.

The children had lost interest now and returned to playing their games, while the women stood in clusters talking.

"Why is she painting your sister's hands and feet?" Mele asked.

"To make them beautiful, of course. And also to keep away evil spirits."

"Is it permanent? I mean, will it wash off?"

"It should last for several weeks. It's henna, you know."

Mele had no idea what henna was. Anyway something else

had occurred to her. "The man your sister's marrying—he's not an old man, is he?"

"I should say not," Darshana said. "He can't be more than twenty-three."

"And he has no other wives?"

Darshana clapped her hand over her mouth to keep from laughing. "Most definitely not. What a thought—Raj with other wives!"

"Then you know him?"

"Of course we know him."

"But I thought Singh said marriage was arranged by the parents—that young people often don't even meet before the wedding."

"That is true. But in this case our parents arranged for Kamala to marry Raj, and Raj is our cousin, so you see we know him very well. We all played together when we were children."

"She's marrying her cousin?" Mele said, surprised.

"It's much better this way," Darshana assured her. "She won't be mistreated by her husband or his mother or sisters. And sometimes she can come home to visit. Kamala is very lucky. Not like our cousin Devi."

"Was she mistreated?"

"They killed her."

Mele stared at her. "How?"

"They burned her. They set her on fire." Darshana said it so matter-of-factly. Was she serious? She certainly seemed to be.

"Who burned her? Why?"

Darshana glanced sideways to see if her mother was listening, then lowering her voice, said, "Most probably they did it so he could marry again and get another dowry."

"Couldn't he have divorced her?" Mele asked, struggling to understand.

Darshana shook her head. "Divorce is a disgrace."

"They murdered her? And that is not considered a disgrace?"

"Oh, they said it was suicide, but everyone knows the truth. All over India when a wife dies by fire they say it is suicide, but everyone knows the truth."

"All over India?"

"That's right. It's quite common actually."

"It's not common," interrupted Sevati, who apparently had been listening to their conversation. "You're exaggerating."

"It happens," Darshana said, shrugging. "You can't deny it happens."

After Peter and Singh returned in the early afternoon, Mele and Peter wandered into the yard, where the preparations for the wedding festivities were underway. He described to her what he and Singh had witnessed, the ritual application of turmeric paste by the groom's female relatives to his hair, his hands, and his feet.

"It was the same with the bride," Mele said.

"You saw it?"

"Yes, and afterwards they painted her hands and feet with beautiful designs."

"That would be the *mehendi* ceremony." He grinned. "You'll have to tell me everything you saw. In fact, could you write it down?"

"Of course." It was funny how excited he was. He was like a kid on Christmas morning.

"This is great. I thought I'd have to make do with what

Singh told me about it, but it's much better if I have a first-hand account. Besides, since Singh is a man, he's probably never seen the ceremony himself."

"So it will help your research?"

"Absolutely."

She saw opening before her a vision of their future. She could be his eyes and ears in the places where only women were allowed. She would be his research partner. This was just the beginning, and in the future, after she had earned a university degree, they would travel and explore the world together. Maybe someday they would even be famous. This was the destiny that was waiting for her. And to think she might have stayed on Ni'ihau her entire life and missed it!

Throughout the rest of the day people continued to arrive for the wedding. Mele and Peter were introduced to grandparents, aunts, uncles, cousins, friends, and neighbors. No one seemed to have any qualms about mingling with them, and whenever Peter protested that they were only there to observe, Mrs. Bhattacharya or one of the aunts brushed his concerns aside as if they had been gnats.

"You are our guests," Mrs. Bhattacharya insisted. "What would people think if we didn't entertain you properly?"

With the influx of so many relatives, Mele wondered where they would all sleep, but when it was night everyone seemed to know where to go. Peter and Singh disappeared into one room with the male cousins and Mele found herself in another with the Bhattacharya sisters and their female cousins, mats spread over nearly every inch of the floor. After she lay down, if she reached out her hand, she could touch Darshana lying next to her. It seemed very strange to be crowded together with so many others, and she wondered if she would be able to fall asleep, but she was tired and soon drifted off.

In the morning the air was electric with excitement from the time she woke up. Chattering, the women decked themselves in their best dresses and saris and helped each other with their hair and their makeup. The two mirrors in the house were much in demand. Darshana and her cousin Shanti, a tall willowy beauty, helped Mele don a purple Indian dress with a purple sari, draped colorful beads around her neck, slipped bangles on her arms, braided her hair, lined her eyes with *kaajal*, and painted a small red dot on her forehead. When they were done and she looked in the mirror, she thought she could have passed for a young Indian woman. The transformation was amazing.

Next came breakfast, and then after breakfast, along with the other women and girls, she watched Mrs. Bhattacharya apply more of the oil and yellow turmeric to Kamala's hair and arms and recite blessings in their language. Then Kamala was bathed again and her long black hair braided and decorated with flowers and jewels. It took several hours in all. When they were finished, Kamala was resplendent in a dark red dress with a sari embroidered in gold. Large gold earrings dangled from her ears, a half dozen necklaces of gold and colored glass hung about her neck, a dozen bangles adorned her arms, and her henna-painted fingers sparkled with rings. Her slender ankles were encircled by silver anklets and her feet were shod in silver sandals. Behind one ear was tucked a white jasmine. A delicate chain of small gems glittered on her forehead, just above her eyebrows, and a fragile gold chain linked a small pierced diamond in her nose to another in her ear. The aunts clucked excitedly as they bustled about her. Last of all came the red veil of beads that would hide her face.

"I think I'm going to be sick," Kamala said, watching them in the mirror as they secured it.

"You're going to do no such thing," said Mrs. Bhattacharya. "Just take a deep breath."

Outside a canopy had been erected in the yard and decorated with flowers. There were people everywhere. Where had they all come from? Mele wondered. Children ran about between the tables. Women sat on chairs in the shade, fanning themselves. She found Peter and for a moment he didn't recognize her in her purple dress and sari. Singh had given him a cream-colored Indian dress coat and matching pants to wear, but with his fair skin and brown hair he did not exactly blend in.

"You look very handsome," Mele said.

"I feel ridiculous," Peter said, "but it's kind of you to say so. I'm surprised the bride allows you to come to her wedding looking like that. Isn't she afraid she'll be eclipsed?" He held up his camera. "May I?"

She smiled, and he snapped a photo of her.

"Any idea what's happening over there?" He nodded toward a cluster of women seated under a banyan tree. "I'm afraid of going over, but maybe you could get close enough to find out what they're up to. I've been watching them for the past fifteen minutes, and I'm dying to know what they're doing."

"They're probably just talking, but I'll see what I can find out."

As Mele started across the lawn, she saw Darshana emerge from the house and decided to enlist her help.

"Do you know what those women under the banyan tree are doing?" she asked as Darshana drew near.

Darshana grinned. "I can guess. Come on. I'll show you." She picked up a plate of pastries from the nearest table and approached the women. They were not speaking in English, so at first Mele could not understand. Sheets of paper and photographs were being passed from hand to hand. Some of the women had put on reading glasses.

Darshana held out the platter to them. "Who are you trying to match?" she asked, her eyes falling on a photograph. "That fellow's nice-looking."

There was an immediate outburst of objections. "Go away," one of the aunts said, flapping her arms. "This is business for married women, not young girls. Maybe it is you we are discussing, Miss Nosy. It is your turn next now that your sister's getting married."

"Well, then please choose someone handsome," Darshana said. "I don't want an ugly husband."

"Shoo," another said. "You'll marry whoever your parents say you should marry."

Darshana and Mele wandered back to the table.

"There, you see," Darshana said. "They can't wait for the next wedding. I dread to think who they'll pick for me." She looked around the crowd of people with a small pout of dissatisfaction, then suddenly brightened. "There's Singh. Let's go talk to him."

It was midmorning when the groom and his party arrived. Although they had been staying with neighbors nearby, they did not simply walk over but arrived with fanfare in a procession accompanied by a brass band. Everyone stopped talking to watch. Children crowded forward to see. As the band approached, Mele saw behind them a gaily decorated open carriage pulled by two white horses tossing their heads as if to shake off their jeweled bridles.

The bridegroom was easy to spot, dressed in gleaming white silk with a jeweled turban on his head that glittered when it caught the light. With him were his two brothers, also splendidly dressed, and in a second carriage his parents. Walking along behind were a number of uncles and male cousins. The rest of his relatives were already at the event.

As the groom and his party alighted, Mr. and Mrs. Bhattacharya greeted them and Mrs. Bhattacharya dabbed a bit of yellow turmeric on his forehead in welcome, after which the groom handed her a coconut.

"It symbolizes fertility," Singh explained. He was standing just behind Peter and Mele.

The crowd parted for the groom and his family to walk with the Bhattacharyas to the wedding canopy, where a Brahmin priest waited. After the sacred fire pot was blessed by the priest, two assistants held up a curtain to prevent the groom from seeing his bride as she was led from the house by one of her uncles. When she had taken her place on her side of the curtain, the priest chanted and everyone tossed rice at the couple.

"That is also for fertility," Singh said. "Everyone wants them to have children."

The curtain was removed then and the bridegroom and bride seated themselves on mats facing each other. The crowd drew closer to watch.

"The fire represents the god Agni," Singh said quietly.

The priest began to speak.

"He's reciting from the sacred texts—from the Vedas."

After a bit the bride and groom tossed small handfuls of rice and butter into the fire.

"Offerings to the god," Singh murmured.

When the bride placed a garland of red roses and white jasmine around the groom's neck and he a similar garland around hers, Mele held Peter's hand tighter. She was surprised to see they gave leis like her people on Ni'ihau and for a moment her vision blurred as tears sprang to her eyes.

As the hours passed, people wandered away and then returned, but always there was a cluster of onlookers around the canopy. In the middle of the afternoon the bride and groom held hands as they circled the fire pot seven times.

Mr. Bhattacharya spoke and the groom's father responded in his deep voice.

"He says he gives them his beautiful virgin daughter," Singh translated. "And the groom's father says he accepts her for his son and as part of his family."

Soon the bride and groom stood up again, held hands, and walked slowly together.

"They are taking the seven steps," Singh explained. "With each step they make a promise. They promise to be kind to each other and to be friends forever."

Mr. Bhattacharya spoke again and handed some small leaves to the groom.

"He has declared his ancestry and he is giving the groom some grains of rice and betel plant leaves. It signifies he's giving the groom his daughter and he agrees to pay the expenses of the wedding."

The groom's father took the bride's hand and placed it in the hand of his son. Then he poured water from a pitcher over their joined hands. The groom fastened a jewel set in gold around the bride's neck.

"It's a *tali*," Singh said. "It symbolizes that she is a married woman now."

They watched as the bride dipped a finger into a small bowl of red paste and then touched it to the groom's brow, making a red dot.

"The *tikka*," Singh explained. "The eye of Shiva."

Then the groom removed his bride's veil of beads and, putting his thumb into the same red paste, solemnly made a matching dot on her brow.

When the sun went down, torches were lit and the celebration continued. It had been a long day, and Mele had had hardly a minute to herself, so, hoping to have a break from all the ritual and the need to smile and make conversation with strangers, she wandered into the garden. She had been there only a few minutes, breathing in the heavy perfume of the flowers and looking up at the stars when she heard footsteps and turned, expecting to see Peter. Instead it was Singh, his immaculate white suit gleaming in the moonlight.

"Do you mind if I join you?" he asked.

"No, of course not. I just thought I'd. . . ."

"You don't have to explain. Hindus must have the longest weddings in the world. Even the bride and groom are probably wondering when it will end."

"It's nice though—having so many relatives and friends around for their wedding."

"Ah. And where you come from, are your wedding customs so different?"

"On my island we have a big celebration on the beach. We cook a pig in a pit we dig in the ground."

"Ah, yes, your island," he said, white teeth flashing. "A pig!"

She wondered if she had shocked him. He was a Hindu, wasn't he? That meant he didn't eat meat. Peter had explained earlier that was why there was no meat at the banquet. Singh probably thought she and Peter were barbarians because they ate meat. She regretted having mentioned the pig.

"I know it's none of my business," Singh said, "but may I ask you a question? How is it that you and your husband . . . ?" He paused, hunting for words. "I mean no offense. You seem so . . . well . . . different."

"I guess we are different," Mele said.

"He reminds me of the British boys I went to school with."

"Peter's not British."

"No, of course not. He's American." That dazzling smile again. "I'm afraid I'm expressing myself badly. What I meant to say is you are more like us."

"Am I?"

"Yes, you are."

They looked at each other.

He smiled. "I don't just mean your skin or your hair. It's something deeper I sense in you. When I look at you, I feel I've known you before."

"But you haven't—unless you've been to Niʻihau."

"Perhaps we met in a previous life."

"I don't believe in previous lives."

"No? Nor future ones either?"

She knew she should go back to the wedding festivities, but she was curious what he would say next. She was intensely aware of how close he was standing. The truth was she was deeply attracted to Singh. He made her wonder what it would have been like to marry someone else. Suppose Singh had come to her island instead of Peter. She might have linked her destiny with his instead of Peter's. She might be Singh's wife standing in this garden with him, and they might have been more suited to each other than she and Peter were. Maybe India was a country where she would have felt at home. She could have worn saris and lots of bangles on her arms every day and painted a red *tikka* between her eyebrows.

"You are very beautiful," he said, leaning forward to kiss her on the lips.

She knew she ought to stop him, but she didn't. He smelled faintly of cologne and unfamiliar spice. She asked herself why she was letting him kiss her. Was it because she had been curious what it would be like to kiss him? Or was it because she wanted him to kiss her? It was almost as if she had willed it. And it didn't seem wrong. Why was that? Could he be right that they were somehow meant for each other? That they had been together in a past life or were meant to be together in future lives? That they might have been destined to be together in this one if she had not met Peter? But of course that could not have happened. If Peter had not come along, she would still be on Niʻihau and would not have met Singh at all. She forced herself to take a step back.

He looked at her. "I should not have done that. Forgive me."

"There's nothing to forgive."

"I was carried away. I thought—"

"You don't have to explain."

He sighed, glancing toward the sounds of Indian music and the babble of voices beyond the garden wall, then back at her. "Your husband is a very fortunate man. I hope he knows that."

She didn't know what to say. She watched Singh turn and walk away. When he was gone, she stood for a moment trying to collect her thoughts. It was as if the earth had tilted on its axis. Had she married one man only to fall in love with another? Had she made a terrible mistake?

Still inwardly churning, she wandered back to the wedding party in search of Peter. She spotted him standing near a table laden with food talking to Darshana's cousin, Shanti. Looking beautiful in a gold and red Indian dress, Shanti held a glass of lemonade in her hand while she gazed up at Peter and laughed at something he had said. Seeing Mele approach, she excused herself and slipped away.

"She's very pretty, isn't she?" Mele said as Shanti rejoined her cousins at the wedding canopy.

"What?" Peter said. "Oh, yes, I guess so. Where have you been?"

"In the garden."

"You got away from this circus, did you? I don't blame you. I don't know how they do it. I'm dying for a break."

"Have you gotten many pictures?" she asked, hoping he would ask no questions about the time she had spent in the garden.

"Tons."

"What are they doing now?" She glanced again toward the canopy.

"Just sitting there as far as I can tell. It would put me to sleep to have to listen to those Sanskrit mantras for so many hours."

"Then I guess it was fortunate we had a much shorter ceremony with no Sanskrit mantras." Mele looked down at the ring on her finger, which she had only been wearing for five days. When she put it on, she had promised her grandmother that she would love Peter forever. She wished she could tell her grandmother about Singh, but, no, even if her grandmother were here, she could not do that. She was married now. She had made a promise. She would have to get Singh out of her mind.

"Are you okay?" Peter asked. "You seem a little preoccupied."

"Look at Mr. and Mrs. Bhattacharya," she said.

The bride's parents stood side by side under the canopy watching their daughter with obvious pride and joy.

"What about them?"

"They seem to love each other, don't they?"

"Yes, I suppose they do."

"Have you noticed how he stands very close to her and whispers in her ear sometimes?"

"No, I hadn't noticed."

"I wonder what he says to her."

"He probably says I wonder when this will end."

"I'm serious."

"Sorry."

"Do you think we'll be like that when we're their age? You know, comfortable with each other?"

"We're comfortable now, aren't we?"

Before she could answer, two ladies approached the food table talking animatedly. When they saw Peter and Mele, they smiled shyly and retreated.

"Do you notice how people stop talking when we're near?" she asked.

"That's natural. There's bound to be some awkwardness. We're outsiders."

"Maybe, but I get the feeling they're talking about something they don't want us to hear."

"You're imagining things."

Was she? Perhaps. It reminded her of how she had felt when she had gone to Kaua'i at the age of fourteen to attend high school. That same feeling of not fitting in, of people talking about things she didn't understand, of secrets kept from her.

"I wish I could be with you tonight," she said wistfully.

"You are with me."

"You know what I mean."

"It'll only be a little longer. You don't really mind sleeping with the unmarried girls, do you?"

How could she explain to him that she felt lonely? The Bhattacharya sisters had gone to great lengths to make her feel welcome, but there was so much strangeness. She missed her family, her friends, her old life. She would have liked to curl up with Peter the way they had in Yang Yi's apartment in Kunming. She wanted him to make her stop thinking about Singh. She wanted to feel again that she had made the right decision. Instead she felt lost and unsure.

Later that night she would lie again surrounded by the sisters and their cousins, listening to their soft whispering in the dark and an occasional stifled giggle, and she would remember how Singh had kissed her in the garden, the feel of his lips on hers, his dark face in the moonlight. Probably she would never tell Peter about that.

Early the next morning when the first light was pouring through the windows, she was awakened by chattering voices. She would have liked to sleep longer. It seemed too early to get up. Surely she had had only a few hours of sleep? But Darshana was kneeling beside her, tapping her arm to wake her.

"Hurry and get dressed."

"What is it?" she asked, raising herself on her elbows. She was surprised to see the other women and girls already up. They were getting dressed, slipping bangles on their arms, vying for the mirror, giggling, and talking in low excited whispers.

"We are going out," Darshana said. "If you want to come, you must hurry."

"Where are you going?"

"I can't tell you. You must dress quickly if you want to come with us and ask no questions."

"Is everyone going?" Mele looked around the room.

"Yes, as you can see, we are all going," Darshana said impatiently. "Now please hurry."

Mele supposed it was a continuation of the marriage festivities from the night before. "What should I wear?"

"Here, put this on." Darshana handed her a yellow cotton Indian dress and a sari.

She stood, stretched, and slipped into the dress. "Is Peter coming?"

Darshana adjusted the sari for her with practiced skill. "There. You look just like one of us."

"What about Peter?"

Darshana held a finger to her lips, and Shanti rolled her eyes. The door was open now, and the young women in front were peeking out. They slipped out noiselessly, one after another. Whatever they were doing, they were doing it on the sly. That made her curious. Maybe it was another of those female rituals from which males were excluded, like *haldi* or *mehendi*. If she went with them, she might observe something that would be useful for Peter's research project.

Once outside, the sisters and their cousins hurried along the street. Several men silently fell into step beside them. Mele recognized two of the male cousins and an uncle. So men were permitted to attend this mysterious ritual after all. In fact, it seemed as if the whole neighborhood was planning to attend. People emerged from their houses as the young women passed. Soon they were part of a stream of people, all flowing in the same direction. Everyone seemed to be going to this event, even the children.

"Where are we going?" she asked Darshana again, but Darshana just shook her head and walked a little faster. Mele supposed she would have to wait until they got to their destination to find out. Maybe they were going to a temple. Maybe it was a holy day. At any rate it seemed like more than just another ritual connected with the wedding festivities. There had been a lot of people at Kamala's wedding, but now the whole community seemed to be in motion.

"Hurry," Shanti urged. "We must get close enough to see."

"To see what?" Mele asked, but no one answered her.

The crowd had grown by now. People pressed against her from all sides as she struggled to stay near Darshana. She was surrounded by a pandemonium of voices, unable to understand what they were saying. The crowd swept her along as they swarmed up a hill. She could not have stopped if she had wanted. At the top they seemed to hesitate. There was no place else to go. All the hillside and the plain below were a seething mass of people. So were the neighboring hills. Where had they all come from? She had never seen so many people in one place before.

"We are too far away," one cousin said in disappointment.

"I brought glasses," Shanti said, pulling out a pair of binoculars. The others murmured their approval of her foresight.

"What is it?" Mele asked. "What's happening?"

"*Sati*," Darshana said in her ear, or at least that was what Mele thought she said.

"What does it mean?"

"It is a wife's ultimate duty," Darshana said solemnly. "It is her *dharma*."

"I don't understand."

Shanti thrust the binoculars into her hands. "Put them up to your eyes."

Mele held the binoculars to her eyes. At first she saw only a sea of people brought closer by the power of the binoculars. "What is it?" she asked, still not understanding. Then, in the midst of all that teeming humanity, she saw something like a parade float. She had seen floats in a parade in Lihu'e on the island of Kaua'i. Like those floats, this one was covered with flowers, but unlike them, it wasn't moving. It was surrounded by people, and on it a man lay sleeping, arms at his sides, face up to the morning sun. As she watched, a young woman in a red sari was lifted onto the float or platform. Her jewels glinted in the sunlight.

"Is it Kamala?" Mele asked.

"Of course not," Shanti said, tossing her head. "Kamala is on her way to Mysore with Raj and his family."

The crowd around them was jabbering in their own tongue and Mele could make nothing of it. The next thing she knew Shanti had snatched back the binoculars and raised them to her own eyes.

"What's happening?" Darshana asked.

"They have put her on the bier," Shanti said.

"Is she struggling?" Darshana stood on tiptoe and squinted.

"Probably they have drugged her," Shanti said. "They usually do. Nevertheless, she is trying to resist."

"Who is she?" Mele asked, filled with a vague dread. "And what are they going to do?"

No one answered. She wished the crowd around her would not press so closely. It was too hot and there were too many people, all trying to see. She wanted to go back.

Whatever was going on down there, she didn't want to see it. But she couldn't move. There was no way of going back, just as there was no way of moving forward. She was pinned where she was, and whatever was happening on the plain below was going to happen.

The binoculars were passed around silently, and soon they were in her hands again. The young woman in the red sari sprang into her view, sitting upright but swaying slightly, surrounded by flowers. Beside her the man slept on. Of course he was not sleeping; he was dead. She knew that now. Maybe she had known from the first, but her mind had not wanted to acknowledge it.

"What are they going to do to her?" she asked as Shanti took the binoculars from her hands. But she knew the answer even before little Parvani said it.

"Burn her."

Mele felt overwhelmed with horror. "But why? What has she done?"

"She hasn't done anything," Jeevana said. "Her husband died. It's her duty as his wife to join him."

"They are lighting the pyre!" someone said.

There was a collective intake of breath. The crowd pressed forward, although there was no place to go. Mele felt as if she would be crushed. When Darshana handed her the binoculars, she shook her head. She didn't want to see any more.

"Just think, she is only nineteen years old!" Darshana said in a hushed voice.

"Her parents should have chosen a younger man," Shanti said.

"Even young men can die."

"Well, let us hope that the husbands our parents choose are young and healthy."

"May I look?" asked Parvani. Shanti handed her the binoculars, and Darshana lifted her so she could see over the crowd.

"Can't somebody do something?" Mele asked. "Can't somebody stop it?"

"It's too late," Darshana said. "They have lighted the fire. And even if they could stop it, they wouldn't."

"It's a terrible custom," Mele said. "Why did you bring me here? Why did you show me this?"

"I thought you'd want to see it," Darshana said. "I thought you were interested in our customs."

"I want to go back," Mele said, feeling she could not stand it another minute. She struggled to turn around, but she was wedged tightly between the people behind her and the sisters in front. Panic began to rise in her. She pushed blindly, but it was like pushing against a wall.

"Stop," Darshana cried. "What are you doing?"

She pushed harder. She felt like she could not get her breath. She had to get out of that crush of bodies or she would suffocate. Hands seemed to paw at her, and her arm was wrenched painfully. She cried out and then everything seemed to slip away as she felt herself falling into blackness. The thought flashed through her mind that she would be trampled to death.

When Mele woke, she was stretched out on a couch in the Bhattacharya's sitting room. She recognized the ceiling fan lazily rotating overhead. An unfamiliar Indian man was looking down at her, his black hair turning gray, kind eyes peering at her through wire-rimmed glasses.

"Ah, the young lady is awake now."

"What happened?" she asked. "How did I get here?"

Peter was beside her, holding her hand. "You fainted."

She remembered now the press of the crowd and the girl in the red sari on the float. No, not a float, a funeral bier. People had set fire to it. The girl was going to be burned alive. That hadn't been a dream, had it? She had to tell Peter. "There was a girl—"

"Try not to think about it."

So he knew. "It was horrible," she said, remembering.

"My daughters were very naughty to take you there," said Mrs. Bhattacharya, also bending over her now. "I have scolded them severely. If I had known they would take you there, I would have stopped them. It's a dreadful custom, of course, dreadful. So backward. You must not judge us by such customs."

"How did I get here?" Mele asked.

"I carried you back," Peter said.

She struggled to understand. "But how did you find me?"

"It wasn't easy. But Singh and I came after you as soon as he realized where you had gone. The girls were trying to get you out of the crowd. You've got some bruises, but the doctor says nothing's broken."

She remembered how panicked she had felt, the overwhelming need to escape the press of people. "I thought I was going to be crushed to death."

"It happens," the doctor said. "You were lucky."

"They should never have taken you there," Singh said. "You should not have seen that."

"Why did they do it?" Mele tried to sit up. She felt lightheaded but didn't want to just lie there with all of them hovering around her.

"It's an old custom," Singh said. "Unfortunately one that has not completely died out."

"Why doesn't someone stop it?"

"Oh, they have tried. The British tried to put an end to it years ago. It's against the law."

"But then why—?"

"*Sati* still happens even though it's been outlawed. Even in other areas it sometimes happens and then they put up plaques declaring the site a place of pilgrimage. The authorities do what they can to discourage the practice, but it still happens. I would of course prefer you didn't mention this to the Alliance. You were not supposed to see it."

"She could have been killed," Peter said, anger in his voice.

"Well, she should not have gone off like that with the sisters," Singh said.

"It's all right." She didn't want them to quarrel. They had both come to her rescue. Peter was her husband; Singh had kissed her in the moonlight. Neither could understand what she was feeling. What she wanted more than anything else at that moment was to go home. She should not have left. In her mind she saw again the young woman in the red sari on the platform surrounded by flowers beside her dead husband. Drugged, Shanti had said. They had burned her alive with all those people watching and no one had tried to stop it. She had never imagined the world could be such a terrible place.

# 7

# Afghanistan, part 1

As they came out of customs in Kabul, they were met by Ahmad, a lean young Afghan. He was their guide, and he was clearly not happy that Peter had brought a woman with him.

"She cannot visit the Forbidden Place," he insisted. "It is out of the question."

"But we have permission," Peter said. "It's been approved by the Alliance. If you don't believe me, call them."

"It does not matter. She cannot come." He glanced with obvious distaste at Mele, who stood a short distance away but close enough to hear. She was wearing jeans and a white top, her hair pulled back in a long ponytail. While they talked, she was looking about the bustling terminal at the other people who were arriving and being greeted by family and friends. Some wore Western attire and others flowing robes and turbans or loose woven shirts and pants.

"Why can't she come? She's my wife, and she has permission."

Ahmad sighed. "I am telling you, you cannot take a woman there."

"Why not? Aren't there women there?"

"Of course there are women there. But they are village women. This is different."

"Well, if she doesn't go, I don't go," Peter said, determined to stand his ground. After what had happened in India, he was not about to abandon Mele in a strange city.

Ahmad shrugged. "Suit yourself. It makes no difference to me."

His attitude irked Peter. "And I will tell the Alliance you refused to take us although they gave us permission."

"I did not refuse," Ahmad objected. "You can't say that. It is a lie."

"We'll have to put up in a hotel until it's time for our next flight. That will cost money and be very inconvenient."

"It is not my problem."

"So you think the Alliance won't mind paying for our added expenses?"

At this Ahmad looked uneasy. "Perhaps I was hasty. I was only trying to say it is a hard journey, especially for a woman. Your wife could stay here in a hotel and wait for your return. I assure you she would be much more comfortable."

"I'm not leaving my wife alone in a hotel in Kabul," Peter said. "We have permission for her to travel with me."

Ahmad shook his head and sighed again. "You Americans think you own the world. Very well, if you insist, I will take you, but"—he threw a dark look at Mele—"she will have to wear a burqa. She cannot go around uncovered. It's too dangerous."

"What's a burqa?" Mele asked, dropping her pretense of not listening and moving closer to Peter.

"It's a sort of head-to-toe covering," Peter said.

"Do your women wear this burqa?" she asked Ahmad.

"They do," he said, reluctant to look directly at her.

"Then I will too."

"Are you sure?" Peter asked doubtfully. "You could stay here if you wanted." While he didn't like the idea of being separated from her, he also didn't like to ask her to wear a burqa. He had the impression they were hot and uncomfortable, not to mention demeaning, especially for a Western woman. Much as he hated to admit it, maybe Ahmad was right about leaving her behind in Kabul.

She looked at Ahmad, who would not meet her gaze. "Do they burn women in the Forbidden Place?"

"Of course not," he said, so surprised he forgot not to look at her. "Why do you ask such a question?"

"Just checking." She turned to Peter. "I want to go with you."

"Well, then, it's settled. We both go."

Ahmad looked unhappy but gave up arguing with them. "Very well, if you insist. But let it be on your head, not mine. I tried to warn you. Remember that. And now we should get started. It's a long journey, and we must find a burqa for your wife."

They found a burqa in a bazaar on the outskirts of Kabul. Then they were on their way. Ahmad's car was an old battered vehicle that belched exhaust, and Peter was not at all certain it was safe for a trip of the length they were undertaking to the remote village that was their destination. What would they do if it broke down on the way? Ahmad waved his concerns aside. "It has made the trip before. It will not be a problem."

For several hours they drove on the highway that led to Kandahar before turning off on a dusty road across the rocky desolate countryside toward the mountains. The burqa lay neatly folded on the seat between Mele and Peter. Ahmad had said she did not have to put it on yet; she could wait until they were closer to the Forbidden Place.

"Not many cars come this way, do they?" Peter observed after they had been driving on the dirt road for more than a half hour and had not seen a single vehicle.

"There is no reason for people to come this way. Besides, it is dangerous."

"Dangerous how?"

Ahmad shrugged. "Robbers, Taliban, criminals who are avoiding the law."

"You mean they stop cars?"

"Sometimes."

Peter wondered if he was just trying to scare them. Surely the Alliance would not have approved their visit here if it was dangerous.

"Your wife might want to take off that ring," Ahmad suggested. "If we are stopped, she could lose it. It is wise not to tempt fate."

Mele glanced down at her grandmother's ring.

"Maybe I should put it in my pocket," Peter said in a low voice.

She nodded, slipped the ring from her finger, and handed it to him.

"Your watch too," Ahmad said. "You should take off your watch before we get there. It is not a good idea to show off valuables like that."

Peter slid his watch off and tucked it into his bag.

They could not travel as fast on the dirt road as they had on the highway, but gradually they drew closer to the mountains. After about an hour Ahmad stopped the car.

"Why are we stopping?" Peter asked, looking around at the barren rocky terrain, where there was no sign of life.

"Soon we will reach the checkpoint," Ahmad said. "It is time to change."

They all climbed out, and Ahmad handed Peter a long-sleeved shirt of a coarse material. Peter took his own shirt off and put on the one Ahmad had provided for him. It hung down to his knees. Next came loose pants, a pair of sandals, and a scarf to tie around his head. Ahmad had quickly changed into a similar outfit himself. Meanwhile, on the other side of the car Mele had unfurled the black burqa and was looking at it in puzzlement.

"How does it go?" she asked.

"You pull it over your head," Ahmad said. "There is an opening for your eyes, a kind of window."

Mele pulled the burqa over her head. "But I can't see! And how am I supposed to breathe?" She flung it off again.

"But you must wear it," Ahmad said, dismayed. "You cannot go through the checkpoint without it. It would be dangerous. I cannot be responsible."

"Dangerous how?" Peter asked again.

"The men at the checkpoint are soldiers. They enforce the Islamic decree that a woman should cover herself."

"But Mele is not Islamic."

"It doesn't matter. A woman must be covered."

"What do they do if she isn't?"

"They have been known to beat women. They might also arrest her. I assure you, you would not want your wife to end up in one of our jails. They are not like jails in your country."

No, they wouldn't be, Peter thought. They would be squalid, filthy places without sanitation, presided over by brutal men, where torture routinely took place unseen.

"I think you'll have to wear it," he told Mele. "It's only until we get through the checkpoint."

"No," Ahmad said emphatically. "She must also wear it in the Forbidden Place. No woman there sets foot outside her house without the burqa. She would be beaten and spit on."

"But she can take it off when she's indoors, right?"

"Indoors, if no one objects, she can wear a headscarf."

Mele didn't say a word. She just pulled the burqa over her head again and climbed back into the car. When Peter climbed in beside her, she was completely hidden by the burqa except for her eyes, which peered out at him through the latticework window as if through the bars of a prison. He couldn't see them clearly enough to guess what she was thinking.

"Are you all right?" he asked, groping for her hand.

"It's hot. I feel as if I'm suffocating, but aside from that, I'm all right."

"I'm sorry. Maybe when we're past the checkpoint, you can take it off."

"Why do your women put up with this?" Mele asked Ahmad as they continued on their way.

"Because it is our way. The holy Qur'an says women should cover themselves."

"And do your men have to cover up too?"

"Yes, of course, but it is not the same for men. Burqas are for women only."

"And why is that?"

Peter hoped she did not antagonize Ahmad. They would need to rely on him when they got to the Forbidden Place, and it would make things awkward if he took offense.

But Ahmad seemed willing to explain his country's customs. "It is a matter of modesty. A woman should not show her skin in public."

"Why not?" Mele persisted, unwilling to let the subject drop. "I saw Afghan women in Kabul who dressed like Western women."

"Kabul is a city of much corruption. You will even see women without headscarves, but they are taking a risk. Respectable women cover themselves. They do not parade themselves before all men like common prostitutes and show bare legs, or bare arms, or hair. Men see these things and feel desire. It can lead to temptation, which can lead to immorality."

"But is it necessary to hide my face like this? I can barely see. I could trip. I could hurt myself."

"Even the face can be a temptation. Some Muslim women wear a half-veil, but you can still see their eyes and even a woman's eyes can tempt a man. The burqa is better. It eliminates all temptations."

"It makes women invisible, you mean."

"Is that the checkpoint up ahead?" Peter interrupted. He had just spotted a small makeshift building in the distance with a tent standing beside it. As they drew closer, he saw a barrier blocking the road.

"Yes, that is the checkpoint," Ahmad agreed. "Now say nothing. Especially your wife must be silent. Let me do the talking."

He stopped the car when they reached the barrier. A guard with an M-16 rifle came out of the building and approached the driver's side of the car, watching them warily. He leaned down and spoke to Ahmad in the local tongue through his open window, glancing in the back suspiciously at Mele in her black burqa and at Peter. Ahmad answered his questions, nodding, offering him a pack of gum. Peter wished he could understand what they were saying and hoped fervently that

Ahmad was doing a good job of explaining. The guard kept glancing at him. Finally he shouted and waved his gun in a threatening manner.

"I'm sorry," Ahmad said, turning. "We must get out of the car."

"Why?" Peter asked, alarmed.

"Just do as I say. Please. Get out of the car."

They did as he instructed. The guard looked at Mele uneasily and said something in his language to Ahmad.

"What's he saying?" Peter asked anxiously.

"Please," Ahmad said. "Let me handle this."

The guard rattled off a stream of words and waved his gun menacingly at them again.

"He wants your wife to go into the tent."

"No. Not unless I go with her."

"She must do it. They want to be sure she is a woman. They must be careful who they let past."

"American?" the guard said, his eyes narrowly watching Peter.

"Yes, American." Ahmad began speaking rapidly again in the local dialect.

"Did you tell him we have permission to visit the Forbidden Place?" Peter asked.

"Just please be quiet," Ahmad said. "You will make everything worse."

"It's all right," Mele said, touching his arm. She walked slowly toward the tent in her flowing black burqa, picking her way carefully across the stony ground in her sandals, and disappeared into the tent.

"They'd better not hurt her," Peter warned.

"They are only checking to see if she is indeed female," Ahmad assured him. "Sometimes men try to sneak past the checkpoints disguised in a burqa."

Peter was not surprised. He figured just about anything could be hidden under one of those shapeless garments, including a rifle or a bomb.

When Mele stepped into the tent, she saw through the latticework window of her burqa a woman wearing a garment much like her own but with no latticework hiding her eyes. She had been reading but laid down her book and stood up when Mele entered. It was difficult to tell her age when only her eyes were visible, but she appeared to be young. The woman spoke to her in the local dialect.

"I don't speak your language," Mele said. "Do you want me to take this off?"

"You speak English?" the woman said in surprise. "Are you an American?"

"Yes."

"We don't get many Americans, except soldiers. You're not a soldier, are you?"

"No."

"I didn't think so. They don't wear the burqa. Their women wear uniforms."

"So what do I do? Do you want me to take this off? I will if you want. I don't like wearing it. I can't see where I'm going. It's hot. It's horrible."

"That's because you are not used to it. With time one gets used to it. In the village where you are going all the women wear them when they leave their house. It is the law."

"That's a strange law."

"It is *sharia*, Islamic law."

"But I saw women in Kabul who did not dress like that."

"They are not so strict there, but many of our people

would like for the burqa to come back again, for us to go back to the old ways."

"Like in the Forbidden Place?"

"Yes."

"Have you been there?" Mele asked, curious to hear about the place where they were going.

"No, and I wouldn't want to go there."

"Why not?"

"It is hard if you're a woman."

"What do you mean—hard?"

"You will see. And now, forgive me, but I must ask you to lift your burqa."

Mele gathered up the voluminous burqa and held it high. She wondered if she would be asked to take off her jeans and top as well.

"Obviously you are a woman. You may put it down now."

But Mele could not resist the impulse to rid herself of the garment and instead pulled it off completely. The woman glanced apprehensively toward the tent opening.

"Sorry. I just couldn't bear it another moment. I'll put it back on in a minute, but first let me breathe." She closed her eyes and took a deep breath.

"You mustn't let him see you like that," the woman said nervously.

"Who? The guard?"

"He's my cousin and he got me this job, but he's quite strict when it comes to women."

"You speak English very well."

"Thank you. That is kind of you. I'm studying English." The woman pointed toward the book she had been reading. "I hope to go to Kabul University next year. I want to be a doctor."

"I'm going to study at a university too," Mele said, "when I go to Boston with my husband."

"You are an American. You can do whatever you want. Here it is not so simple."

"You don't understand. I lived in a Forbidden Place. There was no university."

The woman stared at her. "They have Forbidden Places in America? I didn't know that."

"I think it's the only one."

"I did not think the U.S. would have such places."

The guard outside spoke sharply.

"Hurry," the woman said in a low voice. "Put your burqa back on. He must not see you uncovered."

Mele threw the garment back over her head and tugged it about until she found the latticework window again. The feeling of being suffocated returned. She looked out at the woman through the little squares.

"Be careful," the woman said. "I've heard stories about the village you are going to. I don't know if they are true, but—"

The guard called again, louder, more impatient.

"You must go now. Quickly. Don't say anything. Just get in your car and go."

Peter was relieved when he saw Mele emerge from the tent. At least he assumed it was Mele under the burqa. She stepped carefully over the rocky ground and climbed back into the car beside him.

The guard moved the barrier aside and they drove on.

"It is not much farther," Ahmad said.

"What happened back there?" Peter asked her.

"I met a woman who spoke English. She's going to study to be a doctor."

"There are many women doctors in our country," Ahmad said. "Medicine is one of the few professions open to women. It is frowned on for men doctors to view a woman's body."

Mele leaned close to Peter's ear. "Are there other Forbidden Places in America besides Niʻihau?" she whispered through the cloth of the burqa.

"There's one in Appalachia," he whispered back. "I think that's the only other one. At least the only one I've ever heard about. Why?"

"I just wondered."

"You must be very careful what you say in the Forbidden Place," Ahmad said, glancing at them in the rearview mirror. Maybe he was suspicious about their whispering. "The Pashtuns have very strict customs. Some understand English and they take offense easily. Also they do not love Americans."

"We'll be careful," Peter assured him.

"You must let me do the talking."

"We will." Peter leaned forward. "What's that?" They were rapidly approaching a truck parked sideways in the road.

"This is not good."

"What do you mean, not good?" Peter reached for Mele's hand.

"Just let me do the talking," Ahmad said again.

He stopped the car when they got to the truck. There really was nothing else he could do. Two armed men, their faces covered by black scarves except for their eyes, stepped from behind the truck, automatic rifles pointing at them. Ahmad got out, hands in the air, and began talking rapidly. Two more armed masked men hopped out of the back of the truck. One of the first men looked at a paper Ahmad handed to them. Peter supposed it was a letter of authorization from the Alliance.

The first two men began to argue about the paper while gesturing at the car.

"What's happening?" Mele asked.

"I don't know," Peter said.

"Are they from the village?"

"I don't know."

Ahmad came back to the car and climbed in.

"Is everything all right?" Peter asked.

"We must leave the car here. They will take us the rest of the way." He looked over his shoulder at them. "Your wife must not speak. That's very important. They don't like that you brought a woman here."

"But the Alliance gave us permission. Did you tell them that?"

"It doesn't matter." Ahmad drove the car off the road and cut the engine.

"What about our bags?"

"Bring them along."

"Everything will be okay," Peter told Mele, trying to sound more confident than he felt.

When they got out of the car, the masked men motioned for them to climb in the back of the truck. Peter helped Mele, hampered as she was by the burqa. They sat down on the hard floor of the truck bed with their backs against one side facing Ahmad and two of the masked men. Ahmad was smiling as he offered the men packs of chewing gum from his pocket. Peter wanted to ask him if they were on their way to the Forbidden Place, or if they were being taken hostage by the Taliban, but Ahmad had told him not to talk. He wondered why the Alliance had given them permission to travel to Afghanistan if it was so dangerous. He wished now he had left Mele in Kabul. Ahmad had been right. This was a dangerous place for a woman. He held tight to her hand and vowed he would not let anything happen to her here like it had in India. He had not been vigilant enough before, but this time he would be more careful.

He watched the road behind them fade into rocky barren terrain. They lurched along with nothing to cushion their backsides from the bumpy ride. He hoped Mele was all right. He wondered what she was thinking, but he was relieved she was keeping quiet. He didn't want to anger the two young men in masks.

In twenty minutes they reached the village. Peter knew the instant he saw the flat-roofed mud-brick houses appear that they had arrived in the Forbidden Place. A skinny mongrel dog ran up and barked at the truck, baring its teeth; curious children came running. By the time the truck stopped, they had attracted a small crowd of men, boys, children, and barking dogs. He helped Mele climb out of the back of the truck. The two young men pulled their masks off and suddenly looked far less threatening. Ahmad passed out sticks of gum to the children.

Just as Peter began to relax, a dangerous-looking young man with an ugly scar down the side of his face pushed his way through the crowd, cursing at the children, who parted to let him through. He walked up to Peter, glared at him, then spit on the ground.

"What's that all about?" Peter asked Ahmad in a low voice.

"They do not love Americans," Ahmad said with a shrug. "What did you expect?"

The young man with the scar on his face scowled at Mele standing there in her burqa and started talking rapidly to Ahmad.

"What's he saying?" Peter asked. But Ahmad was busy answering. Peter had to wait until he had finished.

"He asked if she is American too," Ahmad said. "I explained that she is your wife. However, he is not happy you brought a woman along. He says you will have to stay in separate places."

"No, Mele stays with me." He was not going to let her out of his sight in an Afghan village where men wore masks and carried rifles.

"It isn't possible," Ahmad said. "They have no place available. It's a very poor village. You will be staying with the groom's family. It would not be appropriate to take a non-*mahram* woman there. There is only his mother."

"So where would Mele stay?"

Ahmad turned to the young man with the scar and translated the question. He received a curt answer.

"At the bride's home."

"And I can't stay there too?"

"Of course not. A non-*mahram* man in the bride's home—no way!"

Peter glanced at Mele, who had listened in silence from behind the lattice of her burqa. She laid a hand on his arm. "It's all right," she said in a low voice just as she had earlier at the checkpoint. "I don't mind."

The young man with the scar led the way through the dusty streets and the band of children trailed behind them. The compound to which he took them was half hidden behind a mud-brick wall. In response to his shout a woman with covered head and her scarf held across the lower part of her face emerged from the house and met them at a gap in the wall. The young man spoke to her sharply. She merely bowed her head and listened. Then she stepped back to let Mele enter. Mele hesitated, turning toward Peter, but it was impossible for him to read her eyes through the lattice of the burqa. There was only time to give one last squeeze to her hand, hoping it would convey all he could not say, a promise that everything would be all right, but would it? He didn't like leaving her there, but what else could he do? Then she walked through the gap and disappeared with the woman behind the mud-brick wall.

The children followed Peter and the other young men down the narrow street past more mud-brick walls until they came to another gap in a wall at the end of the street. The young man with the scar shouted at the children and they scattered. Then he stepped through the gap, and Ahmad followed.

"Where are we going?" Peter asked.

"Into the house of course."

"But why?"

"Would you sleep in the street?"

"No, of course not. I just thought—"

"He is the groom. You are here as his guest. I thought you knew that."

"No, I didn't. Tell him I'm very grateful for his hospitality."

Ahmad relayed the message, but the young man with the scar ignored him.

"His name is Mustafa," Ahmad whispered. "He is very respected in the village."

"I'll bet." Feared was more like it. He wondered how Mustafa got that scar.

Mustafa led them into a room with rugs covering the floor and a long lethal-looking knife affixed to the wall. A bearded middle-aged man who had been dozing in the corner woke when they came in and looked at Peter with suspicion.

"His father," Ahmad said.

Peter nodded in greeting to the man, who continued to stare at him distrustfully.

Next Mustafa led them to the kitchen, where a middle-aged woman hastily pulled the end of her headscarf over the lower part of her face and shrank back against the wall, eyes lowered. Mustafa spoke to her with contempt. "His mother," Ahmad said in a low voice. Peter tried to catch the woman's eye to smile at her and show her he meant well, but she would not look at him.

Passing through the main room again, they entered a narrow passage with several doors. Mustafa threw one of these open. Inside a young man sitting beside the only window in a small room looked up from the book he was reading. Mustafa growled something in Pashto. Again the contempt in his voice was unmistakable.

"This is his brother Hakim," Ahmad said. "He says his brother is . . . worthless."

"Worthless?"

Mustafa's lip curled with scorn as he let fly a string of insults.

"Worthless, lazy, and a coward," Ahmad translated, glancing nervously at the brother, whose expression did not change.

"Why does he say his brother is a coward?" Peter asked in a low voice.

"Because I refused to fight for the Taliban," Hakim said in accented English, regarding him steadily.

Mustafa released a torrent of invective in Pashto against his brother and indicated with an angry nod of his head that they should leave.

Interesting, Peter thought. One brother spoke English. Did the other? He would have liked to ask Ahmad, but Ahmad was shaking his head and darting warning glances at him. He would have to wait until later when they were alone to ask.

When they were back in the main room, Mustafa turned on them angrily and pointed at the scar on his face, eyes blazing as he spewed out a passionate diatribe in Pashto.

"He says he got that fighting for Allah," Ahmad translated.

"For the Taliban, you mean?"

Ahmad shot him another warning look. "Be careful what you say. Remember where we are. You could put both our lives in danger. Your wife's too. The influence of the Alliance only goes so far."

Again Peter regretted that he had brought Mele with him. He saw the look of hate on Mustafa's face as the other man watched him.

"I didn't know there were Taliban here. Does the Alliance know?"

Ahmad's eyes darted nervously to Mustafa. "Of course they know. They turn a blind eye."

"Why do they allow it to continue?"

"Because they have an arrangement with"—his voice dropped to a whisper—"the Taliban. The Taliban keep the village in the old ways and permit visitors sent by the Alliance—for a fee."

"The Alliance *pays* them?" Peter said, incredulous.

"Shh. What's so terrible about that? Everyone benefits. The Alliance gets a Forbidden Place where the old ways are preserved, and the village makes a little money without sacrificing their way of life."

Peter's eye fell again on the long knife hanging on the wall. Beside it was another object. Stepping closer, he saw it was a whip. An ominous choice of wall décor.

Mustafa noticed his gaze and muttered something with a

twisted grin. Peter did not much care for Mustafa, and he suspected Mustafa did not much care for him.

"He says the whip is for punishing sinners and the knife is for beheading his enemies," Ahmad translated.

"Is he serious?"

"Perhaps. With these *mujahideen* you never know."

Surely they didn't behead people here, Peter told himself. The Alliance would have warned him, wouldn't they? The knife was there for show, a relic from the past. Still, it was an unnerving object to hang on the wall of his home.

"Can I ask him some questions?" Peter asked.

Ahmad translated. "He says ask your questions and he will decide if he will answer."

Peter was tempted to skip the questions altogether after that arrogant response, but he had asked and so he might as well proceed.

"Is it okay if I take notes?" He pulled a notebook and a pen from his bag.

Mustafa eyed the notebook suspiciously, then shrugged.

The three young men sat down on the floor facing each other warily. Mustafa glared at Peter, and Peter glared back, determined not to be intimidated. Mustafa's father, sitting against one wall, did not join them. His eyes were closed as if he were sleeping.

"Will you ask him what is the average age at which people marry?" Peter said.

Ahmad translated the question, listened attentively to a rambling answer from Mustafa, then translated it for Peter. "He says sometimes the bride is young, like thirteen, sometimes older. His wife-to-be is sixteen. He himself is twenty."

Peter jotted down the answer, then hesitated before asking the next question. "Is the, uh, young woman usually a virgin?"

Ahmad stared at him, shocked. "I can't ask that. He would be offended. Of course the bride is a virgin. They live by strict Islamic law here. The women are in purdah. They cover themselves at all times. They can't go out of their house unless they are accompanied by a male relative. No man sees their faces except their brothers and their fathers and their husbands."

"So he has never seen the face of the woman he will marry tomorrow?"

Ahmad relayed this question to Mustafa, who continued to glare at Peter as he answered.

"He says he has never seen her face, but she is as beautiful as the houris of paradise. Everybody says so."

The houris, Peter knew, were beautiful young virgins who were waiting for the faithful Muslim man in their version of heaven.

"Is it an arranged marriage?"

Ahmad posed this question to Mustafa.

"He says, yes, his uncle, the imam, arranged it. She is his reward . . . his payment."

Peter recorded this answer. "What does he mean, payment? I don't understand."

Ahmad translated the question and then Mustafa's response. "He says his uncle arranged this marriage because he has served Allah faithfully."

"Has his uncle seen her face?" Peter asked, knowing he was treading in sensitive territory.

The effect was instantaneous—a torrent of angry words.

"He says of course not. She is in purdah. No one but her family and her husband will see her face."

Peter met Mustafa's outrage with calm equanimity. At least that was the effect he was aiming for.

"How long has he been engaged?"

Another exchange between Ahmad and Mustafa, less heated this time.

"One month," Ahmad reported.

"Is that the usual time?"

As Ahmad translated, Mustafa continued to glare as if he would bore a hole into Peter with his eyes. He was making Ahmad visibly nervous.

"He says, what does it matter—one month, two months, a year? It is Allah's will."

"How many children do married couples usually have?"

Ahmad translated the question. The answer was short and impatient.

"Three or four, sometimes more."

"Do married couples argue much?"

Ahmad hesitated. "Perhaps this question is . . . how do you say? Indelicate?"

"If he doesn't want to answer, he doesn't have to. But ask him."

Reluctantly Ahmad repeated the question in Pashto. Mustafa stared daggers at Peter as he spit out his response.

"He says they do not argue. A husband's word is law. A wife must submit to the will of her husband."

"And if she doesn't?" Peter knew he shouldn't ask, but he did anyway. What was Mustafa going to do—punch him for asking? Grab that lethal-looking knife off the wall and behead him?

Ahmad glanced uneasily from one to the other, took a deep breath, and asked Peter's question. Mustafa's lip curled in a sneer as he shot back his answer.

"He beats her," Ahmad said.

Mustafa sat there like a carved idol, glaring at him, daring him to argue. Peter did not intend to argue. It was information he was after, not a fight. The next question on his list was the one about domestic abuse. He might as well skip that. He already had his answer.

"How about divorce? Do couples ever get divorced?"

Ahmad sighed and translated his question. The answer was flung back in an angry rush of words.

"He says, yes, there is divorce. If a man is not satisfied with his wife, he can divorce her by saying 'I divorce you.'"

"And the wife?" Peter knew he should skip this one too. "Does it work the same for her?" He knew the answer of course. Asking these questions was just a formality.

"Oh, no," Ahmad said, not bothering to translate this question. "She must ask her husband's consent. If he does not give it, there is no divorce. That is Islamic law."

"What about infidelity?"

Ahmad translated the question and Mustafa lobbed back his answer. "He says the punishment for adultery is one hundred lashes for the man or woman who is unmarried, death by stoning if they are married."

"That's harsh."

"Is that all?" Ahmad asked, clearly hoping the interview was at an end.

"No, one more question. Is there a bride-price, something of value he will give the bride's family? It's common in many Muslim cultures."

Ahmad translated his question, then listened politely to Mustafa's lengthy answer.

"He says his gift is his promise to take care of the bride's family. Her mother is a widow, her father died fighting the Americans, and there is no one to feed the family and provide for them except an uncle, who is nearly useless since he lost his hand. After they are married, he will take care of them."

Suddenly Mustafa held up a hand for silence. Like a sound from another world came the eerie chant of the muezzin's call to afternoon prayer.

Mustafa stood and spoke in Pashto to Ahmad, shooting a dark look at Peter.

"He says you may come if you wish, but you cannot enter the mosque because you are an infidel. Only true believers may enter."

"Tell him I'll come," Peter said, curious to see what he could of the customs they were preserving. He didn't think the Alliance would object. After all, he would only be an observer.

Mustafa shouted, summoning his brother from the other room. Hakim emerged and strode toward the door without looking at him. Their father rose from the cushion where he had been sitting, and they set off, joining the stream of men pouring into the dusty street, answering the call to prayer.

"It is required for everyone to attend prayers," Ahmad told Peter in a low voice as they walked. "They are very strict about it here."

"And the women?" Peter asked, noticing there were no women to be seen. "Don't they have to pray too?"

"Oh, women do not come to prayers. They pray at home, where they cannot be seen. That is the custom here, and in many other villages too."

Because the village was small, they did not have far to walk. The mosque was a spare rectangular concrete building with a column on either side of the door and a dome on top. It was the most prominent building in the village, which was understandable considering its role in the life of the community. Peter stopped at the entry and watched the men filing in. They varied in age from smooth-faced boys to gray-bearded old men. The younger men had black beards. All wore some kind of head covering: a scarf, a prayer cap, or a turban. They performed their ritual ablutions at several basins which lined the back wall, splashing water on their face and their arms, and wiping their feet. Then they formed rows behind the imam, an older man with a wiry gray beard and spectacles. They were facing Mecca, Peter knew, the Muslim holy city. When the imam began to recite verses from the Qur'an, the men knelt in unison with him and touched their foreheads to their prayer mats. Peter stood outside alone, watching through the arched open doorway. He was glad he had come. Just seeing this communal act of prayer made the trip worthwhile. He doubted that the marriage ceremony would move him as much. It was an awesome sight. His world had nothing like it. He wondered how it felt to live like this, to devote oneself to prayer five times a day, every day. Did it lose its power through familiarity, or did it gain?

The minutes ticked away, and the imam's voice droned on. Shifting his weight from one foot to the other, Peter wondered what Mele was doing and if she regretted not having stayed in Kabul. He hoped she was all right. He wished he could see her, but he had to be patient. There would be time later for them to be together.

Without his watch, he had no idea how long the prayer session lasted, but when it ended he guessed it was about forty-five minutes. When the men returned home, it was time for the evening meal. They sat on the floor and broke bread into pieces, which they dipped into a stew. The stew had a strange spicy taste that Peter couldn't identify, but he hadn't eaten since morning so he was grateful for any food at all.

"Where is his mother?" Peter asked Ahmad in a low voice, noticing that she wasn't eating with them.

"She eats in the kitchen."

Mustafa said something in Pashto.

"He asks what you think of his brother," Ahmad translated.

"What does he mean?"

Ahmad repeated his question to Mustafa, who gave Peter a hard look as he answered.

"He asks if you think his brother is handsome."

Peter glanced from Mustafa's face with its ugly scar to Hakim's unmarred face. Hakim kept eating as if he had not heard. Their father made what sounded like a half-hearted attempt to avert an argument. Not wishing to be drawn into a family quarrel, Peter thought it best to ignore the question.

For a few minutes they ate in silence. Then suddenly Mustafa's father flung down his piece of bread and broke into an angry rant.

"What's he saying?" Peter asked.

"He is objecting to the food," Ahmad whispered. "He says it is cold."

Mustafa's father got to his feet and went into the kitchen. No one said anything. They heard him in the next room shouting. There was the sound of a blow and his wife pleading. Had he hit her? Peter wondered. Over a bowl of stew that was not warm enough?

Mustafa was watching him, waiting for him to make a move or object. Hakim didn't meet his eyes, stuffing a piece of bread into his mouth and chewing vigorously.

"Do not interfere," Ahmad warned in a low voice. "The Qur'an gives a man the right to discipline his wife."

Hakim sprang to his feet and left the room. Mustafa yelled at him, but he didn't look back. When he was gone, Mustafa's lip twisted in a cruel smile and he spoke to Ahmad in Pashto.

"He says his brother is in love," Ahmad translated. "But

he cannot have the girl he loves because she is betrothed to someone else."

Peter glanced at Mustafa, who was still watching him intently, so he resolved to keep his mouth shut. Clearly Mustafa hated his brother and took pleasure in tormenting him. Peter looked down at his stew. He didn't think he could eat any more of it. Would it be rude not to finish all he had been given? He was about to ask Ahmad when Mustafa's father returned and sat down again. He glanced at the empty space where Hakim had been sitting but said nothing. They finished the meal in silence.

When it was done, Peter asked Ahmad if he could help carry the dishes to the kitchen.

"That is woman's work," Ahmad said. "Men do not clean up the remains of a meal."

As if to prove him right, at that moment Mustafa's mother crept in to gather up the dishes.

"Would it be okay if I walked over to check on my wife?" Peter asked.

Ahmad consulted Mustafa. "He says wait for tomorrow. Tomorrow you can see your wife."

"Is he sure she's all right?"

"Why wouldn't she be all right?" Ahmad said. "You do not want to insult him."

They all paused to listen as the strange and beautiful call of the muezzin came again.

"It's the call for evening prayer," Ahmad said.

"Should I stay here?" Peter asked.

Ahmad glanced at the kitchen door. "No, it would not be proper. You should not be alone here with the woman."

So again they joined the other men of the village on their way to the mosque. Did they ever get tired of it? Peter wondered. Were they ever tempted to skip the ritual? And how did they get anything done when they spent so much time praying? It was so different from the world he came from. Here work and the pursuit of money were not of primary importance. One's relationship with God came before all else.

When they arrived at the mosque, Peter took up his post by the door again as the other men entered. Hakim was one of the last to arrive. He paused briefly beside Peter before going inside.

"Be careful," he warned in a low voice.

"Careful how?"

Hakim glanced at the rows of men and boys waiting for the prayer to begin. "This is a dangerous place."

"You mean the mosque or the village?"

"Both. My brother hates Americans. So do many others. You should leave while you can. Now. Tonight."

Before Peter could question him further he was gone, performing his ablutions and quickly taking his place in the last row of men as the imam began to intone verses from the Qur'an.

Watching the men and boys kneel in unison and touch their foreheads to the floor, Peter wondered what it was like for Hakim living in this remote village. Had he ever thought of leaving? Perhaps he had no place to go. Or perhaps he was content with this life. But it could not have been easy living under the same roof as Mustafa. Hakim did not have to warn him. He knew this was a dangerous place and he was anxious to leave. However, he couldn't leave tonight. He at least had to stay for the wedding tomorrow. He and Mele would leave the following morning unless he could persuade Ahmad to leave sooner. He knew Mustafa disliked him, but he didn't think Mustafa would dare harm him when the village had an agreement with the Alliance. But until he and Mele were safely out of the village, he would be careful.

When they returned to the house, it was time to retire. Peter glanced at the floor where they had eaten earlier and saw all trace of the evening meal had been cleared away.

"We sleep on the floor," Ahmad said, indicating the blankets and cushions which had been laid out for them in a neat pile. "Please do not make a fuss."

"Of course not." He was surprised Ahmad should think him capable of such rudeness. Had other visitors from the outside made a fuss? Or did Ahmad just suspect he would because he was an American?

"Let us get some sleep," Ahmad said, stretching out on the floor. "We must rise early for morning prayer."

"What time?"

"Before dawn."

It was a demanding routine, Peter thought as he lay down on the floor. No lazy mornings lying in bed. The hours of the day carved out for devotions. It was no wonder religion played such a large role in these people's lives.

Mele did not like the idea of being separated from Peter, but there was not much she could do about it. She had no idea what to expect when she passed through the gap in the wall surrounding the strange house. Trying not to trip over her burqa, she followed the woman who had admitted her into the mud-brick home behind the wall. When she stepped inside she found herself in a small dark room lit by a fire. As her eyes adjusted, she saw that sunlight didn't penetrate because the windows had been painted black.

The combination of dim lighting and the limited visual

range offered by the lattice of her burqa made it difficult to see her surroundings. She could make out four people in the room: a pretty dark-eyed girl maybe several years younger than herself who wore a loose long-sleeved garment and a scarf over her hair, a little girl of about five who was clutching the older girl's hand, a boy of perhaps ten sitting in the middle of the floor writing or drawing on a slate, and a lean bearded man who watched her with guarded eyes from a corner where he sat.

The woman who had led her in now dropped her veil and spoke rapidly in Pashto to the others. Mele wondered how she was going to communicate without an interpreter. For at least a minute they just stared at her and she stared back at them through the lattice of the burqa. She wondered if she could remove it now. She did not want to break any rules, but it was hot and claustrophobic under the garment. She attempted to communicate through gestures that she wanted to remove the burqa. They merely stared at her so she gave up her efforts. She would just take it off. If they were upset, she could put it on again.

When she had discarded the burqa, she could see the family more clearly. They were still staring. No one said anything.

She smiled and pointed at herself. "Mele."

For a minute they were silent. Then the older girl smiled back shyly and pointed at herself. "Nasreen." She pointed toward the woman who had led Mele in. "Laila." Then she touched the head of the little girl whose hand she held. "Zohra." She swept a hand toward the boy who sat on the floor with his slate. "Durrani." Finally she gestured toward the lean bearded man in the corner. "Habib."

It wasn't much of a conversation, but it was a start. Now Mele knew their names and they knew hers.

The boy Durrani studied her with solemn eyes. "Are you American?"

"Yes," she said, surprised. "You speak English?"

"I have learned some English at school," he said with obvious pride.

"And your family?" She looked hopefully around at the others. "Do they speak English too?"

"No, only me."

That was a disappointment, but at least there was someone who could understand her, even if it was only a ten-year-old boy.

"Well, then you must be my translator."

The boy nodded solemnly.

"Is it okay for me to take this burqa off?"

He nodded again.

She looked at the girl Nasreen. "You must be the bride."

Durrani translated, and the girl dropped her eyes, bit her lip, and looked as if she might burst into tears. Mele wondered if she had said something wrong. "Isn't she the bride?" she asked the boy.

He glanced at the girl and nodded.

"She's your sister?"

Another nod.

"We are here to watch her wedding," Mele explained.

Nasreen would not meet her eyes. Perhaps it was a custom not to meet the eyes of a stranger? She wished Peter was there so she could ask him.

Their mother Laila spoke to the boy in low tones.

"She asks if you would like some tea," Durrani said.

"Yes, I would like that very much." Mele smiled at the woman and the woman smiled back. "Can I help to fix it?"

The boy translated her offer and received a brief answer.

"She says no, but you can watch."

They crowded around the fire except for the bearded man in the corner, who stayed where he was. A pot was suspended on a hook over the fire. When the tea was ready, Laila carefully poured it into two small bowls. The boy took the first bowl to the bearded man in the corner. The second he gave to Mele. She was thirsty after the long ride from Kabul and felt grateful to have something to drink even if it had a bitter taste.

She was just finishing her bowl of tea when she heard a voice chanting in the distance. It was strange and beautiful, a sound from another world. Immediately the bearded man stood. That was when Mele noticed he was missing a hand.

"What happened to your father's hand?" she asked the boy.

"He is my uncle," Durrani said. "They cut it off."

"Who cut it off?" she asked, not understanding.

"The Taliban."

Ahmad had mentioned the Taliban. She knew they had a reputation for being harsh, cruel even, which was why they were so feared.

"Why did they cut off his hand?"

"They said he stole a pomegranate."

"They cut off his hand because he stole a piece of fruit?"

"It is the law. However, my Uncle Habib says he was innocent. He stole nothing. They cut it off as a warning."

Before Mele could ask, a warning for what, his uncle called to him.

"We must go now," the boy said. "It is time for prayers and we must not be late."

And what happens if you are late? she wondered. Do they cut off hands for that as well? She felt afraid now and hoped Peter was safe. She had a bad feeling about this village and wished she could be with him so he could reassure her that all would be well.

When Durrani and his uncle were gone, Laila and Nasreen brought out a basin of water and splashed water on their faces and hands. Mele settled back against the wall, and the little girl, Zohra, came to sit with her, solemnly watching her mother and older sister perform their ablutions. Mele would have liked to ask them questions, but without Durrani to translate, it was difficult to make herself understood. She had to content herself with watching as they opened their Qur'an and began to pray.

Later, after Durrani and his uncle had returned and the women were cooking the evening meal, she asked Durrani about his father.

"Dead," the boy said. "He died fighting the Americans."

"I'm sorry," she said. "Is that why the windows are painted black?"

"Oh, no. That is so no one can look in."

"And why don't you want them to look in?"

"If they look in, they might see my mother or my sisters."

It seemed to make perfect sense to him, but Mele thought the custom strange. There was much she did not understand about this place. She would ask Peter later and maybe he could explain it to her. In the meantime she would try to find out as much as she could for him about the prenuptial rituals involving the bride.

"Durrani," she said, "I would like to ask your sister some questions. Could you translate?"

He turned his big dark eyes on her. "What do you want to ask her?"

Mele glanced at Nasreen, who was spreading a mat on the floor for them to eat on.

"Ask her what preparations she must do before the wedding."

"What do you mean—preparations?"

"Like her hair or makeup."

Durrani turned and asked his sister, who gave him a short answer in their language.

"She says she will wash herself and pray to Allah."

Remembering the feasts at the two previous weddings, Mele tried again. "Won't there be a celebration—you know, food, music?"

The boy shook his head but translated her question. His mother, who had just bent down to place a bowl of stewed vegetables on the mat, spoke rapidly in her language.

"My mother says she remembers how they celebrated with music and feasting when she was young, but that was many years ago. The Taliban put an end to it. They said it was immoral."

Mele looked at Nasreen again. "Your sister doesn't seem happy about getting married tomorrow."

He shrugged and looked away.

"What is it? What's the matter?"

"Nothing." He spoke low and rapidly to his sister, who glanced at Mele but didn't answer this time.

Mele wished there were no language barrier. She wanted to speak to Nasreen herself and hear the girl's answer. Clearly something was wrong.

"If she doesn't want to get married, can't she say no?"

"No, she cannot say no," Durrani said. "It is all arranged. My uncle agreed to it."

"Your uncle?" Mele looked at the bearded man in the corner, leaning back against the wall, eyes closed, sleeping or praying or just shutting out the world.

"He is in charge of us since my father is dead."

"But why would he agree to this marriage if your sister doesn't want it?"

"It is Allah's will."

"What do you mean?"

He shrugged. "There is nothing anyone can do about it."

This seemed very fatalistic to Mele. "I don't understand. What do you mean nobody can do anything about it? Why not?"

But she could get nothing more from Durrani.

After the evening meal, there was another call to prayer. Durrani and his uncle again left, the women prayed, and then it was time to retire. A mat and blanket were laid out for Mele on the floor. She lay for a while listening to the sounds of the house. She thought she heard Nasreen sobbing, then her mother's low voice comforting her, and the sobbing subsided. She thought of her own mother so far away and wished she could have said good-bye before she left. But of course she could not. Her mother would have stormed and found a way to stop her. She had had no choice but to sneak away. For a while she thought about her family before finally falling asleep.

Sometime in the night she woke. She lay still for a moment, remembering where she was. She thought she heard someone moving about. Opening her eyes, she saw a shadowy figure glide silently across the dark room. For a fleeting second she thought it was a ghost, but then her reason told her, no, it was a flesh and blood person. She doubted Nasreen's mother would be going out in the middle of the night, so she assumed it must be Nasreen herself in a burqa, but where could she be going in the middle of the night? Was she running away to avoid the unwanted marriage tomorrow? Where could she run to when they were miles from anywhere?

The minutes slipped by, and the household remained silent. Mele closed her eyes and tried to fall asleep again, but she found it hard to stop thinking about Nasreen. What would happen if morning came and she was gone? Gradually she drifted to sleep, then woke again much later, her heart racing because she had heard a sound—a door softly closing or a footstep. The mysterious burqa-clad figure floated past her again, returning from her clandestine errand. It had to be Nasreen, but where had she gone in the dead of night? Turning this question over in her mind, Mele fell asleep again.

# 8

# Afghanistan, part 2

When Mele awoke the next morning, her first thought was that today she would see Peter, the wedding would take place, and then tomorrow they would leave this dreadful village where women had to wear burqas and hide behind blackened windows. She wished there were some way to talk to him before the marriage ceremony and tell him something was wrong. But even if she did, what could he do?

As the morning proceeded, everyone in the household seemed anxious and fearful. Nasreen's eyes were red from crying. Her mother hovered near her, trying to console her. Even little Zohra seemed infected by the mood.

Durrani and his Uncle Habib answered yet another call to prayer in the grayness before dawn. Laila and Nasreen prayed together at home while Mele sat with her back to the wall trying to compose a letter to her mother, Zohra snuggled against her hugging a rag doll.

At midmorning Nasreen and her mother donned burqas. Laila spoke to Mele, pointing at her burqa.

"She says it is time to put it on," Durrani told her.

Reluctantly Mele pulled the bulky garment over her head. Immediately she felt smothered as she had before. There wasn't enough air to breathe, she could hardly see, and the long skirt made her clumsy. It is only for a little while, she told herself.

Soon they heard someone shout from outside, and Nasreen's mother slipped quietly out the door. When she returned, she was followed by the imam, looking very dignified and stern in his white turban. Behind him came two young Afghan men, followed by Ahmad and Peter. Although Peter was dressed no differently from the other men, his pale skin and lack of a beard contrasted oddly with their darker skin and black beards. He glanced uncertainly from one burqa-clad figure to another. It was a little frightening to think he couldn't recognize her when she was wearing the burqa, as if it robbed her of her identity.

She recognized the groom as the fierce young man with the scar who had led them here yesterday. The other young Afghan was one of the men who had ridden in the back of the truck.

She moved to Peter's side, hoping to talk to him.

"Are you all right?" he asked in a low voice.

"Yes, but I must talk to you. There's something I have to tell you."

The young man with the scar shot her an angry look. She was not supposed to speak. Women were expected to be invisible in this place.

"Maybe we can talk afterward," Peter said. "I think they're ready for the ceremony."

But that was what she wanted to talk to him about. She wanted to ask if there wasn't some way to stop it. She wanted to tell him something was wrong. Nasreen didn't want to marry the young man with the scar.

Ahmad stepped closer to them. "It is time to begin," he said. "The imam will read from the Qur'an and then they will sign their names."

Nasreen mutely took her place beside the sullen young man with the scar, who didn't once glance at her. The imam began to recite. His strange words inexplicably filled Mele with despair. She looked out at the imam and his Qur'an through the small squares of the burqa's lattice and wanted to cry. She understood now why Nasreen had been reluctant about the wedding. It wasn't just that she didn't love the man she was being forced to marry. Nor was it the ugly scar that disfigured his face. It was because he was full of anger and hate that showed itself in every glance, every word he uttered, every gesture he made. She shivered at the thought of being married to such a man. Poor Nasreen!

It was soon over and a record book produced, which the groom signed, followed by Nasreen's Uncle Habib, who signed awkwardly with his one remaining hand.

"That's it?" Mele whispered.

"It is done," Ahmad said. "They are husband and wife."

"Why didn't Nasreen sign the book?"

"Because her uncle signs for her. That is the custom. If her father were alive, he would sign for her, but since he is not, it is her nearest male relative who must sign. That is her uncle."

Mele looked at Nasreen, who was swaying slightly, her head bowed. The groom had turned away to talk to his friend and the imam, ignoring her utterly.

"If it's over, can't we leave?" Mele asked Peter. "I mean, now, today?"

"We have to stay for the homecoming ceremony," he said,

speaking low so the others wouldn't hear. "That's when the groom takes his new wife home."

"When will that be?"

"In the early evening," said Ahmad, who had overheard the exchange. "The groom will come to claim his wife and take her home."

"Will I see you before then?" Mele asked Peter as the men prepared to leave.

"I don't know. Maybe not."

"But we haven't had a chance to talk, and I really need to talk to you."

"Can't it wait? It's only a little longer."

He reached for her hand and gave it a squeeze. She felt a small surge of anger. Did he care how she felt? Did he have any idea how badly she wanted to leave this place? Did he really have to stay for one more ceremony?

"Everything will be okay," he whispered, leaning close again. "Don't worry."

Through the lattice of the burqa she watched him leave and a sense of hopelessness washed over her. She had not been able to stop the wedding from taking place. She had watched helplessly while Nasreen was married to that horrible man. She had changed nothing.

When the door closed behind them, Nasreen slumped to the floor. Her mother rushed to her, threw her arms around her, and rocked her like a child, murmuring to her. Mele didn't need to understand Pashto to know what she was saying. She was trying to comfort her daughter. She began to tug Nasreen's burqa off until the girl sat before them, tears streaming down her face. Zohra, who had been sitting quietly in a corner, began to cry too. Mele went to the child and held her.

"It'll be okay," she said, although she did not believe that herself.

The uncle uttered something short and fierce under his breath. He sounded like he was cursing. And if so, was he cursing Nasreen or the young man with the scar? Or the Taliban who had cut off his hand? Or the fact that he could not protect his niece from such a fate? He fled the room, as if he could bear to be in it no longer.

"Why must she marry this man?" Mele asked Durrani, who had crept up beside her and Zohra, as if he too needed comforting. "I don't understand. And don't tell me it's Allah's will."

"My mother says she must do it for our family. She must do it so we will have food to eat and so we will all be safe."

Mele shook her head. "No, there must be another way."

She watched as Nasreen's mother helped her to her feet. Clinging to each other, they stumbled out of the room.

Zohra stopped crying and looked at Mele with large round eyes. An enormous pity for the little girl filled her. At Zohra's age she had played on the beach on Niʻihau, the sand coating her bare legs and clinging to her hair. She could hear again their squeals as she and her playmates ran to the water's edge and the waves slapped against them, sometimes knocking them down. Zohra would never experience that. She must pass her whole life in this village of rocks and dust and never see the ocean or know that in other places there were no burqas and women were not forced to marry against their will.

"At what age will she have to start wearing a burqa?" Mele asked.

"When she starts her bleeding," Durrani said.

And at what age would he start taking on that sense of entitlement and power that went with being a man in such a culture? Or would he be able to preserve his natural goodness as he matured? How could boys like Durrani turn out good when they grew up in a society so oppressive to their mothers, sisters, and wives?

Peter had told her to be patient and wait until evening, but she didn't want to spend the rest of the day waiting for the men to return for Nasreen. She wanted to get out of that house, which was little better than a prison, the air stale, the black windows depressing. She wanted to see the sun and breathe fresh air, even if for only a little while. Gently she released Zohra.

"Watch her," she told Durrani.

"What are you doing?" he asked as she moved resolutely toward the door.

"I'm going out."

"You can't," he protested. "Women are not allowed to go out in the streets alone. They will beat you."

She hesitated, almost to the door. "Then come with me."

He shook his head. "No, it isn't safe."

"Why not? Don't you sometimes go with your mother and your sister when they go out?"

"I am not your brother. They will beat you."

It was ridiculous that a grown woman needed a ten-year-old boy to accompany her to leave her house. But even if she persuaded Durrani, did she have the right to put him at risk like that? What might the Taliban do to him if they found him breaking the rules? He was about her youngest brother's age. No, she must not put him in danger. Feeling defeated, she pulled the burqa off and prepared to wait for the hours to creep by until Nasreen's husband appeared to claim her.

The hour for midday prayer came and went. Nasreen stayed in her room, and her mother moved silently about the house as if someone were sick.

With Durrani's help translating, Mele begged Laila for something to do and at last was given a shirt to mend. She wondered how long it would be until the men came. There were no clocks in the house and she had no idea what time it was. When she asked Durrani how much longer it would be, he merely shrugged and said it would be later.

She had finished mending the shirt and was wondering what she could do next when Durrani appeared in the doorway and asked her to come with him. He led her to Nasreen, crouched on the floor of a small room with the Qur'an open in front of her. She was no longer crying.

Durrani sat down beside her and motioned for Mele to do the same as Nasreen began to speak in a low hesitant voice.

"She wants to know about you and the American man," Durrani said.

"You mean Peter? What does she want to know?"

"Is he your brother?"

"No, he's my husband."

Durrani translated her answer for his sister, then waited as Nasreen spoke again.

"She says, do you love him?"

Mele hesitated. Should she explain that she had only known Peter for a week? Should she say she wasn't sure? She looked into Nasreen's brimming eyes and sensed she had to be careful what she said. The girl was ready to clutch at her answer like a drowning person might clutch at a bit of floating debris.

"Yes, of course."

Nasreen smiled gratefully, then rushed on to her next question.

"She wants to know—in your world can all women choose the man they marry?"

How was she supposed to answer a question like that? She had chosen Peter, but of course there were many women who did not marry the man they chose. Not even on Ni'ihau. What if the man you loved did not love you back? What if the man you might love was not on your island? Yet how could she explain all this through a ten-year-old boy? She suspected Nasreen wanted a simple answer, an answer which was for some reason very important to her. But what was the right answer? If she said no, would that confirm Nasreen's belief that happiness was impossible anywhere? If she said yes, would it fill Nasreen with despair that such happiness was denied her?

Nasreen watched her with desperate eyes.

"Tell her that marriages are not arranged in my world," Mele said. "Maybe they aren't always perfect. Maybe love sometimes dies away. But at least a woman has a choice. No one forces her to marry a man she doesn't want to marry."

Durrani struggled to translate this answer, and when he finished Nasreen gave her a trembly smile followed by an avalanche of words.

Mele wondered how Durrani would ever manage to translate it all, but when his sister finished, he confidently launched into the story as if he already knew it by heart.

"My sister says her new husband is a cruel man and she is afraid of him. She doesn't know why he wants to marry her, but she thinks it is because one day he saw her without her veil. She was going to visit a friend that day. Uncle Habib was with her and she was wearing her burqa, but a group of young Taliban, including Mustafa, stopped them on the street. They said her ankles were showing, but they were not. She thinks it was because of Uncle Habib. They knew he would not dare to stop them, so they insulted her and hit her with sticks, but then they said her burqa got in the way, so they pulled it off even though she begged them not to. They knocked her down—two of them holding Uncle Habib back as he swore at them. Once the burqa was off, she says they seemed a little embarrassed at what they had done. They took a few more swipes at her with their sticks, but the only one who really wanted to beat her was Mustafa, and the others stopped him. She knew Mustafa from when they were children. He was mean even then, but since he got his scar he has been worse. He spit on her and then they walked away. Uncle Habib cursed them and said he would tell the imam, but he knew it would do no good. My sister put her burqa back on and they continued on their way.

"It was only a few days later when Mustafa's father and several Taliban showed up at our house to arrange the marriage. Uncle Habib could not refuse. He knew they could kill him, and if they did, what would become of us? We could starve without the money Uncle Habib earns taking care of goats. It isn't much, but it feeds us. My mother cried, but she knew there was nothing we could do. It was bad luck that Mustafa saw Nasreen's face and took it into his head that he wanted her for a wife. She says she is afraid he only wants her so he can beat her, and when she is his wife, no one can stop him."

Mele felt overwhelmed with pity for Nasreen. Surely there was something that could be done.

"You could run away," she suggested.

Durrani shook his head, not bothering to translate. "They would find her and beat her."

"You could come with us tomorrow morning." Nasreen's tearful eyes broke her heart. "There must be a way we could smuggle you out." She had no idea how, but her desire to help the girl made her want to believe it was possible.

"You do not understand," Durrani said.

"I'll go to my husband. I'll tell him about Nasreen and we'll think of something."

"You cannot leave here. I already told you. It's too dangerous."

Nasreen spoke softly to her in Pashto, her eyes trying to communicate what her words could not.

"My sister says you must get away from this place as quickly as you can. You don't know them."

"If I find a way, would she come with us? Ask her."

Durrani and Nasreen had a rapid exchange in Pashto.

"She says she would if someone else could come with her."

They were both looking at her, waiting. She didn't know how she could get Nasreen out and they expected her to get *two* people out? How?

"She says she cannot go without him," Durrani explained.

"Without who?" Mele said, confused.

He looked at his sister and hesitated. She gazed back at Mele steadily.

"There is someone she loves. She cannot go and leave him behind."

In a flash Mele understood. Not only had Nasreen been forced to marry a man she did not love but she had been denied the man she did love. Mele had no idea how she could help Nasreen, but she was determined to try. She knew Peter would say they must not interfere, but they had to. What was happening to Nasreen was wrong. She tried to think what to do. Could they hide Nasreen until the time arrived to leave tomorrow morning? Was there anyone who could help them?

"Does anyone know about this man she loves?"

Durrani shook his head.

"But you knew?"

He glanced at his sister and nodded.

"Does your mother know?"

Another hesitation. Another nod.

"Is there any place in the village where she could hide?"

He shook his head while Nasreen watched her anxiously.

"It'll be okay," she said, reaching for the girl's hand. "I promise."

Nasreen seemed to understand. She broke into speech.

"She asks what she should do."

Mele had no idea how they would get Nasreen and her lover out of the village, but she knew that in the meantime they must keep her away from Mustafa if they could.

"Go get your mother," she said as a plan began to form in her mind.

Durrani sprang to his feet and dashed from the room. A minute later he returned with his mother, who looked anxious and sad.

"Ask her if there is a way to keep Nasreen here tonight," Mele said.

When Durrani translated her question, Laila shook her head, tears welling in her eyes. No, there was no way.

"You could say she is sick," Mele suggested.

To this too Laila shook her head. She spoke rapidly in Pashto to her son.

"She says there is nothing we can do. Nasreen must go. Mustafa is her husband now. She must accept her fate."

"But if she can just wait until tomorrow, maybe we could get her away from here—her and her friend."

This time when Durrani translated, Laila hesitated, turning the idea over in her mind. She spoke to Durrani in a rush of words again.

"She says maybe we could say she is unclean."

Mele looked from one to the other, not understanding. "What does she mean—unclean?"

"Bleeding," Durrani said. "Unclean."

In a flash Mele realized what he was saying. Would that work? Could they say she was menstruating? Would it be enough to delay the consummation of the marriage?

Nasreen looked from Mele to her mother with wild hope in eyes.

Surely it was worth a try.

***

Peter knew he was fortunate to have been able to visit this village and when he was back in Boston no doubt he would see the value of the experience, but for now he just wished it was behind him. Not until he and Mele were safely back in Kabul would he relax. He didn't trust these people, at least not Mustafa and his gun-toting pals. And in spite of all his training to suspend his judgment about other cultures, he had to admit what he saw disturbed him. Being a neutral observer was much more difficult in practice than it was in theory. He had been appalled when Mustafa's father beat his wife. Nor was he comfortable about Mustafa's arranged marriage. Mele had said the bride did not want to marry him. He didn't blame her. What woman in her right mind would want to marry Mustafa? He felt sorry for the girl, but it was none of his business. There was nothing he could do. He was just here as an observer. He had signed an agreement not to interfere. All the same, it disturbed him.

Ahmad chattered nervously as they followed Mustafa and two of his friends through the streets of the village. It was early evening now. The children had all disappeared. Bearded men lounging in doorways watched them pass with wary eyes.

Before they left the house, Mustafa had been upset because Hakim was missing. Evidently he had expected his brother to be part of the little group that would escort the bride home, but Hakim was nowhere to be found and no one knew where he had gone. In the end they had to leave without him, and as a result Mustafa was in a foul mood.

Peter could not help thinking how different this procession to fetch the bride was from the one he had observed in China. Mustafa hardly spoke. His friends, on the other hand, were boisterous as they swaggered down the street, their rifles slung casually over their shoulders. When they arrived at the girl's house, Mustafa shouted and her mother came scurrying out to the gap in the wall, her scarf held over her nose and mouth, eyes carefully averted as she admitted them.

They followed her into the same sparsely furnished room that they had been in earlier in the day for the wedding. It had been dim then due to the blackened windows, but now it was even darker in spite of the fire on the hearth and an oil-burning lamp. Two burqa-clad women stood like shadows against the wall. The slightly taller one would be Mele, the shorter Mustafa's bride. Mustafa barely glanced at them. The bride's uncle, who was missing his right hand, looked Mustafa in the eye and muttered something. Whatever it was, the effect was electric. Mustafa burst into an angry torrent of words.

"What's wrong?" Peter asked Ahmad in a low voice, trying not to draw Mustafa's attention.

"Her uncle says she is unclean."

"What does that mean?"

"It is the wrong time of the month."

Mustafa turned to the girl's mother and shouted at her. She shrank back against the wall, her eyes averted.

"What will happen?" Peter asked.

"Her uncle asked him to wait a few days."

It was impossible to know what the bride felt about the scene playing itself out in front of her because her face was hidden by her burqa. She stood there as still as a statue, waiting for the outcome.

Well, this was an unexpected glitch, Peter thought. A little obstacle nature had set in their path. Perhaps he was not going to witness a homecoming after all. Not that he minded, but he did not look forward to being in Mustafa's company after a setback in his marriage plans. He had been in a bad mood before; now he would be intolerable.

For several more minutes Mustafa ranted at the uncle and the mother, while his friends stood idly by.

"He insists the girl come with him now even if she is unclean," Ahmad whispered when the ranting stopped.

Seconds ticked by. The uncle said something then, and after a slight hesitation, the girl took a step forward. Her mother seemed to shrink even more. Peter hoped Mele did not do anything rash. If she spoke now, Mustafa might unleash his anger against her and it would only make the situation worse.

Mele must have realized this. She stayed where she was and did not draw attention to herself. For that he was grateful. He hated what was happening, but there was nothing either of them could do to stop it. Mustafa let fly one last volley of words, then turned on his heel and stalked out. The girl silently followed and then his friends, more subdued now.

Mele rushed to Peter's side as he turned to go. "We have to help her," she said in a low, urgent voice. "We have to take her with us when we leave tomorrow."

Ahmad had already walked out the door. Maybe he was deliberately giving Peter a minute alone with Mele, but Peter knew he mustn't be long. The others would soon notice he was missing and they might come back. After all the show of temper, he didn't want that. He was not surprised Mele was set on helping the girl, but surely she could see there was nothing they could do. They couldn't take her with them any more than they could have taken little Su-Ling from her home.

Mele's eyes pleaded with him through the latticework of the burqa. She might have been trapped in a prison cell, begging for his help, but he was powerless to help her. He wished they didn't have to wait for tomorrow to leave. He felt guilty about forcing Mele to spend another night in this place, and the idea of spending one more night himself under the same roof as Mustafa depressed the hell out of him. He wanted to be with Mele. He wished he could hold her, reassure her, spend this night with her. It seemed unfair that Mustafa got to spend the night with his new wife, while he had to sleep alone. Well, it was only for a little longer. They would leave first thing in the morning. Ahmad had assured him it was all arranged. Tomorrow he would hold her in his arms and apologize for all of this. When they were back in Boston, he would make it up to her somehow.

"I'll see what I can do," he said, not wanting to dash her hopes.

The bride's mother was still flattened against the wall, as if she feared to move.

"I'm sorry," he mumbled as he passed her.

Ahmad was waiting for him outside by the gap in the wall. Neither said anything. They hurried to catch up with the others.

The journey back was different from the journey coming. Mustafa's friends had loosened up. They fired their guns in the air and uttered wild battle cries. Mustafa's mood seemed to have improved, although he still paid no attention to the girl in the burqa, who trailed behind him like a slave he had bought. Peter, bringing up the rear with Ahmad, felt sorry for her. Poor girl—he didn't envy her the life she had to look forward to.

When they reached Mustafa's house, his friends said goodbye and slipped away into the night. Mustafa headed toward the door without so much as a glance at his bride. She stole behind him like a shadow, followed by Ahmad and Peter.

Once they were inside, Mustafa went straight to his brother's room and flung open the door, but Hakim was still not home. Mustafa's mother tried to calm him, but he lashed out at her, and she fell back, silent. Meanwhile, the girl stood ignored near the door.

Peter wondered what was wrong now but did not dare ask Ahmad. He didn't want to attract Mustafa's attention. It was clear his temper was ready to flare at the slightest provocation.

In the silence following Mustafa's outburst, the muezzin's call to evening prayer wafted through the night. With one last angry outpouring of words, Mustafa stormed out the door. Exchanging wary glances, Ahmad and Peter followed him. Once in the street Peter asked Ahmad what had happened.

"He was angry that his brother was not there to congratulate him," Ahmad said, keeping his voice low so that Mustafa, several yards ahead of them, would not hear.

"Is that so important?"

"Evidently to him it is. And he was angry at his mother for defending his brother. He said she loved him more."

Who could blame her? thought Peter. What mother wouldn't prefer a son like Hakim to one like Mustafa?

He wondered what would happen when Hakim reappeared. Was it always this contentious in their family? Was Hakim so used to his brother's temper that he could ignore it? If this was typical of their home life, he didn't envy Hakim.

By the time they arrived at the mosque, he had decided if he saw Hakim he would warn him that his brother was angry at him. He didn't have long to wait. As before, Hakim appeared at the last minute after the other men had already taken their places on the prayer mats facing Mecca. But Hakim did not stop to talk this time. He gave Peter the barest nod when their eyes met but said nothing.

Disappointed, Peter leaned against one of the columns flanking the door and prepared to listen again to the unintelligible stream of words that would continue for half an hour or more.

When prayers were done and they returned to the house, there was no sign of the bride in the outer room.

"No doubt she is waiting in his room," Ahmad whispered.

Hakim had not yet returned, which was just as well, Peter thought, because the prayer session had not done much to dispel Mustafa's anger. He seemed in no rush to join his new wife in the next room. Instead he dropped into a cross-legged position on the floor, glared at Peter, and fired off a question in Pashto.

"He asks what you think of the village," Ahmad translated nervously.

Peter knew he must be careful how he answered. "Tell him it's a very nice village."

Mustafa did not smile when Ahmad translated this. Glowering, he shot off another question.

"He wants to know what you will write about it when you go back."

"Tell him I'll describe their marriage customs. That's all."

Again Ahmad translated and received in response another question.

"He wants to know if you will say they are ignorant and backward."

"Of course not."

The next barrage of words caused Ahmad to hesitate.

"What did he say?"

"He called you an infidel—an unbeliever."

Mustafa watched him, the corner of his mouth curled in a sneer, a cat playing with a mouse. But Peter had no intention of arguing with him about religion or anything else.

"He says Allah is the true God, that only those who believe in Allah and follow the Seven Pillars shall go to heaven."

"We are from different cultures," Peter said, meeting Mustafa's gaze evenly. "We have different beliefs."

Again the translation, followed by a rush of angry words.

"He says it makes no difference. There is only one God, and He is Allah."

"I'm not going to argue with him."

Mustafa gave him a look of contempt, got to his feet, and stalked away.

"When do we leave in the morning?" Peter asked, relieved that the confrontation was over.

"We must get up early for the morning prayer," Ahmad said. "I think we leave shortly after."

"Good." Peter stretched out on the floor. The sooner he and Mele were out of there, the better. Tomorrow they would fly to Kenya. This place would be just a bad memory stashed in a back corner of his mind. Tomorrow he would see Mele and they would talk. He remembered the feel of her body that night in Kunming. There would be more nights like that. He felt for the ring safe in his shirt pocket and drowsed off thinking of her.

The next thing he knew someone was shouting. He came awake with a jolt, his heart pumping.

"What's happening?" he asked Ahmad, sitting up.

"I don't know," Ahmad said, also sitting up.

They heard a scream. The girl, Peter thought. It must be the girl.

"What's he doing to her?" he said, getting to his feet in alarm.

Ahmad, also on his feet now, put his hand on Peter's arm. "You must not interfere."

They were both looking at the dark doorway leading to the adjoining rooms. Suddenly Mustafa appeared there shouting.

"What is it?" Peter asked. "What's happening?"

In the doorway they saw Mustafa's mother and father, who also had just been roused from sleep. His mother was hastily drawing a scarf over her head.

"He wants to know if his brother is home," Ahmad said. "He says he wants four witnesses."

"There are four of us. Witnesses for what?"

"His mother doesn't count. A woman only counts half. So he has only three and a half witnesses."

Peter did not understand. It made no sense to him.

Mustafa flung open the door to Hakim's room, stormed in, and then stormed out again. Through the open door Peter could see the austere little room was empty.

"Witnesses for what?" Peter said again. Whatever was happening, he could tell it was not good.

"Shh," Ahmad said, shooting him a warning glance.

Mustafa's father hurried away, presumably to find a fourth witness.

Meanwhile, Mustafa herded the rest of them into his room, where the girl crouched on the floor crying. She wore a simple shift; her arms and feet were bare. She had long black hair and looked very young. She was trying desperately to cover herself with a blanket. Mustafa started pacing and each time he came near her she cringed. No one said anything. Mustafa's mother began to cry.

"For god's sake, what's happening?" Peter asked in a low voice.

"Something bad," Ahmad said, also keeping his voice low. "Something very bad."

Mustafa's father was soon back with another man, a rotund middle-aged neighbor apparently awoken from sleep, who looked as if he would rather not be there.

Mustafa pointed at the girl and launched into a passionate tirade.

"He says she lied to him about her monthly bleeding," Ahmad translated. "She is not bleeding, but even worse, she is an adulteress. She has slept with another man. She is not a virgin. We are his witnesses. He wants her to be punished according to the law."

"What's the punishment?"

"Death."

"*What?*" He felt as if he had stumbled into a bad dream. Surely this could not be happening. Things like this didn't happen in real life. Yes, he knew about strict Islamic punishments, but *death*? Would they really put the girl to death because she wasn't a virgin?

Mustafa charged out of the room.

"But she's just a kid," Peter said. "And how can she be an adulteress when she only got married today?"

"It is forbidden for a woman to sleep with anyone but her husband," Ahmad said. "So if she has slept with another man, she is an adulteress. Age does not matter."

Before Peter could argue, Mustafa was back with the whip

from the wall in the other room. Raising it threateningly, he took a step toward the girl, who cowered and flung up her arm to ward off the blow.

"Wait a minute," Peter said. "Tell him—"

Mustafa glared at him and snarled at him in Pashto.

"He called her a whore," Ahmad said nervously. "He asks if you are her lover."

"Of course not. That's ridiculous. I've hardly been out of his sight. When could I possibly have—"

"Then please *shut up*. You will only make matters worse."

The whip came down on the girl's shoulders and she screamed. Mustafa raised it to strike again.

"Can't somebody stop him?" Peter said, looking at Mustafa's father and then at his silently weeping mother and finally at the bleary-eyed neighbor who had been brought in as a fourth witness.

"He wants to know the name of her lover," Ahmad whispered.

The girl was crying and trying to pull the blanket around her to protect herself from the whip.

Suddenly Hakim burst into the room. Peter felt relieved. Surely he would stop his brother. Hakim began to speak rapidly in Pashto and paused only a second when his mother gave a small cry and covered her mouth with one hand. Mustafa struck at him with the whip now and he just stood there. The first blow left a red mark on his neck. Before Mustafa could strike a second blow, his father stepped forward and caught his hand.

There was no need for Ahmad to explain what was happening. Peter understood. Hakim was the girl's lover. That was why he hadn't been at home when Mustafa brought his bride home. He couldn't bear to see his beloved married to his bad-tempered brother. And had Mustafa known Hakim loved the girl? Could that be the reason he had to have her? Not because she was the most beautiful girl in the village, but because his brother loved her? And was that also why he hated her so much?

"What will happen to him?" Peter asked after Hakim had been sent to his room in disgrace. He and Ahmad were back in the main room lying on the floor. The neighbor had gone home. Mustafa's parents had retreated to their room, and Mustafa was sitting with his back to the door of the room where the girl was confined, staring with hatred at the door to his brother's room, their jailer, determined the lovers would have no chance to talk to each other or escape.

"They will kill him," Ahmad said. "He and the girl will be stoned to death. That is the punishment for adultery."

"But his own brother?"

"It doesn't matter. The law is the same for all. And now we should try to get some sleep. It will be morning soon."

Peter didn't see how Ahmad could sleep after all that had happened, but soon he was gently snoring. Peter doubted that anyone else in the house was sleeping, not after what had happened. His ears strained, but there was only silence. He tried to tell himself everything would get sorted out in the morning. Cooler heads would prevail. And in any case he and Mele would be leaving. They would be well rid of this place.

It was still dark when Ahmad shook his shoulder to wake him. In the distance he could hear the muezzin's cry. He must get up, Ahmad said, and join the men at morning prayer. No matter what had happened the night before, prayers must be attended to as usual. With Mustafa, they trudged off to the mosque, leaving behind Hakim shut up in his room and his father, who stayed behind to guard the two offenders. If only he would let them escape while we are gone, Peter thought, but he doubted that would happen. Besides, where could they go? No, Hakim and the girl would be there when they returned. He felt fairly certain of that.

It seemed strange to be walking to the mosque as if nothing had changed. Mustafa stalked several paces ahead, cold and determined. Did the rest of the village know about what had happened last night? Peter wondered. Would no one notice that Hakim was missing from morning prayers?

Again he stood for what seemed an interminable amount of time outside the mosque and waited for prayers to end. He wanted dawn to come. He wanted to get as far as he could from this place. He would not feel safe until he and Mele were out of there.

At last the prayer service was over and the men and boys poured out of the mosque.

"Ask him how soon we leave," he urged Ahmad as they walked back. He meant Mustafa, who was striding ahead of them with one of his friends.

Ahmad gave him an uneasy glance. Peter didn't blame him for not wanting to broach Mustafa. Violent and unpredictable as he was, who knew what would set him off, especially when he was already so angry?

With effort, Ahmad worked up his courage and asked Peter's question. In return he was bombarded with angry words.

"He says we cannot leave until later. We must be here for the stoning. It will be in the early afternoon."

"No, we need to leave this morning. We have a plane to catch in Kabul later today. Tell him we have to leave before the stoning."

Ahmad tried again and got another angry response. "He insists you must be there. You are a witness."

"I don't want to watch anyone get stoned to death," Peter said. "Tell him that."

Ahmad gave him a reluctant look but conveyed the message. Mustafa's response was brief, flung contemptuously over his shoulder.

"I'm sorry," Ahmad said. "It's no use. He says you must watch. And then after that you can leave. Not before. Please. There is no other way."

Peter didn't like it, but what else could he do? It could be dangerous for them all if he continued to argue with Mustafa in his present mood. When they were out of here, he would complain to the Alliance, but for now he had to do whatever was necessary to get himself and Mele safely out of the village. If that meant watching an execution, he would have to do it regardless of how much he hated the idea.

As the morning progressed, he wondered if Mele knew yet what had happened. Men came to the house and consulted with Mustafa and his father in low voices. Peter told himself surely someone would put a stop to this insanity. Where was the imam? Did he know what was happening? But the hours slipped by and nothing changed.

He thought of Hakim and the girl, still confined to their separate rooms, while Mustafa and his friends stood guard outside their doors. Could nothing be done to save them? If he had known the language, could he have reasoned with Mustafa? Ahmad refused to translate for him, sitting with his back against the wall, eyes closed, pretending to sleep.

Peter wondered if anyone would stop him if he tried to walk out the door. If Mele didn't know what had happened, she would be worried about why he didn't come for her and wonder why they weren't leaving in the morning as arranged. Maybe he couldn't stop Mustafa from killing his brother and the girl, but what right did Mustafa have to keep him there like a prisoner? He had done nothing wrong.

When he stood up, Ahmad's eyes flew open.

"What are you doing?"

"I'm going to go see my wife."

"You can't."

"Oh, can't I? Who's going to stop me?"

He headed toward the door, but just as he got to it, the imam arrived surrounded by five or six fierce-looking armed men. The imam gave him a hard look. Ahmad was at his elbow now, gently tugging.

"Please.," Ahmad begged. "You will get us both in trouble."

"Ask then," Peter said, tired of being patient and reasonable. "Ask them if I can see my wife."

Reluctantly Ahmad complied and for his trouble received only a curt *ya*, which meant no, before the imam and his men swept past him. One man stayed behind, near the door, and the warning look he threw Peter was enough to tell him that he had better not try to leave.

"It's no use," Ahmad said. "They say you must stay here."

When the hour came for midday prayer, Peter had to accompany the other men to the mosque again. They all went except for one man who was left behind to guard the lovers. Peter felt thoroughly tired of the ritual now. It no longer seemed awesome to him. All he could think of was the execution that would take place in the afternoon. Every fiber of his being revolted against the thought of it. He told himself he would close his eyes. They could force him to attend, but they could not force him to watch.

After prayers were over, several of the imam's men walked Peter and Ahmad to a rocky field outside of town where the men and boys of the village were gathering. There was excitement in the air as they stood in a circle around three posts, laughing and talking and picking up stones from the ground. Peter attracted glances both curious and hostile. He saw Ahmad squat down and pick up some stones.

"What are you doing?"

Ahmad squinted up at him. "What does it look like I'm doing?"

"You're not going to be a part of this, are you?"

"We already are a part of this, in case you hadn't noticed."

"If you throw a single stone, I'll see you lose your job."

"And if I throw no stones," Ahmad said quietly, "I will very likely lose my life."

"This is insane."

"Is it? To these people your world is insane. And immoral. This, to them, is justice. If they do not punish adultery, others may break the law. This is a warning and a reminder to live by the Sharia laws."

It was their culture, Peter told himself. Ahmad was right. Who was he to judge? But all the same, he didn't want to watch it. Just the thought of what was about to happen made him feel sick.

Another five minutes passed and then two pickups approached in a swirl of dust. When the first stopped, the imam and his men climbed out. The second was the same old dusty pickup that had brought Peter and Mele to the village. When it stopped, Mustafa and his father climbed out. In the back were the condemned lovers. The young woman wore a burqa now. Her hands were tied in front of her and she had to be lifted from the back of the truck. Hakim had a hood over his head and his hands were tied too. As the crowd jeered, they were led and pushed roughly to the posts. Each was then bound to a separate post.

The crowd quieted as the imam entered the circle. He gave a long speech, then read from the Qur'an, his voice strong and authoritative in the open air. Peter felt a wave of despair wash over him. They were really going through with it. Nobody was going to stop them. He imagined telling Mele about it later. He could hear her asking, "Why didn't you do something? How could you just stand there?" There would be outrage in her eyes. He would plead that it had been too dangerous for him to do anything. The outrage would turn to scorn, and rightly so. All the rest of his life he would have to live with the knowledge that he had watched two innocent people die and not tried to stop it. He would never know whether or not he might have saved them if he had at least tried.

Finally the imam ceased to recite and moved away from the lovers, leaving them to their fate. A murmur of anticipation rippled through the crowd.

In another minute it would be too late.

"No!" he shouted. "Don't do this!" He could hardly believe he'd had the nerve to speak up. Everyone was looking at him in surprise.

"Translate," he told Ahmad.

But Ahmad just stood there, staring at him, as if he were deaf. Peter was on his own.

"This is wrong," he said, hoping there were at least a few among the crowd who could understand English. "Surely you know it's wrong. These two people committed no crime except to fall in love."

Mustafa strode toward him, shouting, a rock in his hand raised as if he would strike Peter with it.

"He says if you interfere you will die too," Ahmad said.

Mustafa stood in front of him, glaring at him, his voice steely as he thrust the rock at Peter.

"He says you must throw too or you will die. You and your wife. You are both infidels."

"He can't do that."

"Please. Do as he says."

Mustafa stared at him, the corner of his lip twisting in a sneer, hatred in his eyes. He was taunting Peter, daring him to refuse. It flashed through Peter's mind that he could die in this godforsaken field, and if he died, Mele would too. He saw this in Mustafa's face. If Mustafa had no qualms about killing his brother and his new wife, he would also have no qualms about killing Peter and Mele. He lived in a small brutal world where such horrors were accepted. So Peter took the rock. Mustafa spit in his face, but he merely stared back, determined not to let Mustafa goad him into a rash action. And then the crowd surged forward shouting as they aimed their missiles at the lovers. Peter looked away. The rock fell from his hand but no one seemed to notice. He was forgotten by the crowd in their rush to execute the condemned pair.

Turning away in disgust, he walked rapidly back toward the village, at every step expecting someone to stop him. He tried to block out all thought of what had happened and concentrate on getting to Mele. He was nearly to the mud-brick house where she was sequestered when Ahmad caught up with him.

"Where are you going?" Ahmad asked.

"To get my wife." He was not going to wait for Mustafa to give him permission to leave. He suspected that Mustafa had no intention of letting him go if he could help it. Peter wondered what the Alliance would be told if he died here, how his death would be explained. Would he and Mele simply disappear without a trace? He regretted deeply having brought her to such a dangerous place. He had taken her from her island Eden and brought her to this hellhole where she might die. It was his fault, and now he must do everything he could to save her.

Ahmad placed a hand on his arm. "You must not do this. They won't like it."

"I don't care if they don't like it." Peter shook off the hand. He had reached the gap in the wall that enclosed the house where Mele was waiting.

"You cannot just go in."

Ahmad's words just made him more determined. Mele's life was at stake. Both their lives were at stake. This was no time to worry about customs.

The girl's mother must have heard them coming. She met them at the door, holding her scarf across her nose and mouth. She looked at him with eyes red from weeping.

"I'm sorry," he said.

Still clutching her scarf to her face, she turned, and he followed her into the house, Ahmad close behind him.

When Mele saw him, she sprang up from a cushion near the wall where she had been sitting with the little girl and the boy.

"Is it over? Did they kill her?"

"Yes."

"And Hakim too?" asked the boy.

Peter glanced at him, surprised that he could speak English.

"Yes, Hakim too."

The one-handed man sitting in the corner spoke up in Pashto.

"My uncle says you should leave," the boy said. "If you stay, they will kill you."

"No," Ahmad said from the doorway. "They will take us back now. You will see."

"Get your burqa and your bag," Peter told Mele. He was not going to wait for the Taliban to decide what to do with them. This might be their only chance to escape, before all the men returned.

Mele grabbed her bag and burqa, setting them down again just long enough to hug the children and their mother.

"Do you know where we can get a car or a pickup?" Peter asked the boy.

The boy nodded. "Yes, I know where there is one near here. I will take you."

"What are you going to do?" Ahmad asked nervously as they stepped out into the heat and brightness of the afternoon.

"We're getting out of here," Peter said.

They followed the boy, who took them to a narrow street, hardly more than an alley, where a dusty and dented black pickup stood beside some old tires.

"Thank you," he told the boy. "Now go home and take care of your little sister and your mother. You're a brave boy and I'm sure your father would be very proud of you."

The pickup was unlocked, but there was no key in the ignition or over the visor or in the glove compartment, so Peter fumbled beneath the dash with the wires. He had never hotwired a car before, but he knew the general principle.

"What are you doing?" Ahmad asked again as he tried to decide which wires should be stripped and connected.

"What does it look like I'm doing?"

"If they catch you, they will kill you. Why couldn't you just be a little patient? You Americans are all alike."

"Are we?"

Just then the engine sprang to life, to Peter's immense

relief. Glancing at the gas gauge, he saw there was half a tank of gas and could hardly believe their luck.

"Are you coming with us or not?" he asked Ahmad as Mele scrambled into the front beside him.

Ahmad stood wringing his hands, looking down the street. "If they catch us stealing a truck, they will cut off my hand—maybe both!"

"Okay, stay if you want, but we're getting out of here."

Ahmad looked uncertainly once more down the street. There was still no sign of the returning mob. Evidently that decided him. He hopped into the back of the pickup, and Peter took off with a lurch, charging out of the alley and into the deserted street, which soon led to the dusty narrow dirt road that would take them north to the checkpoint and then to the highway and on to Kabul and safety.

# 9

# Kenya

Their plane touched down in Nairobi in the early morning. When they exited customs, a young African woman was waiting for them, holding a sign with WAPCC printed on it in large letters. She had the face of a model and wore a bright patterned orange dress of a thin material and sandals. Her hair was plaited in a multitude of small braids, and a thin gold band with three dangling gold coins encircled her neck. When she saw Peter and Mele, she broke into a smile that showed perfect white teeth.

"Assalama," she said, holding out her hand, "but just call me Sally. Welcome to Kenya."

"They did tell you there would be two of us?" Peter asked.

"Oh, yes. First they said one, then they said, no, he has a wife with him. Is it a problem? I said, no, no problem." She flashed Mele a smile. "You don't get airsick, do you?"

"I don't think so," Mele said, surprised by the question. "I haven't yet."

"Good. Shall we go then?" She turned and led them

through the crowded terminal toward an exit before Mele had a chance to ask why she had asked about airsickness.

"Your English is very good," Peter said as they emerged from the terminal. Outside it was much hotter. Overhead the sky was blue and bright with wispy white clouds. Cars whizzed by.

Sally grinned. "I studied at Princeton for one year. I would have stayed longer but my mama got sick so I came home."

"What language do they speak where we're going?" Mele asked.

"They are called the Rendille and they speak their own local dialect, but I can translate, don't worry. You got only one bag?"

"Yes, just the one," Peter said.

Mele glanced at him. His bag had been left behind at Mustafa's house. There had been no time to go back for it. He had lost everything—clothes, camera, notes. He said it didn't matter. He could always retype his notes from memory, and they were soon going home anyway so the clothes didn't really matter. The only thing he really regretted losing was the camera. Now he would have no photos to accompany his dissertation.

"Where we're going—is it far?" Peter asked.

"You mean the parking lot?" Sally asked, flashing her smile.

Of course that was not what he meant, as she must have known. He meant the Forbidden Place, the home of the Rendille people.

"We will be there by noon, God willing," Sally said.

Mele had taken a liking to their guide from the beginning. She liked her smile and her necklace and the graceful way she moved. When Sally led them to a yellow jeep in the parking lot, it seemed the perfect vehicle for her to drive. Peter climbed into the front seat beside her, where there was more room for his long legs, and Mele squeezed into the cramped back seat with her bag. As they took off with a squeal of tires, Mele fastened her seat belt. Pedestrians jumped out of their path as their jeep hurtled down the street.

"Have you been a guide long?" Mele asked.

"About a year and a half now," Sally said over her shoulder. "I've been to one childbirth, one funeral, one courtship, one naming ceremony, and one exorcism. The exorcism was very scary, a woman possessed by a lion spirit. It took all the witchdoctor's skills to persuade it to leave. I assure you, you would not want to be possessed by a lion spirit. You are my first wedding, and I am very much looking forward to it."

"Just how isolated is the community we're going to?" Peter asked as they nearly ran down a man who was crossing the street.

Mele looked back and saw the man shaking his fist and shouting after them.

"Oh, very isolated," Sally said. "It was only made a Forbidden Place about five years ago, but hardly anyone went there before that because there's no road, just a trail, and it's surrounded by miles of desert and mountains. Very difficult to get there."

"Do they have much interaction with other people?"

"Only with the people I bring there and nearby tribes who try to steal their camels. But those are their enemies and they speak another language, so there's not really much interaction."

"Good," Peter said. "I very much want to see an authentic ritual."

"Oh, it's authentic," Sally said. "You could not find more

authentic anywhere. The Rendille follow the old ways. They are very ignorant and backward. No TV or cell phones or tap water or toilets. You name it, they don't have it. You should be prepared, as you Americans say, to rough it."

"We are," Peter said. "We understand that these people live as their ancestors did. That's why we're here. That's what makes them unique. That's why their way of life needs to be preserved."

"Mmm," Sally said noncommittally.

"You don't agree?"

"I'm saying I wouldn't want to be a Rendille."

"Why not?" Mele asked, leaning forward.

"Would you want to live in a desert where sometimes there's not enough to eat and just to survive is a daily struggle?"

"Why doesn't someone help them?"

Sally rolled her eyes. "Because then they would stop being the Rendille. I don't know what they'd be, but they wouldn't be the Rendille anymore. You take away their traditions and what would they be?"

"But surely people could help them without taking away their traditions?"

"Sally's right," Peter chimed in. "Contact with civilization can be the worst thing to happen to indigenous people. It undermines everything they believe in. It robs them of their sense of self-worth and identity and gives them nothing of value in its place. Look at Native Americans, look at the aborigines of Australia, look at the Inuit. Everywhere civilizations have been destroyed in the name of progress."

In Hawaii too, Mele thought. Like every other child of the islands, she had learned about it in school. The Westerners came and they destroyed the sacred sites and outlawed the old ways. So much was lost. It was a wonder anything of her ancestors' culture had survived.

She watched the crowded streets of Nairobi sweep past. Throngs of people filled the sidewalks, cars and buses jammed the streets, tall buildings towered overhead. It was not so different from Honolulu or any other big city, she thought, except the people were darker-skinned. The jeep had to slow down until they were past the most congested areas. Twenty minutes later they were bumping along an unpaved road on the outskirts of the city, headed into a flat area where the buildings were low-rise and more spread out.

Their destination turned out to be a small airport. Sally drove toward the hangar, then stopped short near a small plane gaily painted with pictures of animals and birds.

"Well, here we are."

"We're flying in that?" Peter asked, eyeing the plane skeptically.

Sally rolled her eyes. "Did you not hear me say there is no way to the Rendille except a trail that goes over the mountains? If we could just drive there, so could everybody else, and then soon it would be just like Nairobi. Would you want to go there then? No."

"Can you fly it?" Mele asked, excited at the prospect of flying in such a wonderful plane. She had never seen anything like it before. It was like a child's toy, only larger. Why didn't all planes have pictures painted on them? That Sally could fly seemed perfectly natural. After all, she had been to Princeton. Why shouldn't she be able to fly a plane? Mele decided she would add learning to fly to her list of things she wanted to do. But it turned out Sally was not going to fly them.

"Are you kidding?" she said. "For that we have Mike." She indicated a tall lanky young man in a red cap emerging just then from the hangar, wiping his hands on a cloth. He walked toward them flashing a smile as broad and friendly as Sally's.

"So here you are again, pretty lady," he said to Sally as he came up to them. "What's it going to be this time?"

"A wedding. You want to go?"

"Yeah, right."

"There'll be lots of food and pretty girls."

"*Rendille* girls. No thanks."

"What you got against Rendille girls?"

"Nothing, but I'm not partial to camels."

They both laughed.

Mele was mystified by this exchange. She wondered if Peter understood.

"Well, climb aboard," Mike said. "She's got a few years on her, but she can get you where you're going."

"Did you paint the pictures?" Mele asked.

"Yeah, you like them? They add a little something, don't they? She looked so naked before." He glanced at Sally, who was trying not to laugh. "What?"

Mele was surprised at how small the plane was on the inside. There were only four seats, two in front, two in back. Sally slipped effortlessly into the front seat beside Mike while Mele and Peter climbed awkwardly into the seats behind them. Mele saw Peter strapping himself in and followed his example. The engine was loud, and when they started to move, she was surprised how flimsy the plane seemed. She felt a prick of fear and wondered if it was safe as it accelerated. Just when it looked as if they might run out of runway, the plane lifted off the ground like a clumsy bird taking flight.

It was very different from flying in a commercial jet—a lot noisier for one thing, and the plane tilted precariously for another, rattling and shaking at times as if it might fly apart.

She gripped her armrests and glanced at Peter, but he was gazing obliviously out the window next to him with no apparent concern for their safety, so she decided they must be in no danger and tried to relax.

Sally was talking to the pilot, leaning close to his ear and shouting to be heard, but Mele could not make out what she was saying over the roar of the engine. Mele looked out her window at the landscape spread out below them as they rose. It was a patchwork quilt of green and brown squares. How small everything looked from up here! It was like some child's pretend world, with miniature cars and houses, or a game board where you threw the dice to see which square you would land on.

It was an hour before they reached the mountains, which lay below them in soft brown folds. Beyond them lay a desert that stretched for miles. Just as she was beginning to wonder how much farther they would fly, Sally turned and grinned at them.

"Look," she shouted through cupped hands and pointed down.

At first Mele could see nothing. Then she noticed small brown spots on the ground. "What are they?" she shouted.

"Camels," Sally shouted back. "That means we're getting close."

"Is that it up there?" Peter asked.

Sally looked where he was pointing. "Yes, I think so. Landing will be a little bumpy so brace yourselves."

Mele clung to her armrests again as their small plane swooped down. When the wheels touched the ground, they were jolted by the shock and the plane shimmied on the desert floor. Gradually they slowed and finally shuddered to a stop. The pilot grinned back at them.

"Everyone okay?"

"Kind of a rocky landing, wasn't it?" Peter said, unfastening his seatbelt. "Is it always like that?"

"It's hard on the tires, but what can I do?" Mike said cheerfully. "Who would build a runway in a place like this? Besides, if we had a real runway, we wouldn't be able to keep out the tourists."

"Where are we anyway?" Peter asked as he climbed out of the plane. He squinted at the horizon. As far as the eye could see, there was only barren desert. Overhead the hot sun beat down from a flawless blue sky.

"It's not far," Sally assured him, strapping on her backpack.

"Isn't your friend coming?" Peter asked, glancing back at the plane and Mike, who was still sitting in the cockpit.

"He'll be back for us tomorrow. Come on. We don't want to stay here in the hot sun."

Mele was in agreement with that. Already she felt as if she were baking.

"Where's the village?" Peter asked, looking all around.

"That way," Sally said, pointing. "We can't land too close. It would scare the camels. The Rendille too. Besides, it's Alliance regulations. We're not supposed to get within a mile of them with our plane. But they saw us come down. They'll know we're coming."

"What about our clothes?"

She grinned. "You mean, should you dress like the Rendille? You can if you want. Just take off all your clothes."

"I'm sure they must wear something," Peter said. "Don't they?"

"Even if you put a little goatskin over your privates, you'd still stand out," Sally said. "With your white skin, there's no way you're going to look like a Rendille."

"Do the women go naked too?" Mele asked.

"*Half* naked," Sally said.

Mele pondered this but decided not to ask which half.

The Rendille were nomads who moved every few months Sally explained as they trekked across the dusty land. They had herds of camels and goats which they moved about the desert seeking scarce spots of greenery where they could feed and water. The young men and boys were given the task of tending the animals, which meant living apart from their families for much of the year. But they would generally be within a day's walk of the village and would make the journey back every few months.

"There it is," Sally said after they had walked about a mile.

Mele stared in the distance but saw nothing, just scrubby growth and flat terrain stretching away to the mountains in the distance. Five minutes later she could make out small huts and a cluster of camels. As they drew nearer, she saw the camels were enclosed in a pen a little apart from the village. When she caught a whiff of a foul odor, she realized why the camels were kept apart. It was not a pleasant smell to live close to.

"They are probably the bride-price," Sally said. "The groom must pay the bride's family eight camels."

Mele would have stood longer watching the camels if a group of Rendille children had not run up and surrounded them. The children wanted to touch them and to touch Sally's backpack and Mele's bag. Adults came running too. Mele could understand nothing of the strange language that everyone was speaking all at once around her, but she smiled back and tried to look friendly. The crowd pushed an old man forward and fell silent while he delivered a short speech to welcome them.

Sally made a short speech to him in return and gave him a small metal box that she pulled from her backpack. Everyone crowded closer as he opened it and oohed and aahed.

"What was that you gave him?" Peter asked.

"We cannot come here without gifts," Sally said. "Gifts are expected."

"But what about the Alliance's rule not to introduce foreign objects into native cultures?"

"They have seen gold wire before. It's hard to come by, but we are not introducing something they have not seen before."

A bowl of milk was brought out of the nearest hut by a village woman and carefully handed to Sally. She tipped it to her mouth, drank a few sips, thanked the woman, and then passed it to Mele.

"What is it?" Mele asked.

"Camel's milk. You must drink it but not too much. They are being generous, sharing what they have with us."

Mele took a sip. It had a strange taste, quite different from cow's milk. "I didn't know milk could come from camels," she said, passing the bowl to Peter.

"It's their main nourishment," Sally told her, "which is why their camels are so important to them. Camels give them food, drink, and soft skins for their beds. Their lives revolve around their camels."

"It's supposed to be very healthy," Peter added. "But I have to say I don't much care for it."

Sally had been right about how the Rendille dressed, Mele thought as she looked around at the men, naked except for a loincloth, and the women, who wore longer goatskins than the men but left their breasts bare. The people were urging them forward now.

"They want to show us the hut they have built for the bride and groom," Sally said. "It's where they will spend their wedding night and where they will live together."

Several women were smiling, nodding, and speaking rapidly in Rendille.

"The women built it. It's made of camel and goat skins and poles. When it's time to move, they will take it down, pack it on their camels, and carry it to their next site."

When they came to the hut, Mele thought it looked exactly like all the others—cone-shaped and patched together with animal skins and sticks.

"Very nice," Peter said to the women.

They giggled and bobbed their heads, pleased.

"Can we look inside?" he asked.

"Of course," Sally said. "They would be disappointed if you didn't."

Peter ducked his head and squinted into the dim interior, then stepped aside for Mele to look. There was very little to see. The hut was empty except for some skins on the ground which would serve as a bed for the newly married couple.

"I wish I had my camera," Peter said.

Mele touched his arm. "Perhaps the Alliance can get it back for you."

"I doubt it. And even if they could, it'll be too late for here."

He was right of course, she thought. There would be no pictures of these cone-shaped huts or the gentle Rendille people for his dissertation. What he had to say about them would have to be conveyed in words alone, and how could words capture the strange and lonely beauty of this place?

"Come," Sally said. "I want you to meet a friend of mine."

With a small group of women and children at their heels, they passed half a dozen huts before stopping at one.

"Wait here," Sally told them, then stooped and entered

Peter was holding Mele's hand, and now she felt

something touch her other hand and looked down to see a little Rendille girl of five or six years of age looking up at her with big dark eyes.

"Who are you?" Mele asked.

The child just looked at her, then smiled shyly.

"I think you found a friend," Peter said.

Just then Sally stuck her head out of the door of the hut. "You can come in now but no pictures."

"That's not a problem," Peter said. "We don't have a camera."

When Mele entered the hut, the little girl who had been holding her hand hung back, reluctant to enter. It took a few seconds for Mele's eyes to adjust to the dim interior. When they did, she could see a young woman lying on some skins with a baby and an old woman sitting with her back to the wall of the hut. The only source of light was the open door.

Sally spoke to the young woman in Rendille, then turned to Peter and Mele. "This is my friend, Natunya. I was here for her courtship ceremony last year."

The young woman—barely more than a girl—was thin with circles under her eyes and her face beaded with perspiration. Like the other Rendille women and girls, she was bare breasted. She looked at them with feverish eyes and spoke a few words in a breathless voice but did not attempt to sit up. The baby waved his small fists in the air.

"She says you can hold him if you want," Sally said. "Go on. Pick him up."

Mele carefully lifted the naked infant. "Hey, there. What's your name?" The baby made gurgling sounds and tried to catch hold of her hair. While she cradled him, Sally talked to her friend.

"Is she sick?" Mele asked.

"Yes, she's sick."

"What's wrong with her?" Peter asked, frowning.

"Who knows? An infection, dengue fever, Ebola virus, malaria. It could be anything."

"*What?*" he said, taking a step back. "Are you serious?"

Sally shrugged. "Nobody else seems to have it, so don't worry. You probably can't catch it. You are perfectly safe. And even if you catch something, you can find a doctor to cure you once you get back to your country." She sounded bitter.

"Look, if she could have something as serious as dengue fever or Ebola virus, we shouldn't be here." He retreated a few more steps toward the door.

"Maybe we could take her back to Nairobi with us," Mele suggested, gently bouncing the baby and patting its back, just as she used to do for her younger brothers and sisters.

"They would never let her go," Sally said.

"Can't they bring a doctor here?" Mele asked. "They could fly here, like we did."

"They can't," Peter said, "because if they bring a doctor here for this, then they will have to bring one for other things, and eventually the village would lose its traditions. The old ways would not be preserved."

Mele was getting tired of this argument. Surely saving a sick woman should matter more than preserving traditions.

"That's right," Sally said dully, looking down at her sick friend. "Those are the rules."

Sweat shone on the woman's forehead and her glassy eyes searched their faces.

"I think we should leave," Peter said, glancing toward the open door of the hut. "Just in case she is contagious."

Sally squatted beside her friend and spoke to her in Rendille while she stroked the woman's hand. Finally she stood up.

"Here, give me the child."

Mele kissed the baby lightly on its forehead before handing him to Sally, who returned him to his mother's side. As they were about to leave, the old woman sitting in the shadows spoke. She had said nothing until now, and Mele had forgotten she was there.

"She wishes to meet you," Sally said. "Come. I will introduce you."

Mele looked more closely at the old woman. Her eyes gazed past them, a look Mele knew well. Like her grandmother, the old woman was blind. Dropping to her knees, she placed the old woman's hand against her face.

The old woman spoke to her in Rendille.

"What did she say?"

"May your ancestors watch over you."

"What does it mean?"

"It's just a saying. It doesn't mean anything."

Mele looked at the old woman and wished she could speak her language.

"They believe their ancestors visit them," Peter said, still standing near the door. "They believe their ancestors are around them and watch over them."

"They are very superstitious people," Sally said. "Very backward and ignorant. Your husband is right—we should go now. My friend's illness may be contagious. I will come back later to talk to her."

The little girl, who had waited patiently by the door, slipped her hand back in Mele's as they stepped out of the hut. Once outside they immediately found themselves again surrounded by a cluster of Rendille, all of whom seemed to be talking at once.

"They want us to see the bride," Sally said.

"Where is she?" asked Peter, looking around.

Like a river the crowd bore them along toward the center of the encampment where a girl sat on a small stool between two women. Like the other women and girls of the village, all three were bare-breasted. The girl's breasts were small in contrast to the pendulous breasts of the two women. It seemed strange to Mele that they were so unself-conscious about their nakedness. The women smiled at them as they approached. At first Mele thought they were applying makeup to the girl, but looking closer, she saw they were pricking fine points in the girl's face from her brow to her jaw and then brushing a white powder on the tiny bleeding cuts. The girl sat patiently, not objecting, although it must have hurt.

"What are they doing?"

"They are making her beautiful for her wedding tomorrow," Sally said. "They use a thorn as a needle to make tiny dots in her skin and then cover it with a mixture of chalk and ashes. The markings will show that she is a Rendille and a married woman."

"I'd love to get a picture of this," Peter said wistfully.

"I'm not sure they'd give you permission," Sally said. "They're very shy about being photographed."

"Does it wear off later?" Mele asked, remembering the henna tattoos painted on Kamala's hands.

"No, it's permanent. That's why they must do it so carefully."

"She doesn't mind?"

"Of course not. I told you. It makes her beautiful."

"Lots of tribes mark themselves," Peter told Mele. "They scar their faces or their chests. It's like wearing jewelry, only permanent. This isn't really extreme. Not like the Ndebele people, who put metal rings around their necks to stretch them or the Murzi, who put plates in their lower lips or their earlobes to stretch them."

"Why do they do that?" she asked, still watching the girl.

"Because their culture considers it beautiful."

She thought of little Su-Ling with her broken feet and shivered. Maybe she would never understand.

"How old is she?" Peter asked.

Sally repeated his question in Rendille for the two women.

"Fourteen or maybe fifteen. I'm not sure because they measure time differently than we do. They count in camel cycles."

"Is it an arranged marriage?" Mele asked. "Or does she get to choose who she will marry?"

"Oh, it's always arranged. But she doesn't mind. That's just the way it is. It's the way it's always been."

Just then there was a shout in the distance and suddenly the crowd that had gathered was in motion again. The two women started talking excitedly. It looked as if they were torn between continuing their work and following the crowd.

"What's happening?" Peter asked.

"The bridegroom has come home from herding camels. The villagers will welcome him back. Shall we go watch?"

By now the bride was having difficulty containing her excitement too and the delicate task of marking her face had to be halted while the women scolded her.

Sally, Peter, and Mele followed the crowd to the edge of the encampment, where the camels were tethered and two young Rendille warriors stood, dusty and grinning.

"The one with his hair dressed is the groom," Sally said, pointing out the young man whose black hair had been braided into many small pigtails and dusted with red powder. "The other is his best friend."

"What makes his hair red?" Mele asked.

"Red ochre. It's what makes the soil red. You know, iron in the soil."

As they watched, a bowl of camel's milk was brought out and offered to the returned warriors. Meanwhile the children began to leap about in a spontaneous dance.

"Now the party starts," Sally said with a grin.

The atmosphere was infectious. Everyone was laughing, smiling, talking, and dancing to the beat of half a dozen different drums that had suddenly appeared. A bowl of murky liquid was passed around which Sally warned them not to drink.

"*Banjo*," she said and grimaced. "Camel's blood mixed with camel's milk. I don't recommend it. We'll say you aren't thirsty, you will drink later."

After the sun went down, a fire was lit but people gradually drifted away. Mele's little companion had long since left her to join the other children and was nowhere to be seen.

"Tonight the young warriors will be invited to join the elders around the sacred fire," Sally said. "It's a great honor and a sign that they are becoming men and will soon take up new responsibilities."

"Can we watch?" Peter asked.

"No, I'm sorry. It's not permitted."

"So what do we do?"

"They have given us a hut to sleep in. The family who lives there will sleep with others for these two nights. If you are ready, we can go there now."

"It looks like the party is over."

"Don't worry. It all starts again in the morning."

The hut in which they were to sleep was much like the other huts they had visited. There were animal skins to sit and lie on, but not much else. Sally pulled a thermos of water out of her backpack and passed it around. It wasn't cold, but Mele didn't mind. She hadn't realized how thirsty she was. Next Sally shared flatbread and bananas she had brought with her. Mele thought food had never tasted so good.

While they were eating, a tall thin man with missing teeth came to their doorway and spoke in Rendille, bobbing his head as he talked and smiling at them.

"He says you are invited to join the elders around the sacred fire," Sally told Peter.

"Really? That's great!"

"Can I go too?" Mele asked.

Sally shook her head. "No, only men can sit in the sacred circle. You and I must stay here."

Peter glanced at Mele uncertainly.

Of course she was disappointed, but she was not going to make a fuss. "Go on," she told Peter. "That's what you're here for."

"Thanks." He gave her a kiss on the cheek.

"He's really really lucky," Sally said after Peter was gone. "They don't usually let outsiders observe."

"But without you there to translate, he won't be able to understand anything they say."

"No, but he can *watch*." Sally made it sound like that was something fantastic. Maybe it was, but Mele felt her stubborn streak rising. That was what her father called it—a stubborn streak that he said she got from his side of the family.

"Watching only goes so far. I'm sure he would like to know what is said."

"Well, he must get by without me," Sally said, throwing up her hands. "They won't allow a woman to sit in their circle."

"Don't the women ever try to sneak up and hear what they're saying?"

"I have no idea. And if you're suggesting we should sneak up on the elders, forget it. I don't want to lose my job."

"What do you think they talk about?"

Sally took a swig of water from her thermos. "Tonight they will praise the bridegroom and they will talk about the importance of their ancestors and they'll tell stories like how their ancestors came to this land. There are so many stories. Every tribe has its stories and tells them over and over to pass them on to the next generation."

"My people have stories too. Our ancestors believed in many gods and we have lots of stories about them."

"Who are your people?"

"Hawaiians."

"And do they still believe in many gods?"

Mele pondered this. "Do you mean, are we Christians? Yes, we are Christians and believe in God, but we also honor the old gods and tell their stories. We don't think it has to be one or the other."

"Then you are just as superstitious as the Rendille," Sally declared, putting her thermos away.

"Your people don't tell old stories you believe in?"

"They tell stories, but I don't believe in them. I've been to Princeton, and I know better."

Mele had not been to Princeton or any other college for that matter, although going to college was precisely what she hoped to do when they got to Boston. She thought perhaps she should not say anything more on the subject. She didn't want Sally to think she was ignorant and backward. When she had attended high school on Kaua'i, she had learned to keep her beliefs to herself. Other students could be very cruel about differences of belief, and her teachers only had to look appalled the first few times she let slip some local bit of lore or custom before she learned to keep quiet about what she had been taught. She wondered if marrying Peter meant she would have to give up her old beliefs. She hadn't really thought about that before. The idea of not believing in Kane and Lono and Pele bothered her, but they also seemed far away. The old gods of her people were not here in this place. Other strange gods that she had no knowledge of lived here. Hers were a part of the land, the rocks, the sea, and the sky of her islands. Thinking about them made her feel homesick.

"Look, it's okay if you believe in old stories," Sally said, touching her arm. "I shouldn't have said anything. I keep thinking about Natunya and it's making me a little crazy. Listen, would you mind if I left you alone—just for a little while? I want to go see her. She may not be here the next time I come."

Mele knew by the tears that had just sprung to her eyes that she was worried her friend might die.

"Of course, go to her. You don't need to stay with me."

"I won't be gone long. Are you sure you don't mind?"

"I'll be fine," Mele assured her. "Don't worry about me."

After Sally was gone, she lay down on her bed of animal skins and stared at the ceiling of the hut. She was tired but wanted to stay awake until Peter came back, although she had no idea when that would be. Maybe he would come back while Sally was still out and they could make love. It seemed as if they were destined never to be alone together. She wondered about the people who lived in this hut. What would it be like to be a Rendille woman and make love with your husband in a hut like this? Were the Rendille happy? Was it so terrible to be cut off from the world beyond their desert? Did they need to know about life in other places? Or was this enough, raising their children in an arid land, tending their camels and goats, preserving the old ways and the old beliefs? Peter had said that without the Alliance their way of life would be lost. That struck her as sad, but wasn't it also sad if Sally's friend died because they had no access to doctors or antibiotics? Niʻihau was a Forbidden Place too, but there a sick woman would not have been left to die. A helicopter would have been called in to transport her to a hospital on another island. On Niʻihau no one had to die to preserve the old ways. Surely that was better.

When they emerged from their hut the next morning, they saw children running. Within minutes the whole village seemed to be in motion, all heading in the same direction.

"What now?" Peter asked.

Sally called out to a woman running by and asked her. "She says they are going to watch the sacrifice of a camel."

"Why are they sacrificing a camel?" Mele asked.

"For the wedding feast. It will provide the meat."

Mele stared at her, shocked. "You mean they're going to eat it?"

"Of course. But first they will ask its forgiveness. Camels are very important to them, as I told you before. Without their camels, they could not survive."

"I don't think I want to see a camel sacrificed," Mele told Peter. "You go and watch if you want. I'll just hang around here."

"Are you sure?"

"I'm sure." She wondered what else there would be at the feast because she did not want to eat camel meat. She watched as Sally and Peter headed toward the camel pen on the other side of the village. Then she wandered about among the huts until she came to a group of women preparing balls of dough.

When she gestured that she would like to help, they smiled, nodded, and showed her how to roll the dough into balls. As they worked, she talked to the women, who responded in their own language, a friendly back-and-forth even if they could not understand each other. That was how Peter and Sally found her when they returned half an hour later.

"You can be glad you didn't go see the business with the camel," Peter said. "The ceremony beforehand was interesting, but the actual killing was pretty bloody, although they know how to do it fast without making the camel suffer much. They cut its neck—"

"I don't want to know," Mele said, stopping him.

"The first time I saw it, I thought I would throw up," Sally said, "but now I have seen three camels killed and it seems to me not so different from killing a chicken or a goat. It's just bigger."

Mele remembered the camels as she had seen them the day before as they approached the village. They were such strange and ungainly animals, with their odd hump and long necks and heavy-lidded eyes which looked back at you with timeless indifference. It seemed a shame to kill such harmless creatures. No, she was not going to eat any camel meat.

Sally spoke to the women in Rendille, and they smiled and bobbed their heads. "I asked them if we could borrow you."

Mele looked around for something to wipe her hands on.

"Do like this." Sally squatted, took some sand in her hands,. and rubbed them together. "They don't have soap and they must save their water for drinking."

"I'm looking forward to a good long soak in a hot tub when we get back," Mele said as she rubbed sand between her hands.

Sally grinned. "Me too. Now let's go see the bride."

They found the bride in front of her family's hut, surrounded by women adorning her in beads. Her hair had been intricately braided and many strands of white beads hung around her dark neck and fell over her breasts. Massive hoop earrings dangled from her ears and brass armbands encircled her arms. She gazed straight ahead like a goddess to whom they were paying homage. The markings from yesterday were pinpoints of white running in a graceful curve down both sides of her face.

After speaking with the bride's mother for a few minutes, Sally turned to Peter and Mele. "She says this is her first daughter to marry. She's very happy today."

"Tell her we are grateful to the village for allowing us to be here," Peter said.

A minute or two later after more conversation with the bride's mother, Sally turned to them again. "She asked if you are married. I told her yes, and she asked how long."

Peter glanced at Mele. "Nine days."

Sally again translated. "She says she wishes you many children."

"Tell her we wish her daughter many children too," Mele said.

Just then an old woman hobbled up carrying something small wrapped in a cloth. The other women took a step or two back.

"Now we must leave," Sally said. "We may not watch the next part of the ceremony. Only the closest female relatives of the bride may be present."

"What happens?" Peter asked.

"They will cut her," Sally said as she moved away. "They will make her a woman."

"You mean, circumcise her?" He glanced back over his shoulder.

"Yes, it's the most important part of the ceremony."

"What are they going to do to her?" Mele asked uneasily.

"Never mind," Sally said. "I will explain it later."

Mele noticed that others were walking away from the hut too. Women were shooing children away. She paused to look back. Nothing had changed. The girl still sat there. Her mother was there and the old woman and two other women.

"Why will they cut her?" she asked, catching up with Sally and Peter.

"To make her a woman," Sally said again.

"I don't understand."

Sally rolled her eyes and sighed. "It's a very ancient tradition which used to be practiced all over Africa. They say it goes back to the Pharaohs of Egypt. In some places they do it when the girls are very young, but the Rendille do it at marriage."

"What did you mean, they circumcise her?" Mele asked Peter. "I've heard of baby boys being circumcised, but how can a girl be circumcised?"

"I told you," Sally said, impatient now. "They cut her. It's a very small cut really, just a little flesh cut away, but they believe it's necessary in order to become a woman. The blood she sheds joins her to her ancestors. It connects the present and the past."

"Does it hurt much?" Mele asked doubtfully.

"It hurts like hell, but she will try not to cry out to show that she can endure the pain life will bring."

At that moment there was a scream from the direction of the bride's hut. Sally walked faster. Peter took Mele's hand. Behind them they heard a protracted wail. So much for enduring pain, Mele thought.

"Why do they do it?" she asked as they caught up to Sally. "Why do they hurt her?"

"I told you. It's a custom. A very old custom."

"But what about her wedding night? How can she—?"

Sally whirled on her. "Do you mean, how can she have sex? Simple. She doesn't. In fact, she will not for a long time because she needs time to heal. Three months maybe. That is, if she doesn't get an infection. Sometimes the cut gets infected. Sometimes she dies. It can't be helped. They don't have antibiotics."

"It sounds horrible."

"Horrible to you, but not to them. To them it's a rite of passage. Today she leaves behind childhood and becomes a woman. It's a cause for celebration. Look around you."

Mele saw it was true. All around them people were beginning to dance and sing. They laughed and called out to each other. She spotted the groom with his funny little red ochre braids dancing with the others. It seemed unfair to her that he should get to celebrate while his bride had to endure a painful cutting ritual.

"Don't think about it," Peter said.

But how could she not think about it? Her eyes kept wandering back to the hut where the young woman was undergoing her ordeal. How could they have a wedding without a bride? Her little friend from the previous day ran up and took her hand again. Looking down at her, she could not help but think how the little girl would grow up and experience the same cruel ritual as the bride had today. Was Sally right—that she should respect the custom because it had been handed down through many generations? Did the fact that it was a custom make it right?

"Look," Peter said. "Over there." He was trying to distract her by pointing out a group of children who were shaking themselves and waving their arms, imitating the dancing of their parents and older brothers and sisters.

But what about that poor girl in her hut, she wanted to say. However, there seemed no point in saying it. She felt he didn't understand. How could he just ignore what they had done to the bride? How could he pretend everything was okay? She watched the villagers dancing, but she could not stop thinking about the girl who had been cut. Not just a cut that would heal, but flesh had been cut away, Sally said. It made her feel sick to think about it. Nothing Peter could say could lighten her mood. No food they offered could tempt her to eat. She was just waiting for it all to end.

Toward evening the villagers lined up in two rows and held up long sticks to make an arch.

"Now the bride will come out," Sally said.

All eyes were on the doorway of the bride's hut. The people cheered when she emerged, smiling bravely, her mother on one side and another woman on the other. She walked stiffly and haltingly, her face a mask of pain. Then the groom stepped forward, the women fell away, and the couple passed side by side under the arch of long sticks. When it was over, the bride retreated again to her hut and the festivities continued without her.

Peter and Mele sat together on the ground as it turned dark and watched the fire and the dancing Rendille and listened to the hypnotic beat of their drums.

"I wonder where Sally is," Peter said, looking around once the moon had risen and the stars were out. "She seems to have disappeared."

"I think she's gone to see her friend," Mele said.

"The woman with the baby? The one who may have some deadly disease?"

"Yes."

"You'd think she'd have the sense to stay away from the woman when she doesn't know what's wrong with her. She could end up catching something fatal herself."

"I think she knows that."

"Yeah, I suppose she does." He looked at her. "This hasn't been much fun for you, has it?"

"It'll be over soon."

"Yes, I guess so." He glanced away and looked pensive. "Do you think you'll like Boston?"

She thought about that. How could she possibly know when she'd never been there? She hoped she would like it. And if she didn't . . . ?

Peter glanced at her, waiting for her answer.

"They don't kill camels there or cut women, do they?"

"No, they don't. Although we do have muggers and our fair share of criminals and the occasional serial killer."

"I know it's going to be different."

"That it is. I just hope you'll give it a chance."

She smiled at him and squeezed his hand. "I will."


That night, lying on her bed of animal skins beside Peter, she dreamed her grandmother was calling to her. She woke up sobbing and he tried to comfort her.

"I have to go home. Something's wrong."

"It was just a bad dream."

"No." She shook her head. "My grandmother is calling to me. I have to go home."

"Is everything all right?" Sally asked sleepily from several feet away in the dark hut.

"Mele had a bad dream. She's all right now. Go back to sleep."

"I could hear her so clearly," Mele said. "She was calling my name. I have to go back. Something's wrong."

"Nothing's wrong,. You're just feeling homesick."

"I shouldn't have left. I don't know why I thought I had to leave."

He kissed her forehead. "Look, try to get some more sleep. You'll feel better in the morning."

She stared at the dark ceiling of the hut above her and felt a great emptiness inside her. He didn't understand. He thought dreams were just dreams, but for her people they were messages, warnings, signs. Her grandmother had called out to her and she had not been able to answer. She should not have left her alone. Her grandmother was old and blind. I would have stayed if she had asked me, Mele told herself. Why was I so eager to leave? What am I doing so far from home among people whose customs I don't understand?

She lay in Peter's arms, and gradually the fear and panic ebbed and she fell asleep again. In the morning, as he had predicted, she felt better. They shared the last of Sally's flatbread and drank water from her thermos. When Peter asked her about her grandmother, she merely shook her head and refused to talk about it.

Then it was time to say good-bye to the Rendille. The little girl who had followed Mele about held her hand until they reached the edge of the village. They shook hands with their hosts and she kissed the child on the top of her head before taking a last look at the camels, standing so patiently in their pen, ignoring the commotion around them. Then they started their trek back into the desert.

"They are good people," Sally said as the village receded behind them. "Very backward, but good."

"There's a primitive beauty about living like they do,"

Peter said. "Everyone knows what is expected of them. No one is really alone. Everyone is surrounded by people who care. In a way I envy them."

Mele glanced back at the cluster of cone-shaped huts surrounded by barren desert. She wondered if the Rendille would survive even with the Alliance trying to protect them from the outside world. They might have survived for many generations, but they were small in numbers and their life was hard. A single deadly disease sweeping through their village could wipe them out.

"Are you all right?" Peter asked, touching her arm.

She nodded. How could she explain to him how she felt? Her feelings were so confused. She didn't understand them herself. Her heart went out to these people, living in such a lonely and inhospitable place, where the sun beat mercilessly down on them and there was never enough food or water. She wished there were something she could do for them.

"I know you were upset about the circumcision ritual," he said, "but it's just an initiation ceremony. The boys go through one too."

She stared at him, shocked that he had no idea what was going through her mind, shocked that he understood so little about what young Rendille women suffered in the name of tradition. Then she looked at Sally, who was squinting up at the sky, watching for the plane. "It's not the same, is it?"

Sally ignored her.

"Of course it's not the *same*," Peter said. "I wasn't suggesting it's the same."

They started walking again.

"I just doubt it's as bad as all that. Primitive initiation rituals can seem violent and senseless to outsiders, but they are a part of indigenous people's traditions and cultures."

"It should be stopped," she said. "Someone should stop it."

"Well, they have stopped it, of course, in other places," Peter said. "There are laws against it now."

"You don't understand," Sally said, turning on Mele. "You come here from your own safe world and you judge these people. What right do you have to judge them? Who are you? What makes you any better than us?"

"You think it's all right for them to cut their daughters? You don't think that's cruel?"

"Cruel? What is cruel? Do you mean it hurts? Yes, it hurts. Do you mean it's dangerous? Yes, it's dangerous. Sometimes they bleed to death or their wound becomes infected and they die. But does that mean you have a right to come here and tell them they can't do it?"

"Surely you see that it's wrong," Mele said. "You studied at Princeton. You're educated. You're not a Rendille."

"I was cut too, as was my mother before me and her mother before her. This tradition has been ours in Africa as long as anyone can remember. It's the way of our ancestors."

For a moment no one said anything. Peter looked intently at a point on the horizon.

"You were cut like that?" Mele said. "But you're not married, are you?"

"I was ten years old when I was cut."

Mele struggled to understand. Ten! How could anyone do that to a ten-year-old?

"Some are cut even younger."

She felt sick. How many were cut like that? How widespread was this dreadful practice? Why did no one stop it?

"Don't feel sorry for me," Sally said. "I know what people from your world think about it. You think it's barbaric. You think it's disgusting. But I'm not ashamed. I'm glad I was cut. I'm proud of it." Her eyes shone with tears. "What would you know about it? What would either of you know? These are not your people. Do you think you know about them from reading books? Do you think you know from watching a wedding ceremony? From drinking the milk of their camels? From sleeping two nights in one of their huts? You don't know anything."

"We're sorry," Peter said. "We didn't mean to offend you."

Sally shielded her eyes with her hand and scanned the sky. "I'm sorry too. I didn't mean to lose my temper. I'm upset about my friend back there. I have been here six times, and I've gotten to know her. She's like a sister, but now she's dying and there's nothing I can do." She wiped tears from the corners of her eyes. "It doesn't seem fair, you know? She's only sixteen years old."

# 10

# Boston

Of course Peter should have told his family about Mele before he got back to Boston. And he should have told Rosemary. Especially Rosemary. There was really no good excuse for not having told her. He could have called during their layover in London. He could have called even when they were 30,000 feet over the Atlantic. But instead he kept telling himself it would be easier to explain in person. In fact, he owed it to Rosemary to explain in person, didn't he? As for his family, well, he was twenty-seven years old and he had a right to marry when he chose and whomever he chose. If they didn't like it, that was just too bad. And he knew his mother wouldn't like it. It had taken her more than a year to resign herself to Rosemary, but now that she had, she wasn't about to change her mind overnight. It wouldn't matter that Mele was beautiful and spoke flawless English; she would be as foreign in his mother's eyes as a Rendille girl from the remote deserts of Kenya. But then when did his mother approve of anything he did? The problem was that he was still living at home and, aside from his fellowship, had no income. If she refused to let Mele stay at her house, where would they go? He told himself he would cross that bridge when he came to it. Surely it couldn't be that hard to find a small apartment somewhere, something cheap enough to afford on his fellowship until he had time to finish his dissertation and land a job.

Mele had asked him at least half a dozen times on the flight home if his family would like her. Each time he assured her they would. How could anyone not like her? She was sweet, good-hearted, intelligent, beautiful, and sexy. She had eyes that could melt your heart. They just had to get to know her. He did not tell her about his mother. He thought there would be time later for that, like right before they arrived at the house. He didn't think his mother would be rude to her face. That was not his mother's style. No, she would be polite and gracious. Maybe Mele wouldn't even notice the disapproval. It would be subtle, held in check at least until his mother could get him alone.

He had told his family not to bother picking him up at the airport, he would get a taxi, so he was surprised to see Susan when they exited through the sliding glass doors at Logan. She was standing there at the curb in jeans and a pale yellow T-shirt, her blonde hair pulled back in a ponytail.

"What are you doing here?" he demanded.

"Welcoming you back," Susan said, flinging an arm around his neck so she could pull him down and give him a quick kiss on his cheek. "And besides, I just couldn't resist being the first to congratulate you." She turned to Mele and held out her hand. "I'm Susan. You must be Peter's wife."

Mele took her hand and they smiled at each other.

"I thought you'd be younger," Mele said.

Susan rolled her eyes. "Peter thinks I still play with Barbie dolls."

"How did you find out?" he asked as they stood there bonding. "And does anybody else know?" He meant Rosemary, of course. Why hadn't he called her before they left Honolulu? What had he been thinking? Wasn't it a hundred times worse if she had to hear that he was married from someone else?

"Oh, *everybody* knows," Susan said cheerfully.

His heart sank. "How?"

"Well, Rosemary told Mother."

So much for breaking the news diplomatically. "And how did Rosemary find out?"

"Your Professor Rinehart told her, I believe."

And how had that happened when they barely knew each other? They had only met once, at a department reception for graduate students. He had introduced them over wine and crackers. They had hardly exchanged a dozen words. How on earth had she heard about his marriage from Rinehart? Well, however it had happened, there was nothing he could do about it now. And maybe it was for the best. Now she knew. She would have some time to get used to the idea before he saw her again. Hopefully it would make things less awkward.

They climbed aboard a crowded shuttle bound for the parking lot.

"How's Mother taking it?" he asked after they had found poles to hold on to and the shuttle had taken off with a lurch.

"Oh, you know Mother."

Yes, he knew Mother.

"Was she surprised when she heard we're married?" Mele asked cautiously.

"Oh, she was surprised all right. We *all* were."

While no one, including Peter himself, had expected him to get married when he took off on his trip, was it really so inconceivable that he should decide to get married? He had been under the impression that getting married was precisely what everyone wanted him to do.

"I'm looking forward to meeting her," Mele said.

Peter knew he should warn her about his mother right then, but he couldn't do it. What was he going to say—that she might not be welcome at his home? He couldn't, not after they had flown so far and she had sacrificed so much. Better to leave her clueless a little longer.

"Well, was the trip a success?" Susan asked. "I mean, aside from the fact that you fell in love and got married?"

"Yes, of course." He wondered how long he would be able to hide the fact that falling in love had not preceded getting married. How could he ever explain to Susan that it hadn't happened like that? He hadn't been in love with Mele when he married her. At least he didn't think he had been. Nor had she been in love with him. He had been a means for her to leave her island. And she had been—what had she been for him? A chance to throw caution to the winds and do something he would never have done in Boston? A chance to experience at first hand a people he had only read about in books? No, he could never explain it. It would sound all wrong. And anyway he was in love with her now, wasn't he?

"I'm dying to hear all about it," Susan said. "What you saw, what you did."

"We can tell you all about it later," he said quickly before Mele could open her mouth. He was hoping they could wait until they were home or at least in the privacy of Susan's Camaro before they started revealing some of the more unsavory parts of their visits.

But it came out in bits and pieces as they rode the shuttle, then walked the rest of the way to Susan's car, first Mele talking, then Peter. He tried to explain that these were of course cultural customs and so it was important to keep an open mind, but when Susan seemed just as outraged as Mele, he gave up. He was outnumbered. Once they were in Susan's Camaro, he just sat back and let them talk, interrupting from time to time to point out landmarks they passed, which Mele barely glanced at before continuing her account of what they had seen. He had thought she would be impressed by Boston, but instead she seemed indifferent. The buildings were very tall, she agreed, and there were a lot of cars, but then there had been tall buildings and many cars in Honolulu, Kunming, Bangalore, Kabul, and Nairobi. She was no longer as easily impressed as when she first left her island.

Meanwhile, the closer they got to home, the more nervous Peter became. He hoped his mother would be out, that they could just slip into the house unnoticed and nap until dinner. But of course that was not to be. They were scarcely in the door when she came gliding down the stairs like royalty to greet them. She had probably been lying in wait, watching for them from an upstairs window.

"You must be Mele." She proffered a hand in her best hostess manner, a smile plastered on her face. She was wearing a beige suit, matching heels, and a string of pearls at her throat. Her hair looked as if she had just been to the hairdresser's and her face looked recently botoxed.

Peter was tempted to step between them, an impulse to protect Mele, but refrained. Sooner or later they had to meet. They might as well get it over and done with.

"I hope you had a smooth flight," his mother said, expressing just the right degree of polite concern.

"Smooth enough, but long," he said. "We're both exhausted." It was meant to be a hint. He was still hoping they could escape upstairs and rest before being grilled. But of course his mother was not going to let him off that easily.

"I hear you've got some news," she said, looking expectantly from him to Mele.

Okay, he thought, let's get this over. "We're married, but then you already knew that."

"I heard you had married, but I wasn't sure it was true since I didn't hear it from *you*. Usually a mother isn't informed via the grapevine that her only son has gotten married."

As usual, he had fallen short in his filial duties, and as usual she was the patiently suffering martyr in this little drama—the neglected mother.

"It happened very fast," he conceded. "And then I was busy."

"Obviously." She turned to Mele and gave her that benign hostess smile. "You must be tired, my dear. You'd probably like to freshen up."

"Yes, I would."

"Susan can show you up. Peter, I'd like a word with you."

There didn't seem to be much point in delaying the inevitable, so with a sigh he followed her into the dining room, where a bowl of pink roses sat on the polished mahogany table. She closed the door behind them as carefully as if they were about to discuss matters related to national security.

"Honestly, Peter," she said, dropping the polite hostess act. "Have you lost your senses?"

"I don't expect you to understand," he said, slumping on to the nearest Queen Anne chair.

She remained standing, her back stiff, a general facing his mutinous troops. "What about Rosemary? Did you think about her? You've broken that poor girl's heart. You ought to be ashamed."

He already felt guilty enough about Rosemary. He didn't need her rubbing it in. "I'll explain it to her," he said wearily. First thing tomorrow, he promised himself, after a hot shower and a good night's sleep.

"Oh, you will? And how will you do that?"

"I'll tell her I changed my mind. It was a mistake for us to get engaged."

"It was a mistake, was it? I'll tell you what was a mistake. Marrying that girl upstairs was a mistake. How long did you know her before you married her? One day? Two days? Did it occur to you that you knew nothing about her? That you came from two totally different worlds? Whatever possessed you? This isn't like you, Peter. To jump into a marriage with a complete stranger, someone with whom you have nothing in common. I just don't understand it. And I have a strong suspicion that young woman upstairs is the one to blame. On your own, I really don't think you would have done this."

"I don't expect you to understand, but Mele and I love each other." He was proud of himself. He was taking a stand against his mother. It was something he should have done a long time ago.

She held up her hand. "There's no point in discussing this. It's clear what has to be done. You'll just have to get an annulment."

"What? I'm not getting an annulment."

"It's only been—let's see—two weeks? You can say it was a mistake. There should be no problem getting it annulled. It would be best for both of you. She can go back where she came from and you can marry Rosemary, just as you planned. I'm sure Rosemary will eventually forgive you, although I wouldn't blame her if she never spoke to you again. Oh, Peter, surely you can see it wouldn't work out. You're too different.

She doesn't belong here. You would just be making both of your lives miserable. And if you can't get it annulled, you can get a divorce. Lots of people get divorced nowadays. The main thing is to admit it was a mistake and try to fix it before you ruin both your lives."

"I'm not going to get it annulled. I love Mele, and she loves me." He crossed his arms and scowled at the bowl of pink roses. He was determined not to let his mother intimidate him.

"Two weeks ago you thought you loved Rosemary."

That barb hit its mark. It was true he had told Rosemary he loved her before he left on his trip two weeks ago. He had to tell her he loved her—they were engaged—but he hadn't been sure he really did love her, and now he knew he didn't, but how could he explain that without sounding like an idiot?

"I changed my mind."

"Well, change it back again."

They glared at each other. Did she really expect him to give in? Did she think she could tell him how to live his life?

"I'm not going to. Mele is my wife whether you like it or not."

"You can't seriously want to be married to a girl who's probably semi-literate, not to mention totally lacking in social skills."

"For your information, Mele *is* literate. In fact, she's quite bright and wants to go to college."

"Oh, she does? And did it occur to you that maybe she married you to get that?"

He wanted to shout at her that Mele married him because she loved him, but he couldn't. She would have known right away that he was lying. She had a sort of radar for detecting when he was not being completely truthful.

"I don't care what you think. Mele is my wife, and that's that." He was gaining confidence now. For once his mother was not going to have her way. He had managed to do something totally beyond her control and she would just have to accept it.

Her eyes narrowed as if she were reading his thoughts. He stared back, determined to hold his own.

"I will not have that young woman under my roof."

"Fine. I'll look for an apartment tomorrow."

"I will not have her under my roof *tonight*." Her voice was cold as steel.

His spirits sank at the idea of leaving the house when they had just got back home from such a long flight and were so tired. Where would they go? How would he explain to Mele? He could see that small smile of triumph curl the corner of his mother's lips. He knew she wouldn't back down. She thought she had found a way to thwart him.

He stomped upstairs to his bedroom, where Susan was sitting on the bed and Mele was unpacking her bag.

"Don't bother to unpack. We're leaving."

"Are you kidding? Mother's kicking you out?" Susan looked at him with wide eyes.

"Looks that way." He glanced around the room and wondered what he should take. The pile of books on the floor beside his bed? His old laptop? Clothes? He hauled a suitcase from his closet and dumped the entire contents of his underwear drawer into it. Then he started pulling shirts from hangers and tossing them in. He didn't give a damn if they got wrinkled or not. He couldn't have cared less what they looked like.

"What happened?" Mele asked.

"Nothing." He unplugged his clock radio and dropped that in too.

"Where will you go?" Susan asked.

"I have no idea. To a motel I guess."

"It's because of me, isn't it?" Mele said.

She looked so stricken that he stopped and put his arms around her and kissed her, ignoring Susan.

"Look, none of this is your fault. I should have told you about my mother. I should have warned you."

"I'll go down and talk to her," Mele said.

"No. It won't do any good. Her mind's made up."

He felt terrible taking Mele to a motel on her first night in Boston. They stopped on the way and had dinner at a Denny's. When they got to their motel room, they showered and fell into bed almost at once.

"I didn't mean to cause trouble for you," Mele said for about the hundredth time that evening, snuggling up against him.

"Don't worry. Eventually she'll come around."

"What if she won't?"

"It's not going to stop me." He kissed her forehead. "You're my wife. I love you. She can't do anything to change that."

Mele sighed. "I didn't know it would be so complicated."

"Are you sorry you married me?"

"No," she said, but there was a slight hesitation in her voice.

She was right, of course. Their marriage had turned out a lot more complicated than either of them had foreseen. It was not going to be easy to make this work.

\* \* \*

The next day he looked for an apartment, a task that turned out to be very discouraging. He couldn't believe how expensive apartments were. And then when he called, either they were already taken or they had something major wrong with them— heaters that didn't heat, faulty plumbing, stoves in need of replacement, year-long leases, ridiculously large deposits. He looked at two apartments, neither of which he could imagine taking Mele to. One smelled suspiciously of backed-up sewer odor and the other was in a bad neighborhood. He kept seeing in his mind his mother's smug smile of satisfaction, as if she were looking over his shoulder.

In the middle of the afternoon he gave up and went to Professor Rinehart's office. The professor was reading a book when he arrived but immediately laid it aside and invited him in. Peter sat down on the chair facing his desk, as he had so many times before.

"I must say you surprised me," Professor Rinehart said, looking at him over the rims of his glasses. "I hardly expected you to come back married."

"Neither did I," Peter admitted, shaking the hand held out to him.

"It took a bit of negotiating, I can tell you, to persuade the Alliance to let you take the young lady along with you, but when I pointed out that what was done was done, no use crying over spilled milk, they agreed and were good sports about it."

"Thank you for all your help," Peter said. "It was very kind of you to intercede for us."

"And where is the young lady now?" Professor Rinehart glanced at the doorway as if expecting her to be standing there.

"She's—" He was about to say at our motel room, waiting to hear if he had found an apartment, but he felt reluctant to explain to Professor Rinehart how they found themselves in this predicament. It would mean telling him about his mother, and at the moment he didn't trust himself to speak on that subject, so he just said, "She's not here. I mean, she's not on campus, but she is here, in Boston, that is." He could not have tripped over his words more if he had tried.

Fortunately Professor Rinehart didn't ask any more questions. "Well, bring her by. I'd like to meet her. I'd like to see this young woman who could persuade you to drop everything and marry her on the spot. She must be quite something."

Peter wondered if he was being ironic, but those intelligent little eyes, as usual, looked benign and inscrutable. He thought maybe he should apologize for the trouble he had caused. "I'm sorry if I—"

Professor Rinehart held up a hand to stop him. "No need to apologize. You got carried away. Sometimes it happens to the best of us."

The way he said it made Peter snap to attention. The best of us? Had *he* ever gotten carried away? Peter had always wondered if something had happened to Professor Rinehart among the Yanomami. More than once a chance remark of his had made that question flash through his mind. "Did you ever—?" He stopped himself. What was he going to ask the professor? If he had ever crossed the line between observation and involvement? Had there been a woman—? No, he couldn't ask the professor that. It was too personal. It was none of his business.

"Ever what?" Professor Rinehart watched him closely. He looked amused.

"Never mind."

"Of course I hope this isn't going to throw you off track. You're still going to finish your dissertation, aren't you?"

"Yes, of course."

"And the young lady? What's she going to do, if I may ask?"

"She's going to enroll in classes next term if the college will accept her."

"Excellent. Let me know her name and I'll put in a good word for her."

Peter thanked him. "There's one other thing. I heard Rosemary. . . ."

"What about Rosemary?"

Suddenly he felt awkward. "I heard that you told her about—"

Professor Rinehart raised both hands in surrender. "You didn't tell me not to. She came by my office quite concerned about you. You weren't returning her calls. Naturally she was worried something had happened to you."

"I should have told her," Peter admitted. "I kept meaning to call, but I wasn't exactly sure how to explain."

"I understand," Professor Rinehart said, all empathy. "And to tell the truth, I never thought Rosemary was right for you."

"You didn't?" This surprised him. Why had the professor thought Rosemary wasn't right for him? He was hoping his mentor would explain, but he didn't.

"Anyway, bring the young lady by. I'd like to meet her."

When Peter went back to the motel, he was surprised to see Rosemary's black Lexus parked directly outside the door to their room. He could not imagine how she had found them or why she would be there. His next thought was that she might take out her anger on Mele. Just how angry was she and what was she capable of? He leaped out of his car and charged into their room, half expecting to see Rosemary pointing a gun at Mele. Instead Mele was perched casually on the bed and Rosemary was seated in the one armchair the motel provided. There was no sign of a gun. In fact, they seemed to be getting along very well when he burst in.

"Rosemary," he said.

"Peter," she responded.

"I see you've met Mele."

"I have indeed. You shouldn't have hidden her away here. At the very least you could have taken her over to the campus."

"How did you find us?"

She smiled sweetly. "I have my ways."

"Nobody knew we were here."

She sighed. "I called your house and Susan told me your mother kicked you out. She said you would probably be in a motel not far from campus. I called around. It wasn't hard to find you."

"It's only temporary. Until we can find an apartment."

"Of course."

He looked at Mele, but there was no sign that Rosemary had upset her. She smiled back at him and patted the space beside her on the bed, inviting him to sit.

"You should have told me," Rosemary said. "I would have understood, you know. How could you not fall in love with her? She's adorable."

Adorable? It was not the word he would have used to describe Mele. Beautiful, rather naïve—which was to be expected, considering her background—generous, strong-willed, curious, unpredictable, maddening at times, but adorable? No. He sat down beside Mele and held her hand, wondering how they could get rid of Rosemary without appearing to be rude.

"You're not upset?" he asked as she sat there beaming at them like a fairy godmother.

"Of course right in the beginning, yes, I must admit, I was a little upset," she conceded. "After all, we were engaged."

He didn't look at Mele, just held firmly to her hand. He still wasn't so sure Rosemary might not have a concealed weapon. If she pulled out a gun, he would have to throw himself in front of Mele. As her husband, it was his duty to protect her from crazed ex-girlfriends.

"I mean, imagine how it felt to be told by your adviser that you had married," Rosemary continued, still smiling.

"I'm sorry. I should have called."

"Well, what's done is done," she said, echoing Professor Rinehart's words. Is that what he had said to her? "No use crying over spilt milk. Right?"

Peter could not believe she was taking it so well, but then ranting and raving would have been so unlike her. She was being sensible about it, just as she was sensible about everything. He had worried unnecessarily about how she would take it. Of course she would take it in stride. Rosemary was not the sort to pine away in her room over any man, including him.

"Anyway, I'm glad I came. I wanted to meet your . . . new wife." She hesitated only a fraction of a second over the words 'new wife.' In fact, maybe he only imagined she hesitated. "And now that I've seen her, I *understand*."

He wondered what that was supposed to mean. What did she understand? Was she inferring he had been blinded by Mele's beauty? Was she suggesting he had been taken in by her exoticism? Whatever it was, he had the feeling it wasn't good.

"I just wanted you to know there are no hard feelings. I see no reason why we can't all be friends."

"Yes, you're right," Mele agreed eagerly.

Peter was a great deal less sure about this than Mele. It seemed to him that being friends with Rosemary might not be such a good idea now that he was married to someone else.

"I can hardly wait to show you around Boston," Rosemary gushed. "And I want you to have my phone number." She pulled a business card from her pocketbook and held it out to Mele. "If you need anything, call me. I know you'll need a friend and I hope I can be that friend to you. It must be awful not knowing anyone here, except for Peter of course." She flashed him an overly bright smile.

Mele took the card. "It's very kind of you."

"I know we're going to be great friends," Rosemary said.

Not if he could help it, he thought grimly just as the motel phone rang. It was Susan, who had also tracked him down. She wanted to let him know that a letter had come for Mele. As soon as he was off the phone, he told Mele. He thought she would be pleased, but instead she looked anxious.

"I hope nothing's wrong," she said.

"Why should something be wrong?"

"I just have a bad feeling. And that dream. . . ."

"What dream?" Rosemary asked, leaning forward.

"We'll go over right away and get the letter," he said quickly before Mele could start telling Rosemary about her dream, which was none of Rosemary's business. This would also give them the chance to get rid of her.

Rosemary took the hint and stood up. "Call me," she urged Mele. "We'll have lunch together. I'll show you around."

"I'd like that," Mele said.

He could tell by the small furrow on her brow that her mind was not on some future lunch with Rosemary but on the phone call, and she would not relax until she knew nothing was wrong at home.

They all left the motel room together. Peter opened his car door for Mele and then walked over to Rosemary's Lexus. She lowered her window as he approached. He knew he owed her an apology.

"I'm sorry," he said.

She smiled at him brightly. "You already said that. It's okay. I understand. Really."

"We weren't right for each other."

"You thought we were right enough for each other before you left on your trip." She tilted her head, still smiling.

"No, I didn't."

"Peter, it's silly for us to argue about this, here, now. Let's have coffee next week and discuss it. What do you say? Surely you can spare half an hour to have coffee with me? You owe me that much, don't you?"

He knew he had been unfair to Rosemary, but meeting her for coffee might give her the idea that there was still something between them.

"Mele's my wife now," he said, determined not to let her forget that.

"Well, surely she wouldn't object to you having coffee with an old friend?" She made it sound so harmless.

"I'm sorry. I can't."

Her smiled wavered. She sighed. "But surely you see she's not right for you, Peter."

"I see nothing of the sort," he said, then turned before she had a chance to say anything else and walked back to his car, where Mele was waiting.

When Peter stopped in front of his house, the door flew open and Susan, who had been watching for them, ran out to meet them.

"Mother's still on the warpath," she said, leaning down to his open window and thrusting the letter at him. "Hi, Mele. Sorry I can't invite you guys in."

"That's okay," Mele said. "I understand."

"Oh, and Rosemary called."

"I know," he said. "She found us."

"She seems to be taking it well."

"Yes, she does," he agreed because it seemed mean-spirited not to. He would have to keep Mele and Rosemary apart, although he wasn't sure how he would do that. He didn't trust Rosemary after that remark about Mele not being right for him. Was Rosemary coping as well as she wanted people to think? It struck him as a very fast recovery from a broken engagement. Had he really meant so little to her? He supposed that sounded unfair. After all, he had thrown her over with hardly a second thought. Why shouldn't she get over him just as easily? But he knew Rosemary. She wasn't the type to let go of anything easily. If he hadn't broken her heart, he had at least disrupted her grand plan for them, and he knew she didn't like to have her plans disrupted.

"Did you find an apartment?" Susan asked, bringing him back to the here and now.

"Not yet."

"Do you need money?"

He made a face at her. It was humiliating to think his little sister was offering him money. But if his parents cut him off altogether, he might have to resort to borrowing from whomever he could. His credit cards would not hold out forever and he didn't have much money in his account.

"Thanks for the offer," he said, "but don't break open your piggy bank just yet."

She made a face at him. "Keep in touch. Let me know

where you are so I don't have to call every motel in Boston to find you." She glanced back at the house. "Well, I'd better go back in before Mother notices you're out here and calls the police."

"I'll call you," he promised.

"You better."

She ran back to the house then, her ponytail bobbing. At the door she turned and waved before disappearing inside.

It was early evening by now, and he thought they would get something to eat before going back to the motel.

"Hungry?" he asked Mele.

The envelope was lying unopened in her lap.

"Aren't you going to open it?"

"I'm afraid."

He didn't see why she was so certain this was bad news. They had talked about that dream she had had their last night in Kenya, but nothing made any difference. She could not seem to shake her anxiety about her grandmother. He hoped this letter would finally reassure her.

"Would you like me to open it?" he offered.

She nodded.

He took the envelope and tore it open.

"Do you want me to read it?"

"Yes, please."

The letter was from her mother. The handwriting was difficult to decipher, the spelling iffy, and the grammar fractured, but after only a few sentences he knew that her grandmother had died. Mele had been right. It was bad news.

"I'm sorry."

"My tutu," she said, tears springing to her eyes. "My sweet dear tutu. I should never have left. I was so selfish."

He put his arms around her and held her while she cried,

comforting her as best he could. When the initial storm of tears had passed, he turned the car around and they headed back. He didn't want his mother charging out of the house to confront them or to be still parked in front of the house when his father got home. He knew he could expect no sympathy from his father, who had always been disappointed in him. His marriage to Mele was not likely to change that.

After reading the letter, Mele was in no condition to go into any restaurant or fast food outlet, so in the end they got Chinese takeout and drove back to their motel room.

Later she cried for a long time in his arms as they lay in their motel bed until finally she fell asleep, exhausted.

Later still he woke to find her no longer beside him. He pushed himself up and looked around the dark room. Then he saw her in front of the window in her nightgown. She had thrown open the curtains and was swaying in the moonlight—no, not swaying but dancing slowly, languidly, her bare arms and hands graceful as they traced signs in the air, her body moving to unheard music. It was like the hula the bride on Niʻihau had danced for her new husband on the beach in the firelight with the surf breaking in the background. But he knew she wasn't dancing for him. She was dancing for her grandmother. She was dancing for herself. She was dancing because it was the only way she knew to ease the ache inside her. It was strange and beautiful, and he marveled once again at the mysterious way they had been brought together and how much his life had changed since the day he met her, and he wondered if this love they had found would last or if it would turn out to be as insubstantial as a dream.

## 11

## Boston, seven months later

Mele missed her grandmother. Not a day went by that she didn't think of her, although she cried less now, and that was as it should be, as her grandmother would have wished it to be. She knew her grandmother wouldn't have wanted her to drown in grief. Still, she wished she could sit beside her beloved tutu one more time and hold her hand, or lay her head on her lap and feel her fingers stroke her hair. It was hard knowing she would never see her again.

Niʻihau seemed far away now, almost like a dream. Did it still exist? She thought if she didn't receive an occasional letter from her mother telling her what everyone was doing, she would doubt it really existed. Sometimes she felt as if she had been in Boston forever, surrounded by tall concrete buildings, living among strangers who were always in a rush and had no time to speak to each other. It was cold now. There was snow on the ground. She felt chilled to the bone in spite of the sweater she wore and the insulated jacket Peter had bought for her. She didn't like it there, but she tried not to complain, for his sake. She felt as if she were living in exile, but she knew she must get used to that. If only it weren't so cold. She shivered and her teeth chattered from the cold. When she exhaled, her breath hung in the air like smoke. And yet she had to admit, the first time she saw snow one day in November, she thought it was one of the most beautiful sights she had ever seen. It drifted down in delicate flakes, dusting her eyelashes and melting in her hands when she tried to catch it. Peter laughed at her for being so excited. For a while it was like that every time it snowed. But now she was tired of snow. There was too much of it and the magic was gone. It lingered in dirty patches and overhead the sky looked relentlessly gray and bleak. It was as if the sun had been blotted out, and something deep within her cried out for something more than this awful grayness. Peter told her to be patient, spring would come, but she felt trapped in this moment in time like the prehistoric person frozen in a chunk of Alpine ice that she had read about in her anthropology class and wondered if she would ever be warm again.

She liked to think that her grandmother was looking down on her, watching over her, and that if she was, she would approve of what Mele was trying to do. She was a student at the university now, just as she had wanted so badly to be, going to classes and listening to professors lecture and reading until her eyes ached and her mind felt numb. She knew it would be a long time before she graduated, but she was determined to do this. And now she was not just doing it for herself. After what she saw on her journey with Peter, she knew what she wanted to do with her life. Somehow she was going to make the lives of women in this world better. She was not sure how she would do that, but that's what she wanted to do.

And what of her marriage? What of Peter? He was kind and good and said he loved her, and yet they were so different she sometimes despaired that they would ever understand each other. Sometimes they quarreled and she felt so alone and thought it was a mistake to have married him. Sometimes he drove her crazy with his logic and his caution. She wished they had more time to find out if they were right for each other before the baby arrived, but now there were only a few months left. Whether they were ready or not, it was coming. She could feel it kicking inside her, and she was beginning to show. Soon she wouldn't be able to hide her condition with bulky sweaters. Already this child seemed real to her. She talked to it. She tried to reassure it that everything would be all right, that she would take good care of it when it came into the world, that she would protect it. She didn't tell it she was scared, although she was. If only her grandmother were there and could give her advice as she used to do.

She wore the ring on her finger that her grandmother gave her the night she left Ni'ihau. She had often wondered why her grandmother hadn't tried to talk her out of marrying Peter. Perhaps she knew it would do no good. Mele had always been so impetuous and stubborn. Even her grandmother might not have been able to stop her. She had been so young, so headstrong, so determined to go her own way. She felt older now, years older, although it had been only seven months.

Not that it had been a mistake. Peter was good to her. He had made sacrifices too. His mother still wouldn't speak to him. They lived in a little apartment now, with neighbors above who made a great deal of noise on the ceiling, and a shower that took five minutes for the hot water to come through. But they managed, and soon Peter would start his new job and they would be able to afford some place bigger.

## FORBIDDEN PLACES

His sister Susan came often to see them. She was very excited about the baby and had done a lot to help Mele get settled into her new life; she had taken her to shop for clothes and explained all the things Mele didn't understand when she didn't want to ask Peter.

Perhaps everything would change when the baby was born. Perhaps Mele would change. Perhaps then she wouldn't feel so confused and lost and have such strange thoughts. Not just strange thoughts—crazy thoughts, thoughts that made no sense. But she was not crazy. She was not imagining things. She knew what she had seen. She couldn't explain it, but she was as certain of what she had seen as she was that she was in Boston and not in her old bed on Niʻihau dreaming. She had seen a watcher. Yes, in this place where there should be no watchers, she had seen one.

She had been in her astronomy class in the lecture hall, where more than one hundred students were listening to a professor talk about the stars when she noticed an athletic-looking young man with short sandy hair wearing a green shirt. On his finger was a gold ring that glinted in the light from the window nearby. Maybe it was the ring that caught her attention first. He sat about ten seats away from her, and she could only see the back of his head until he turned for a split second and looked directly at her. It was as if he knew she had been looking at him. His eyes were green, like his shirt. She knew at once that he wasn't a student, that he didn't belong there any more than she did. She wasn't sure how she knew it. Maybe his hair was cut a little different. Maybe it was the greenness of his eyes, or his cool appraising stare as if he were looking over the animals in a zoo and finding them interesting but of course they were just animals. He had the look of someone who was only observing and confident none of it could touch him because he was only there temporarily, he was only there to watch. She had seen a lot of watchers when she was a guide on Ni'ihau. Even when you dressed them like the locals, they never quite blended.

That evening she waited until they were about to sit down for dinner to tell Peter about the watcher. She expected him to be surprised and intrigued, but instead he simply didn't believe her.

"It's not possible," he said. "There are no watchers in Boston. It's not a Forbidden Place."

"Nevertheless," she said, setting two glasses of water on the table, "I saw a watcher." She sat down across from him and waited for him to ask questions.

"Your imagination was playing tricks on you. It's probably one of those odd side effects of being pregnant, something caused by hormonal changes."

She glared at him. "It was not my hormones. I know what I saw."

"You're serious, aren't you?"

"Of course I'm serious. Do you think I would joke about this? Do I look like I'm joking? Why don't you believe me?"

He reached across the table for her hand. She pulled it away, in no mood for hand-holding if he didn't believe her when she said she had seen a watcher.

"Look, if it makes you feel better, I'll go to class with you tomorrow. You can show me this guy and. . . ."

"And what?"

"I'll check it out."

"He was a watcher. I swear it."

"And where was he from?" he asked in that maddeningly patronizing way he sometimes talked to her, as if she were seven years old.

"I don't know," she said irritably. "How am I supposed to know?"

"Well, did he look Russian?" Peter sat there, the epitome of adult reasonableness. "Or Chinese? Or African?"

"He looked neutral," she snapped. "He looked like everybody else and yet different." Even to her ears it didn't sound very convincing.

"Neutral," he repeated softly, trying not to smile. Now it sounded not only unconvincing but ridiculous.

"Yes, neutral," she insisted, tempted to throw her water glass at him if he said another word. Fortunately for him, he didn't.

After that, they ate their meal in near silence, carefully avoiding any further mention of what she thought she had seen. Nor did they talk about it later as she sat on the sofa studying and Peter worked on his laptop at the table. He was revising his dissertation, a project that looked as if it might never end.

She could hardly sleep that night wondering if the watcher would be there again the following day.

The next day Peter insisted on going with her to class, although she told him it wasn't necessary. If the watcher did not appear again, Peter would chalk it up to her overactive imagination and ignorance, and it would crop up in quarrels. He would say, "Remember that time you thought you saw a watcher in your astronomy class?" and she would hate him for not believing her. It would drive a wedge between them, and the wedge, with time, would become a wall. How much hope was there for their marriage if they had walls between them?

By the time they got to the astronomy class, Mele didn't really expect the watcher would be there. He would have observed all he needed to the previous day and there would be no reason for him to return. But when they walked in, there he was, wearing the same green shirt and sitting in the same seat.

Feeling vindicated, she pointed him out to Peter. They could only see the back of his head from where they sat. From the back he looked very much like the other young men in the lecture hall. But he wasn't, she saw again. She had been right. He was a watcher.

"There's nothing unusual about him," Peter said, scrutinizing the back of his head. "I don't see why you think he's a watcher."

She wished the young man would turn so they could see his face, but he didn't. The instructor launched into his lecture for the day. He was attempting to explain the nature of the universe. Peter quickly lost interest, opened a book he had brought along, and started reading to pass the time. The minutes ticked away. It was frustrating that she had no way to convince him the young man was a watcher. She was so sure, but how could she prove it? Then when it was almost time for the class to end, the young man in the green shirt finally turned and looked directly at her again in that amused and superior way he had the day before. She had the feeling he had known all along that she was watching him. She nudged Peter with her elbow to get his attention, and just at that moment a girl sitting beside the watcher also turned, as if to see what he was looking at. Their eyes met. Mele felt a flash of recognition. She knew exactly what the girl was doing because she had done it so many times herself—looked about to keep a watcher safe and to keep her people safe from him. She was a guide.

"Do you see?" Mele asked Peter.

He did. His book was forgotten now. They stared at the young man and the girl, and the young man and the girl stared back at them. Then the bell rang and the lecture hall exploded into motion. The aisles filled with students swarming for the exit at the back of the room.

"Quick," Mele said. "They'll get away."

Grabbing his book and his jacket, Peter pushed into the aisle and struggled to catch up with them. She pulled on her jacket and followed more cautiously, not wanting to risk a jab in her stomach from an elbow or a stray book.

As she emerged from the building, the cold air struck her like an Arctic blast. As usual, the sky was gray. She spotted Peter just as he caught up with the girl and laid his hand on her arm. Students passed them, but the girl's companion was nowhere in sight. She said something, shook off his hand, and broke into a run. Peter just stood there looking after her. Mele could have cursed him for letting her get away.

"What did she say?" she demanded when she got to him.

"She told me I was crazy and said if I bothered her again she'd report me to campus security."

"She's his guide."

"We don't know that. She could be just a girl in your class, a student like any other. In fact, that's probably all she is."

"So you don't believe me?"

He looked at the students jostling past them on their way to classes. Their breath hung like small clouds of fog in the air and she was shivering. It was cold, so cold.

"It makes no sense," he said, frowning. "Why would there be a watcher here? Where's he from? What's he doing?"

"Observing. What else would a watcher do?"

Peter put his arm around her. "Whoever he is, he's gone now."

Just then she felt the baby kick and automatically put a hand to her stomach. "Maybe Boston *is* a Forbidden Place. Maybe you just don't know it."

***

While Peter didn't know what to think about the guy in the green shirt in Mele's astronomy class or the girl who may or may not have been with him, he didn't think they were a watcher and a guide. A foreign student and his American girlfriend maybe, but there were no watchers in Boston, as he kept trying to explain to Mele. Who in their right mind would want to observe a boring college lecture on quasars and black holes or whatever it was the lecture had been about? He could think of hundreds of things more interesting. But there was no reasoning with her. She was so sure, and when he tried to discuss it with her calmly and logically, she just turned on the TV, some crime drama when he knew she didn't like crime dramas, and refused to listen to him. Later he noticed she wasn't really watching the show, she was crying, and he felt guilty. Also he had a nagging doubt in the back of his mind.

The truth was the young man had seemed strange to him too, although he couldn't pinpoint why. It was when he turned and looked at them that it struck Peter. For a fleeting second he thought Mele might be right. Something about his eyes. Maybe he was wearing tinted contacts. People just didn't have eyes that green. And he didn't really look like a student, more like a male model or an actor. Too handsome, too flawless. A touch of arrogance about him, royalty mingling with the peons. And when Peter caught up with the girl, well, she was just an ordinary girl and understandably reluctant to be stopped by a stranger, but still—she didn't wait to find out what he wanted. She seemed to know and was determined to avoid him. He could understand why Mele thought they might be a watcher and a guide, but of course they couldn't be.

However, as the evening wore on, he became more

uncertain as he turned the whole thing over in his mind. He thought about calling Professor Rinehart and discussing it with him. He was pretty sure the professor would laugh about it and that would end whatever doubt he had. He wanted someone else's opinion, someone intelligent and educated whose opinion he respected, but he was reluctant to call him with Mele there. If she overheard him talking about the incident, she might get even more upset with him than she already was, and in her hormonally unbalanced state, who knew what she might take it in her head to do—make him sleep on the couch? Leave him? Still he couldn't shake the idea of talking to Professor Rinehart once it had taken hold of him. He knew he could just as easily wait until the next day, but then it would be on his mind all night, so he told Mele he was going out for a newspaper and would be back in a little while. When he left, she was still sitting in front of the TV clutching a pillow in her arms.

Of course he could have phoned Professor Rinehart. He really didn't have to drive over to his house, but by the time he left the apartment he was looking forward to talking to him face-to-face. It wasn't just the watcher and his guide that were bothering him. He wanted to talk to the professor about Mele too. The professor had been married. Maybe he could give him some advice.

Professor Rinehart's house was only about twenty minutes away in a nice but not ostentatious neighborhood. On this cold wintry night, there were warm lights in the windows and SUV's in the driveways. Streetlights cast a pale glow over the patches of crusty snow on the lawns.

When Peter rang the doorbell, he could hear it distantly chime. Although Professor Rinehart wasn't expecting him, he didn't think the professor would mind if he showed up unannounced on his doorstep. The professor was almost like a second father to him and much more understanding than his own father had ever been.

He had to ring a second time before Professor Rinehart opened the door. He looked surprised to see Peter. In fact, for a minute he just stood there staring.

"Peter!"

He nodded, hoping the professor would invite him in. It hadn't occurred to him that he might not. And then the awkward moment was past, the door swung wide, and the professor was inviting him in.

"What on earth brings you here in the middle of the night? I hope nothing's wrong?"

Peter assured him it wasn't. Professor Rinehart was wearing a white bathrobe, which made Peter wonder if he had interrupted him on his way to take a shower. Again he had a feeling of awkwardness as they stood there in the entryway.

"I probably should have waited until morning," Peter said and realized that he probably should have, but he was here now and so he would tell Professor Rinehart about the young man with the strange green eyes and the girl. They would discuss the odd pair and maybe Mele as well. The professor would put it all in perspective for him and set his mind at rest.

"I hope you're not going to tell me you're making some major change to your dissertation," Professor Rinehart said. "Not now when you're so near the end. If you are, it's just dissertation cold feet, something like marriage jitters. Just hang in there and it'll pass."

"Oh, no," Peter said, "it's nothing like that."

"Well, that's a relief," the professor said. "It would be a shame to get this far and then not finish it. So what's this all about?"

Peter was surprised that Professor Rinehart didn't ask him to sit down. It was strangely unlike him. It was as if the professor expected him to just blurt out what he had to say instead of building up to it gradually over a glass of scotch, as he had anticipated. He saw the professor glance nervously over his shoulder, and it occurred to him Professor Rinehart might not be alone, but he knew the professor's wife had left him and the idea of his having any woman in the house who wasn't his wife seemed preposterous. The professor gave him a fatherly and benevolent smile that swept these thoughts from his mind. Maybe he would offer the glass of scotch after he heard what Peter had to say.

"Mele thought she saw a watcher," he said, getting straight to the point.

The professor raised an eyebrow. "Oh?"

"And a guide."

The professor waited patiently for him to continue. "A guide?"

"Of course I know it's not possible. She's just imagining it. It's probably got something to do with being pregnant."

"That's what you came here to tell me?" Professor Rinehart asked, looking amused. "In the middle of the night?"

It was not the middle of the night, it was only a little after nine, but Peter was starting to feel foolish. He tried to defend himself.

"Of course I didn't believe it when she told me. But then I saw them myself—"

"You *saw* them?" the professor said, eyebrow raised again. Peter wasn't sure if he looked skeptical or amused, or both.

"Yes, I saw them. I went with her to her astronomy class and there they were."

"Let me get this straight. You saw a watcher and a guide in

an astronomy class? And how did you know that's what they were?"

"I don't, but they might have been. There was something weird about the guy . . . something I can't quite put my finger on . . . like he didn't belong here—like he was visiting. And the girl—Mele was right—she was like his guide." Now that he had said it, he began to feel more convinced himself. He had expected Professor Rinehart to laugh but instead he frowned and looked thoughtful.

"Is it possible?" Peter asked.

"Anything is possible."

"But it makes no sense. Why would a watcher be here in Boston? Where would he be from?"

"Where indeed? That's the question, isn't it?"

"Then you do think it's possible?"

"Why not? We go to the Amazon and China and Africa to observe civilizations different from our own. What's to keep others from someplace different and possibly more advanced than we are from visiting us?"

"But from where? There are no societies more advanced than our own. Boston isn't a Forbidden Place."

Professor Rinehart smiled. "You're right, of course. The idea is absurd."

Just then in the corner of his eye Peter caught a movement in the hallway behind him. The professor turned to see what he was looking at. A woman stood there in a matching white bathrobe. Not a woman. Rosemary.

Peter could hardly believe his eyes. She was the last person he expected to see at that moment. She looked embarrassed for about two seconds, then stood straighter, chin lifted. His mind was struggling to understand what he saw. Rosemary and Professor Rinehart? How was that possible? He thought she disliked him. How many times had she complained about him? And Peter thought the professor didn't approve of her. Hadn't he hinted that she was too controlling? When had this happened? Peter had thought Rosemary wasn't over him. Had she turned to Professor Rinehart on the rebound? In some twisted way had she expected to get at him through the professor? No, that made no sense. *They* made no sense. He was twice her age and had no interest in the law. They had nothing in common.

Professor Rinehart cleared his throat. "This is a little awkward," he said, which was certainly an understatement.

"Hi, Peter," Rosemary said, as if they had simply met on the street and she were not wearing a bathrobe.

He wanted to ask what she was doing there, but it was pretty obvious.

"Peter had something he wanted to tell me about," Professor Rinehart explained.

He did not want to stand there while the professor repeated it all to Rosemary. It was bad enough to think the professor would tell her all about it after he was gone. He could imagine them laughing about it together. 'Thought he saw a watcher. Can you imagine?' 'A watcher from where?'

"I'd better go now," Peter said. "Mele will be expecting me back."

"We can talk about this tomorrow," Professor Rinehart said. "Drop by my office."

"All right."

But he had no intention of dropping by the professor's office tomorrow. He stepped back out into the night and hurried down the icy walk to his car. Just before he got in, he looked up at the night sky. It was too overcast to see stars, but he did see the small blinking light of an airplane. Maybe they were being watched, but maybe it didn't matter where the watchers came from. Maybe what mattered was what the watchers saw. If they are anything like us, Peter thought, they are probably just as imperfect as we are, although they might consider themselves superior. In the end, we are all just trying to muddle through our lives, searching for love and happiness, doing the best we can in the little time we have. Suddenly he knew where he wanted to be. He wanted to be back in that cramped little apartment with Mele. The watcher didn't matter. His dissertation didn't matter. What Mele and he had together—that was what mattered.

# ABOUT THE AUTHOR

Deanna Madden has taught literature and creative writing at various colleges on the U.S. mainland and in Hawaii. Her publications include short stories, essays on literature, the novella *The Haunted Garden*, and the novels *Helena Landless*, *Gaslight and Fog*, and *The Wall*. She lives in Honolulu with her family and is at work on her next novel.

Made in the USA
Charleston, SC
11 February 2017